Matt Jensen:
The Last Mountain Man
The Eyes of Texas

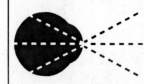

This Large Print Book carries the
Seal of Approval of N.A.V.H.

Matt Jensen:
The Last Mountain Man
The Eyes of Texas

William W. Johnstone
with J. A. Johnstone

WHEELER PUBLISHING

A part of Gale, Cengage Learning

GALE
CENGAGE Learning

Detroit • New York • San Francisco • New Haven, Conn • Waterville, Maine • London

GALE
CENGAGE Learning·

LIBRARY OF CONGRESS CATALOGING-IN-PUBLICATION DATA

Johnstone, William W.
    Matt Jensen, the last mountain man : the eyes of Texas / by William W. Johnstone with J.A. Johnstone. — Large Print edition.
        pages cm. — (Wheeler Publishing Large Print Western)
    ISBN 978-1-4104-5391-4 (softcover) — ISBN 1-4104-5391-X (softcover)
    1. Large type books. I. Johnstone, J. A. II. Title.
PS3560.O415M3845 2013
813'.54—dc23   2013005554

Published in 2013 by arrangement with Pinnacle Books, an imprint of Kensington Publishing Corp.

Printed in the United States of America
2 3 4 5 6   17 16 15 14 13

Matt Jensen:
The Last Mountain Man
The Eyes of Texas

CHAPTER ONE

The Byrd Ranch, Las Animas County,
Colorado

Matt Jensen was coming back from town with gifts for Amon Byrd and his wife, Bernice. Amon Byrd was one of Matt's oldest friends, and for a while the two of them had been residents of the Soda Creek Home for Wayward Boys and Girls, an orphanage of sorts. The gifts, a decorative blue and white vase for Bernice and a sheepskin coat for Amon, were thanks for them having given Matt a place to stay for a while.

Matt Jensen was a man who wandered around, always ready to go to the next town to "see the elephant." Although he was never totally dissatisfied with where he was, or with what he was doing, he was always happiest saying good-bye, with someplace else to go.

He was a lone wolf who had worn a deputy's badge in Abilene, ridden shotgun for a stagecoach out of Lordsburg, scouted for the Army in the McDowell Mountains of Arizona, and panned for gold in Idaho. He had rescued a governor's niece in Colorado, saved a ranch in Idaho, defended an editor in the Dakota Territory, rescued a young Winston Churchill in Wyoming, and taken a herd of Angus through a blizzard in Kansas.

Matt was a wanderer, always wondering what was beyond the next line of hills, just over the horizon. He traveled light, with a Bowie knife, a .44 double-action Colt, a Winchester .44-40 rifle, a rain slicker, an overcoat, two blankets, two spare shirts, socks, two extra pairs of trousers, and extra underwear.

Because he was a wanderer, he often dropped in on old friends, though never without contacting them first, and never without leaving them with a gift of thanks.

Dismounting in front of the house, Matt very carefully removed the vase, then wrapped it up in the sheepskin coat and went inside both to deliver the gift and tell his friends good-bye.

"Amon," he called. "Amon, where are you?"

"Matt!"

There was something about the voice, a

strained urgency that caught Matt's attention right away.

"Amon, where are you?" Matt repeated.

"In the kitchen." Matt noticed then that not only was the voice strained, it was weak, and he pulled his pistol and went cautiously into the kitchen. The first thing he saw was the naked body of Bernice Byrd. She was lying on the floor in a pool of her own blood.

"Amon!" Matt shouted again.

"Over here."

Amon was on the other side of the wood-burning cooking range. He was sitting up, leaning back against the wall, holding his hands over his stomach. His hands were covered with blood, as was the front of his shirt and the top part of his pants.

"My God, Amon, what happened?" Matt asked, quickly putting away his pistol, then kneeling beside his friend to see what he could do to help him. When he pulled Amon's hand away from the wound, he saw his friend's intestines hanging out.

"Bernice?" Amon said.

Matt didn't know if he should tell him or not, but he knew that his friend wasn't going to make it, and he figured he had a right to know the truth. He shook his head.

"I'm sorry, Amon. She didn't make it," Matt said.

Amon was quiet for a moment. "I thought as much," he said. "I kept calling out to her, but she never answered. Ahh, I'll see her in a few more minutes anyway, 'cause I'm not going to make it either."

"Who did this, Amon?"

"I don't know, I never saw them before. There was two of them, rode up, said they was hungry and asked if we could give 'em anything to eat. Bernice invited them into the kitchen, was goin' to cook 'em some bacon and eggs, when one of 'em took a knife to me. I must've passed out, 'cause next thing I knew, they were gone and I couldn't get Bernice to answer me."

"You say there were two of them. Can you describe them?"

"Yeah, one of 'em was kind of short and stocky. Oh, and he had a real bad scar come down across his left eye. His eyelid was puffed up real bad. His hair was cut real short, and looked to me like the hair was kind of red. Oh, wait, I do know his name. The other fella called him Mutt. I don't know if it's his real name, or just somethin' he was called, 'cause he wasn't all that big. The other man was tall, with long dark hair, and a dark beard and moustache. I never heard his name said."

"Did you see which way they went?"

"I didn't see 'em, but I heard 'em. They was goin' south when they left here."

Matt walked out to the front of the house and saw tracks of two horses heading south. One of them was riding a horse with a tie-bar shoe. Smiling at his luck, Matt went back inside.

"We're in luck, Amon. One of them is riding a . . ." Matt stopped in midsentence. His friend was dead.

"I'll find them for you, Amon. I promise you, they will not get away with this," Matt said quietly.

Matt went into the bedroom and took a sheet off the bed, then brought it back into the kitchen to spread it over Bernice's nude body. Then he rode into Trinidad, the county seat of Las Animas County, and also the nearest town to the Byrd Ranch. There, he stopped at the sheriff's office to report what happened.

"My God! Both of 'em?" Sheriff Carson asked in disbelief.

"Both of them. And I'd better warn you, Sheriff, it's not a pretty sight."

"I'll go have a look around."

"I've got a lead on who did it," Matt said. "I want you to deputize me so it'll be legal when I bring them back."

Sheriff Carson pulled a badge from his

desk drawer and pinned it on Matt, then told Matt to raise his hand.

"You swear to do a good job?"

"I do."

"You're deputized. I guess, from what you tell me, that I should take Tom Nunnelee with me to bring the bodies back."

"That would be a good idea," Matt said.

Mutt Crowley lay on top of a flat rock, looking back along the trail over which they had just come.

"Is he still there?" Coy Ashford asked.

"Yeah," Crowley growled. "Still there."

"Who is it that's a' trailin' us?" Ashford asked.

"How the hell am I s'posed to know? I ain't seen him close enough to identify, even if I did know him," Crowley said. He rubbed the scar on his eyelid, a habit he had acquired since he picked up the scar in a knife fight with a Mexican three years ago.

"Well, I'll say this for him," Ashford said. "Once he gets his teeth into you, he don't give up. We've tried ever' trick in the book to shake him off our tail, but he's still there."

"What are we goin' to do about that sidewinder? We can't shake him off," Crowley growled.

Ashford looked back toward the rider. "All

right, let's go up through that draw," he said, pointing.

"That's a dead-end canyon," Crowley replied

"Yeah, I know it's a dead-end canyon, but it's got two or three good places in there where we can hide. All we got to do is let him follow us in there, then ambush him."

"What if he don't come in? What if he just stays back at the mouth of the canyon and waits us out?" Crowley asked.

"The way this fella has been doggin' us, I don't think he'll wait for nothin'. If he knows we're in there, he'll come after us. That gives us the edge."

"Yeah, maybe you're right," Mutt said. "Best thing to do with someone like that is to lie in ambush, then kill 'im. Let's just do it and get it over with."

"Come on, I know the perfect spot," Ashford said.

Three Dog Canyon

When Matt trailed the two men into the canyon, he pulled his long gun out of the saddle holster, then dismounted and started walking into the canyon, leading Spirit. The horse's hooves fell sharply on the stone floor and echoed loudly back from the canyon walls. The canyon made a forty-five-degree turn to the left just in front of him, so Matt stopped. Right before he got to the turn he slapped Spirit on the rump and sent him through.

The canyon exploded with the sound of gunfire as Crowley and Ashford opened up on what they thought would be their pursuer. Instead, their bullets whizzed harmlessly over the empty saddle of the riderless horse, raised sparks as they hit the rocky ground, then whined off into empty space, echoing and re-echoing in a cacophony of whines and shrieks.

From his position just around the corner from the turn, Matt was able to locate them. They were on the south side of the canyon, squeezed in between the wall itself and a rock outcropping that provided them with a natural cover.

The firing stopped and, after a few seconds of dying echoes, the canyon grew silent.

Matt studied the rock face of the wall just behind the spot where he had located them; then he began firing. His rifle boomed loudly, the thunder of the detonating cartridges picking up resonance through the canyon, then doubling and redoubling in intensity. Matt wasn't even trying to aim at the two men, but was instead firing at the rock wall behind them, knowing that even if the ricocheting bullets didn't kill them, they would make things awfully uncomfortable for them. He emptied his rifle. Then, as the echoes thundered back through the canyon, he began reloading.

"Mister!" a strained voice called. "Mister!"

"What do you want?" Matt called back.

"My pard's been kilt. I want to give up."

"All right, come on down with your hands up."

A man moved out from behind the rock and started toward him.

"Drop your gun and put both hands up," Matt shouted.

The man did as Matt ordered, then continued toward him, holding both hands over his head. From his size and the very obvious scar on his face, Matt knew that this was the one Amon had said was Mutt.

Matt, with his own pistol in hand, started toward him.

"Now, Mutt!" another voice called, and Mutt Crowley threw himself to the ground. Coy Ashford stepped out from behind the rock outcropping and fired at Matt, the bullet whizzing by so closely that Matt heard the pop as it passed by his ear.

Matt returned fire and Ashford crumpled to the ground with a bleeding hole in his chest. Matt hurried to check on Ashford; then, satisfied that the would-be ambusher was dead, he turned back toward the other man, who was still holding his hands in the air.

"What's your name?" Matt asked.

"Crowley. Mutt Crowley. Is Ashford dead?"

"If you're talking about this man, yes, he's dead."

"He's the one that done it," Crowley said. "All I wanted to do was steal a little money and go on, but Ashford, I don't know, he went crazy. First he cut the rancher's gut open, then he cut the woman's throat. He done it all. I didn't have nothin' to do with it."

Matt looked down at the body. "Where's the knife?" he said. "Or did he borrow yours?" He pointed to the hunting knife hanging from Crowley's belt.

"I . . . I ain't goin' to talk no more," Crowley said.

"I don't want you to talk, I want you to run."

"What? What do you mean you want me to run?"

"I want you to run, Crowley," Matt said. "Please, try to run away from me."

"You're . . . you're crazy!" Crowley said.

16

"I ain't runnin' and I ain't fightin' back. You got to take me in alive."

"All right. I guess I'd rather see you hang anyway."

CHAPTER TWO

Trinidad, Colorado

At Mutt Crowley's trial, Matt's testimony was damning. He told how he had found Amon and Bernice Byrd, that Amon had still been alive and had given a physical description of his killers. He told also how he had tracked the two men from the Byrd Ranch to Three Dog Canyon, where he'd engaged in a shoot-out with them, killing Coy Ashford, and placing Mutt Crowley under arrest.

Mutt Crowley did not deny being there, but he tried, unsuccessfully, to blame everything on Ashford.

It was now time for the prosecutor to wrap up the case, and he was doing so with his concluding remarks.

"There is no question but that Mutt Crowley was at the Byrd Ranch. In his dying declaration, Amon Byrd gave a vivid and accurate description of the animals who attacked him and then raped and murdered his wife. Mr. Matt Jensen, a man who is well known throughout the West for his tracking ability, honesty, and integrity, legally empowered to do so, tracked Mutt Crowley and Coy Ashford from the Byrd Ranch until he located them at Three Dog Canyon. There, in a deadly gunfight, he killed Coy Ashford and brought Crowley back to stand trial."

The prosecutor turned toward Crowley, who was sitting, defiantly, at the defendant's table.

"And Crowley admits to being there!" The prosecutor boomed out those six words. "He claims that it was Ashford who killed the Byrds, even though both Mr. and Mrs. Crowley were killed with a knife, and Crowley was the only one of the two men who had a knife. Also, Crowley's clothes were covered with blood when he was brought in, but Crowley had not been wounded, and Coy Ashford suffered only the single shot that killed him. Where did the blood that was on Crowley's clothes come from?

"It's very clear that the blood that was on him came from Amon and Bernice Byrd. Despite Crowley's claim that it was Coy Ashford who did the actual killing, it is clear from the evidence presented during the course of this trial that Mutt Crowley was the murderer."

The prosecutor held up his finger to make the next point.

"But, prosecution is willing to drop that part of the assertion. We are willing to say that it might have been Ashford, and not Crowley, who wielded the knife that ended the lives of two of this county's most revered citizens."

The prosecutor looked back toward Crowley.

"Mr. Crowley, if you say you didn't do it, we will accept that."

A big grin spread across Crowley's face, and he nodded triumphantly.

The prosecutor turned his attention back to the jury. "Evidently, Mr. Crowley does not understand the law. We don't have to prove that he is the one who killed Mr. and Mrs. Byrd. All we have to do is prove that he was there. The Colorado Penal Code allows that a person can be convicted of any felony, including capital murder, 'as a party' to the offense. 'As a party' means that the person did not personally commit the elements of the crime, but is otherwise responsible for the conduct of the actual perpetrator as defined by law, to include encouraging its commission, or being present and making no effort to stop it, or, following such commission, failing to report the crime. Therefore, by association, and by his own admission, Mutt Crowley is guilty of murder, and should face the hangman's rope."

There were several in the gallery who applauded the prosecutor's summation, but the judge used his gavel to call the court to order.

At the conclusion of the summation, the judge charged the jury, then sent them back to the jury room for deliberation.

There were one hundred spectators in the gallery, and that many more standing outside the courthouse. Those who were closest to the open windows were able to carry on a running commentary of what was going on in the courtroom.

Less than fifteen minutes after the jury retired, a man who had posted himself near the open window, shouted the news to the others who had been waiting outside.

"The jury's comin' back! The jury's comin' back!

"Oyez, oyez, oyez, this here court of Las Animas County, Trinidad, Colorado, will now come to order, the Honorable Judge Tom Murchison presiding. All rise."

There was a scrape of chairs, a rustle of pants, petticoats, and skirts, as the spectators in the courtroom stood.

Judge Murchison was a dominating figure with brindled hair, a square jaw, and piercing blue eyes, who, by appearance and demeanor, could immediately make his presence known. He moved quickly to the bench, then sat down.

"Be seated."

The gallery sat, then watched as the defendant, his hands in shackles, was brought back in to the courtroom.

"Gentlemen of the jury, have you selected a foreman?" Judge Murchison asked.

"We have, Your Honor. My name is Frank Tanner, and I have been selected as foreman."

"Mr. Tanner, has the jury reached a verdict?"

"We have, Your Honor."

"Then if you would, please, publish the verdict."

"Your Honor, we, the people of this legally selected and appointed jury, find the defendant, Mutt Crowley, guilty of murder in the first degree."

"So say you one, so say you all? Let me hear from the jury, by the word aye."

"Aye!" the jury shouted.

"Are there any in opposition?"

There was no response to that question.

"Very well. Mr. Defense Attorney, please bring the prisoner to stand before the bench."

"Yes, Your Honor."

The prisoner was brought before the bench, and he stared defiantly at the judge.

"Do whatever you are going to do, you son of a bitch. Just don't keep me standin' here for all the peckerwoods to gawk at," Crowley said.

The gallery gasped at his gall and lack of respect.

"Oh, I will, sir. Believe me, I will. Mutt Crowley," Judge Murchison began. "Tonight the sun will set, and as it so often does, it will spread the western sky in brilliant hues of scarlet and gold, until, finally, it sinks below the horizon. But you, Mutt Crowley, will not see it.

"Tonight, the dark velvet of a midnight sky will be filled with all the stars of the cosmos, coyotes will sing their lonesome call, and the innocent will sleep peacefully in their beds.

"But neither are you innocent, nor will you sleep peacefully.

"At the break of dawn tomorrow these beautiful Rocky Mountains, as they do

23

every morning, will gradually emerge from the shadows of their slumber, and the sun will reach into the canyons and draws to push away the last remnants of the purple haze. There will be in the air the delightful scent of pine needles to perfume the new day. Fish will swim in the cool water, and birds will fly in the air.

"But, Mutt Crowley, this will be of no concern to you.

"By noon, the sun will flood the earth with its golden light, even as a few white clouds will hang in the brilliant blue sky, all this the work of a beneficent God, as men and women, boys and girls, will be enjoying their midday repast.

"But you, Mutt Crowley, will not be sitting down to lunch.

"By tomorrow afternoon the birds will sing, squirrels will leap from tree limb to tree limb, honeybees will drink the sweet nectar of wild flowers, and beavers will continue with their amazing engineering feats.

"But, Mutt Crowley, you will take notice of none these things.

"You will not be here because I hereby order the sheriff of Las Animas County to lead you to the gallows and there, to hang you by the neck until you are dead. Afterward, your body will then be taken down and buried so that it becomes food for the maggots. But you won't even be there for that, because by then your condemned soul will have left your body, and it will be writhing in the eternal torment of hell.

"Sheriff, get this worthless dreg of humanity out of my sight," Judge Murchison said with a concluding rap of his gavel.

4:17 p.m.
Deputy Boyle came back to stand just outside the bars, and to look at Crowley, who was lying on his back, with his hands folded behind his head.

"Sheriff Carson said I was supposed to ask you if you wanted anything to eat. They had a good apple pie over at the Chatterbox Café and the sheriff told me to bring a piece over here just in case you wanted it."

Outside the cell, the sound of the gallows being tested floated across the town square, and in through the tiny barred window. As the weight slammed down against the trap door, Mutt Crowley jumped. Deputy Boyle laughed.

"Kind of scary soundin', ain't it?"

Crowley didn't answer.

"What about it, Crowley? You want a piece of apple pie, or not?"

"No."

"I don't blame you. More'n likely all you'd do is shit it out when you get your neck stretched, anyhow. But if you don't mind, I'm goin' to say that you did want it, so's I can have it for myself."

Crowley glared at the deputy, but said nothing.

"Look at it this way," Deputy Boyle said. "Gettin' hung like this, in front of all those people that's gatherin' to watch . . . why, boy, this is goin' to make you famous. There's little kids out there now that, when they are old men, will be tellin' their grand-kids that they seen Mutt Crowley get hisself hung. Why, I would think you'd be right proud of that."

Deputy Boyle put his fist alongside his neck, tilted his head to one side, and made a gagging sound. Then he laughed out loud. "You sure you don't want that pie, 'cause it's sittin' out there on the sheriff's desk, right now."

"I said no," Crowley said.

"Good, then I'll be enjoyin' it myself. But don't worry, I ain't goin' to leave you out. I'll be thinkin' about you while I'm eatin' it."

Outside, they continued to test the device, and, over and over again, the trapdoor would spring and the rope would sing before the sandbag hit the ground with a violent thud.

Although the trial, verdict, and execution were scheduled to happen on the same day, so sure had everyone been that Crowley would be found guilty and sentenced to hang that visitors had come from miles around to watch him "dance in the air." As a result, there were a lot of strange faces in the town, most of them gathered on the square.

The gallows stood in the center of town, its grisly shadow stretching under the afternoon sun. The hanging was not to be until five, and it was now only three-thirty, but the crowd was already thick and jostling for position. Murchison had specifically chosen the time of the hanging so the people would be able to watch it after they got off work, then talk over their dinner about justice being done.

Several hundred people were gathered around the gallows, men in suits, shirt sleeves and overalls, women in long dresses and bonnets; children, who didn't quite understand the significance of the event, were there as well. The younger ones stood silently, grasping the hands of their mothers. A couple of older boys approached the cell and tried to peer in through the window, but a woman called out to them and they returned to the crowd.

A photographer paid a farmer two dollars to allow him to establish his camera tripod in the bed of the farmer's wagon, and he was there now, sighting through the camera to get the picture set up just right.

Inside the jail, there was the sound of keys rattling in the lock of the door.

"Go away. I've got at least half an hour left," Crowley said without looking toward the cell door. "I don't plan to go out there and stand in front of all those folks any longer than I have to."

"Of course you can stay here if you wish," a voice said. "But I would think you might be ready to leave, about now."

"What?" Crowley said excitedly. Looking toward the cell door he saw that it was wide open, and his brother was standing there with a big smile on his face.

"Prichard! What are you doing here?" Crowley asked, shocked, but very happy to see his older brother.

"It was brought to my attention that you had gotten yourself into a bit of trouble, so it became incumbent upon me, as your older brother and guardian, to come over and see what I could do to extricate you from the situation."

"The jailer and the deputy?" Crowley said.

"You needn't concern yourself about them," Prichard replied.

"Really?"

"We had best hurry," Prichard said. "If someone should see them in their present state, they're likely to get a little suspicious."

"You got horses?"

"They're out back."

Hurrying out back, the men mounted their horses then rode away slowly, with their hats pulled low.

"Hey!" someone shouted, and Mutt Crowley felt a quick tinge of fear. "You two boys ain't leavin' now, are you? Don't you want to see the hangin'?"

"No, thank you, I find hangings to be brutal and inhumane," Prichard said as the two men continued their slow ride out of town.

CHAPTER THREE

One year later — Shady Rest, Texas

Seconds earlier, the Ace High Saloon had been peaceful. A card game had been in progress in one part of the room; the teases, touches, and flirtatious laughter of the bar girls had been in play in another; and a piano player had been banging away on a beer-stained and scarred, out-of-tune instrument at the back of the room. But all that changed in an instant when Ethan Scarns shouted out, "By God, Moore, I paid to have this woman sit by me, and if you don't get up and go to another table, I'll kill you right where you are sitting."

The music, conversation, and laughter stopped, so that now the loudest sound in the saloon was the ticking of the grandfather clock that stood next to the piano. There were at least two dozen people in the saloon counting the bartender and the four bar girls. At the moment all eyes were directed toward the table where Scarns, the bar girl, and a cowboy named Moore were sitting.

"You paid for a drink, you didn't pay for the woman," Moore said.

Ethan Scarns was a small, gnarled-looking man. In a world without guns he would barely draw a second look. But this was a world with guns and Scarns was a perfect example of the saying, "God made man, but Sam Colt made them equal." Scarns had to be taken seriously because he had proven his skill with the pistol, as well as a propensity, almost an eagerness, to use it.

"Did you hear what I said, Moore?" Scarns asked. His voice was a low, evil hiss. Slowly and deliberately, he pulled his pistol and pointed it at Moore. "I told you to move to another table."

"I like this table," Moore replied calmly.

"Move, or so help me, I'll blow your brains out."

"You're crazy! You're both crazy," the bar girl said and she started to get up.

Scarns reached out toward her and pulled her back down in the chair. "You ain't goin' nowhere," he said. "I bought you."

"You bought a drink, you didn't buy me."

"It's the same thing," Scarns said.

"Leave the girl be, Scarns," the bartender called. "What do you want to go shucking her for?"

"You just stay the hell out of this, Reese. This ain't none of your concern," Scarns said. He looked back toward Moore. "I thought I told you to get."

"I ain't goin' nowhere," Moore said.

Scarns cocked his gun, the action making a double click as the sear engaged the cylinder and rotated a new bullet under the hammer. "I ain't askin' you again. I'm goin' to count to three and if you ain't out of that chair by the time I get to three, I'm goin' to blow your head off. One," he said, beginning his count.

"This ain't goin' to turn out good for you," Moore asked.

"What the hell are you talking about? Two," Scarns said, continuing his count.

Suddenly there was a loud bang and a curl of smoke rose from beneath the table. When Moore lifted his right hand from under the table, his fingers were curled around a Colt .44.

Scarns looked down in surprise at the hole the bullet had just punched in the middle of his chest.

"Uhnn!" he grunted, standing up and taking a step back. He dropped his gun and put his hand over the wound. "You . . . you killed me," he gasped.

"Yeah, I did," Moore answered easily. "Are you upset that I didn't wait until you got to three?"

Scarns collapsed. One of the men nearest him hurried over, then knelt beside him and put his hand on his neck. He looked up at the others.

"He's dead," he said.

"Yeah, that's sort of how I planned it," Moore said.

"What happened here?" Red Gimlin asked, coming into the main room from his office in the back. Gimlin, whose once-red hair had turned white, was the proprietor of the Ace High Saloon.

"Moore just killed Scarns," Reese said.

"Is that right?" Gimlin asked.

"Mr. Gimlin, he didn't have no choice. Scarns was about to kill him," the bar girl said.

"I need a whiskey," Moore said.

"Reese?" Gimlin called.

"Yes, sir?"

"Give Moore a whiskey, on the house." He looked down at Scarns. "Scarns was a worthless peckerwood anyway."

Marshal Jarvis came running in then, drawn by the sound of the gunshot. His own gun was drawn and after a quick glance around the room, he saw Scarns lying on the floor.

"What happened?" he asked.

"I see you're a day late and a dollar short, as usual," Gimlin said. "As you can see, Scarns got hisself killed."

"Who did it?"

"What difference does it make who did it? Scarns is dead, no matter who did it."

Marshal Jarvis walked over to Scarns's body and stared down at it for a moment. He kicked the body lightly, then a little bit harder. Scarns did not respond. Then he kicked him so hard that it moved his body slightly.

"You're right," Jarvis said. "He's dead."

There was a spattering of nervous laughter.

Jarvis looked around the saloon, returning everyone's curious gaze with one of his own. "So, is anyone going to tell me who did it?" he asked.

"I killed him," Moore said.

"Why?"

"Because it seemed like the thing to do at the time," Moore said easily.

"Go on about your business, Marshal," Gimlin said. "There's nothing for you to do here."

"I'll, uh, send Ponder down for the body."

"You do that. And you tell Ponder that

the Ace High won't be paying for the burying. He'll have to get the money from the
town."

"Yeah," Jarvis said. "The town is going to
run out of money if the killing doesn't slow
down."

The Ace High Saloon was one of three
saloons, a whorehouse, a couple of dance
halls, a gambling house, and half a dozen
prostitute cribs that occupied an area of
Shady Rest called Plantation Row. It was
called Plantation Row because it was just
the opposite of what one thought of when
thinking of plantations. Plantation Row,
which was really First Street, was one of
two cross streets of the main street in town,
which was called Railroad Avenue. Railroad
Avenue was as inaccurately named as Plantation Row, for no railroad served the town
of Shady Rest.

The most successful of all the businesses
on Plantation Row was a saloon called Pig
Palace, and it was run by a man named
Jacob Bramley. Bramley was a vain man
who almost always dressed in black, with a
low-crowned black hat, around which was a
band of silver. He had dark, brooding eyes,
and a neatly trimmed van dyke beard.
Because of his greed and corruption, Bramley was the recognized head of Plantation

Row. And his saloon, though the most successful, was in appearance typical of the other two saloons of Plantation Row.

The bar of the Pig Palace was made of pine and painted with a flat, red paint. There was no brass foot railing, and no cushions in the chairs. There were four women who worked the Pig Palace, and all four of them had been "on the line" for several years now. The dissipation of their profession had taken a severe toll on their looks.

Just after dark on that same day a man named Quince Calhoun rode into Shady Rest. The street was dimly illuminated by squares of yellow light, which spilled through the doors and windows of the buildings. High above the little town stars winked brightly, while over El Capitan Mountain, the moon hung like a large, silver wheel.

He tied his horse off, then went into the Pig Palace Saloon. The barkeep slid down the bar toward him.

"What can I get you?"

"Whiskey," Calhoun said. "And leave the bottle."

"What kind?"

"The cheapest."

The bartender took a bottle from beneath the counter. There was no label on the bottle and the color was dingy and cloudy. He pulled the cork, then poured a glass.

"That'll be a nickel," he said.

Calhoun took a swallow, then almost gagged. "Goddamn!" he said. "This tastes like horse piss."

"It's all in the way you drink it," the bartender said. "You don't just bolt it down. This is sippin' whiskey."

"Sippin' whiskey, you say?"

"Yeah, just go easy on it. You'll get it down, and it'll get you drunk, if that's all you want."

"That's all I want," Calhoun said. He took a smaller swallow and grimaced, but got it down.

"See what I mean?" the bartender said.

As Calhoun raised his glass to take another sip of his whiskey, he saw, in the mirror, a man step in through the swinging batwing doors. The man was wearing a badge, and he was sure that the star-packer had recognized him.

"Who's the lawman?" he asked the bartender.

"His name is Jarvis. He's the city marshal."

"How long has he been your marshal?"

"Only about a month. Why do you ask?"

"No reason," Calhoun answered.

In fact, Calhoun had a good reason. Calhoun was wanted for the murder of a railroad messenger up in Howard County. Jarvis had been a deputy sheriff up in Howard County at the time.

Calhoun tried to avoid the marshal, but when he looked into the mirror again, he saw that Jarvis was looking at him. He also saw, by the expression on Jarvis's face, that he had been recognized.

"Calhoun?" the marshal called.

Calhoun drew his pistol even as he was turning. Jarvis saw that Calhoun had a pistol in his hand, and he tried to draw, but it was too late.

Calhoun fired, the loud and unexpected gunshot surprising everyone. Jarvis went down.

"Ever' body, get back against the wall!" Calhoun shouted, waving his pistol. "If I see any of you goin' for your gun, I'm goin' . . ."

Calhoun' declaration was interrupted by an even louder explosion, and he was suddenly launched forward to crash over a table that was in front of him. His back was opened up by buck and ball shot, the gaping wound so deep that the white bone of his spine could be seen protruding through the wound.

Harry Durbin, the private security man for the saloon, came walking toward Calhoun's body, carrying a smoking shotgun.

"How's the marshal?" Durbin asked.

"Dead," someone replied.

"Son of a bitch. That's what, three marshals in the last three months?" one of the other patrons asked.

"Yeah, somethin' like that."

Durbin opened the barrel of his shotgun, pulled out the empty cartridge and replaced it with another. Snapping the barrel closed, he walked back to the high chair where he had been sitting, observing all the activity of the saloon.

"You know what? We've had three people kilt in town today," someone said. "That's a lot, even for Shady Rest."

Chapter Four

The name Shady Rest had been chosen specifically to appeal to the railroad officials of the Texas and Pacific, when the town made an application for the railroad to pass through their community.

Passengers and settlers will opt for this shady island in the open spaces of West Texas and that will, no doubt, prove to be mutually beneficial, bringing progress to our area and additional business to your railroad. We earnestly appeal to you to give our town every consideration as you choose the western route for your great railroad.

Despite their sincere petition, the town was bypassed when the T&P chose to go through Van Horn, some forty miles south. Shady Rest survived, though its name took on a more sinister tone when a newspaper in San Angelo wrote a very unflattering article about the town.

Deadliest Town in America

The community of Shady Rest, Texas, located in the shadow of El Capitan Mountain, has earned the unenviable reputation of being the deadliest town in Texas, if not in the entire United States of America. The name Shady Rest suggests a peaceful cemetery, and indeed, the population of the cemetery is growing nearly as fast as the population of the town, which seems bent upon reducing its number through almost daily murders.

Shady Rest has become a town of wild saloons, debauched "houses of pleasure" and disagreements too frequently settled by gunfire in the streets. It is said that the decent citizens of the town, if there be any remaining, are prisoners in their own homes.

On the very day the article appeared in the San Angelo newspaper, two young men passing through the town stopped in front of the Crooked Branch Saloon. Swinging down from their horses, they patted their dusters down.

41

One of them started coughing. "Sum bitch, Pete, you're like a pure dee sandstorm there," one of them said.

"Yeah, well, I know what will take care of it. Come on, Johnny, let's have us that beer we been talking about."

"You ain't goin' to get no argument from me," Johnny replied.

The two young men went into the saloon, then stepped up to the bar. The saloon was relatively quiet, with only four men at one table, and a fifth standing down at the far end of the bar. The four at the table were playing cards; the one at the end of the bar was nursing a drink. The man nursing the drink was unusual looking, in that he had no hair, nor did he have eyelashes or eyebrows. His head was almost perfectly round, and it sat upon his shoulder with no perceptible neck. His skin was white, and there was so little color in his eyes that they looked almost like clear glass.

"What'll it be, gents?" the bartender asked, stepping over in front of them.

Pete continued to stare at the strange-looking man.

"Pete?" Johnny said. "The bartender asked what'll we have."

"Oh," Pete said. "Uh, two beers."

"Two beers it is," the bartender replied.

He turned to draw the beers.

"And I'll have the same," Johnny added.

The bartender laughed. "You boys sound like you've got a thirst."

"Yeah, you might say that," Pete said. He continued to stare at the strange-looking man.

"Hey, Johnny," he said. He tried to whisper, but the words were spoken too loudly to be a whisper. "Look at that fella. You ever seen anything that looks like him?"

"Shh, Pete," Johnny said.

"Yeah, you're right. I don't have no business starin' at him, but I swear, I ain't never seen anyone looks like that.

"Mister, I don't mean to be buttin' in where it's none o' my business," Pete continued. "But was you born like that? Or was it some fire or somethin' that took off all your hair. Hey, do you have hair around your pecker?" Pete laughed at his question, and, though Johnny had been trying to caution him to be quiet, he laughed as well.

"Hair around his pecker," he said.

The bartender put the beers in front of the two boys and they each picked up one.

"I'd like to buy a drink for my new friend down there," Pete said, putting another nickel down on the bar.

The bartender picked up the nickel, then

put a drink in front of the man who had so caught Pete's interest.

"There you go, mister, I bought you a drink," Pete said. "Now, that you 'n me's friends, why don't you tell me how come it is that you look like that."

"I don't drink with sons of bitches like you," the man said, speaking for the first time, and sliding the drink back toward him.

"What the hell did you call us, mister?" Pete asked, bristling at the man's comment. He turned away from the bar to face the man.

"Easy, Pete," Johnny said, reaching out for his partner. "Maybe he's just real embarrassed by how he looks, and he don't like it that you brought it up."

Pete glared at the man, but the expression on the man's face didn't change. In fact, Pete didn't know if the man's expression could change.

"I just don't intend to stand here and be insulted by that hairless, glass-eyed, chalk-faced peckerwood." Pete said. He put up his fists. "I'm going to mop the floor with his sorry ass."

The hairless man smiled, or at least, his mouth moved in that expressionless face into what might have been a smile, though if it was a smile, it was certainly a smile without mirth.

"You're wearing a gun, cowboy. If we're going to fight, why don't we make it permanent?" he asked. He stepped away from the bar and turned toward Pete.

"Now wait a minute!" Pete said, pointing at him. "Hold on! There's no need to carry things this far. This isn't worth either one of us dying over."

"Oh, it won't be *either* of us, cowboy. It'll just be you," the man said. "Well, actually, it will be both of you," he added, looking at Johnny. "You came here together, you are going to die together."

"Wait a minute. Are you saying that you are willing to go up against both of us? One against two?"

"Well, that's not quite what I'm saying," the hairless man replied. "Wade, are you up there?"

"Yes sir, Mr. Foster, I'm up here," Wade replied. Wade was sitting in a high chair overlooking the saloon. He was holding a rifle.

"What? Wait a minute!" Pete said. "This ain't right. If there's goin' to be two of you, you should both be down here."

"There aren't two of us, cowboy," Foster said.

45

"What do you mean there aren't two of you?"

"Actually, there are three of us," Foster said. "Luke, are you following this?"

"Yes, sir, Mr. Foster, I'm ready," Luke answered. He had been one of the four men sitting at the table when Pete and Johnny first came in. The other three at the table had moved out of the way, leaving only Luke. Luke was no more than twenty feet away from the two boys, and to their side. He already had a pistol in his hand.

"You feel better now?" Foster asked. "Luke is going to be a part of this fight, and he is down here with us."

"But, that's — that's three to two!" Pete said. "And both of them are already holdin' guns."

"Well, they are holding guns, because that's what I pay them to do," Foster said. "You see, I own this establishment."

"No!" Johnny said. "This is gone too far now. Look, we're sorry if we offended you, but me 'n Pete will just be on our way now."

"It's too late for that," Foster said. "I'm afraid you two boys have already brought this to a head."

"We ain't goin' to draw on you. If you shoot us, it'll be in cold blood, in front of all these witnesses."

46

"What witnesses would that be?" Foster asked, looking over toward the three men who, earlier, had been sitting at a table with Luke, but were now standing back against the wall. "I don't see any witnesses," he added.

Taking their cue, the three men hurried out the front door, followed by the bartender. Pete's knees grew so weak that he could barely stand, and he felt nauseous.

"Please, Mr. Foster, we don't want no trouble," Pete said. "Why don't you just let us apologize and we'll go on our way?"

"Like I said," Foster said. "Pull your guns."

"The sheriff," Pete said. "How are you going to explain this to the sheriff?"

"Oh, the sheriff don't even come to Shady Rest," Foster said with what could be called an evil smile, if indeed it could be called a smile at all. "He says it's too dangerous for him."

"What about the marshal? Don't this town have a marshal?"

"I don't know whether we do or not. We keep killin' them off, you see. Luke, do we have a new marshal yet?"

"Not yet, we ain't," Luke answered. "Our last marshal got hisself kilt down at the Pig Palace, last week. Remember?"

"Oh, yes, I do remember. Well, this is going to work out just fine, isn't it?" Foster asked. "The sheriff never comes to Shady Rest, and we don't have a marshal. I don't reckon we're goin' to be bothered by anyone at all." His evil smile grew broader. "So, anytime you're ready, cowboys."

"Please," Pete said, his voice now nearly a whimper.

"Pete," Johnny said. "These sons of bitches are goin' to kill us, and there ain't nothin' we can do to stop it. And I don't plan on goin' out like any kind of a snivelin' coward. So buck up. Let's at least go down fightin'."

Pete took a couple of deep breaths to get hold of himself. Then he nodded.

"Yeah," he said. "Let's do it."

The two young men looked at each other; then, with an imperceptible signal, they started their draw. They were badly overmatched in this fight, not by the skill of their adversary, but by the way the odds were stacked against them. It was two to three, but not even that told the story. Two of three men they were going against were more favorably positioned, and, they both already had their weapons in hand.

Pete and Johnny made ragged, desperate grabs for their pistols.

So unfavorable was their position that the first shot, a rifle shot from Wade, who was standing up on the landing, struck Pete in the chest even before Pete was able to clear his holster. Johnny went down when Luke shot him in the temple from almost point-blank range.

Although Foster drew his gun, it wasn't necessary because both men had already been shot. Foster walked through the cloud of gun smoke and quickly looked through the bodies of the two men. From Billy's pocket he took a twenty-dollar gold piece, and twenty dollars in paper money. Johnny had no gold pieces, but he had sixty dollars in cash. Foster's men divided the money, and the three were calmly sipping their whiskey by the time a few of the citizens of the town got up the nerve to look inside.

On the afternoon of the day that the shooting occurred, the Shady Rest Merchants Association held an emergency meeting. It was attended by most of the business owners in town, though the owners of three of the four saloons were absent. So, too, were the owners of the dance hall and gambling house, as well as Abby Dolan, the whorehouse madam.

Gerald Hawkins was there. He owned the

Texas Star. The Texas Star was not to be confused with, or compared to, the Ace High, the Crooked Branch, or the Pig Palace. Fist fights were a daily occurrence in those saloons, and knifings and shootings happened with alarming regularity. The bar girls in those three saloons generally came from a whorehouse, the saloons being their last stop before they were no longer able to ply their profession.

There was one woman present at the meeting, and that was Annabelle O'Callahan. Annabelle was an attractive, and some said "feisty," redhead in her mid-twenties, who owned the Elite Shoppe, a dress-making shop in Shady Rest. Because she was a business owner, she was very active in the Shady Rest Merchants Association.

The first time she attended a meeting of the Merchants Association, Jacob Bramley, who had on that day made one of his rare appearances at the meetings, had protested.

"What's she doin' here, anyway? I mean, women can't even vote."

"We're not voting for the president, congress, or even the mayor," Annabelle had said. "We are discussing how to improve business for Shady Rest merchants, and that involves everyone who owns a business.

Now, if you don't want me to participate, I can always move my store outside the town limits, and pay no taxes at all to the town."

"Miss O'Callahan is right," Mayor Trout had said, defending her, and also the rather substantial municipal taxes she paid. "She has as much right to be here as any other legitimate businessman."

"Or business*woman,*" Annabelle had added. That had been two years ago. Now Annabelle was not only a regular attendee of the Merchants Association meetings, she was also a most welcome member, since she often came up with solutions to problems.

The problem they were discussing today, though, didn't seem to have an immediate solution. They were discussing the incident that had happened in the Crooked Branch earlier in the day, when the two young men who had been just passing through town had been shot dead.

"Gene, where are the bodies now?" Melton Milner asked. Milner owned the Milner Hotel.

"They are down at my place," Gene Ponder said. Ponder was the undertaker.

"Do you know who they are, or where they came from?"

"Foster said they called each other Pete and Johnny. He never heard their last

51

names, or where they came from."

"Did they have any money on them?" Roy Clinton asked. Clinton owned the apothecary.

Ponder shook his head. "They didn't have one thin dime," he said.

"Which is damn hard to figure out," Milner said. "I mean, those boys obviously weren't from around here, which means they were traveling. And who travels with no money at all?"

"If they didn't have any money, who's paying for the burying?" Gary Dupree asked. Dupree owned the emporium.

"Mayor Trout said I could sell their horses and tack. That will be enough to pay for the burying."

"That's right," Mayor Trout, who had been silent so far, said. "I told him he could sell the horses and tack. I got the approval of the city council."

"But, if we don't know who they are, or where they came from, we won't be able to contact their folks to tell them what happened," Annabelle said. "That's such a shame."

"They'll be but two more of more than a dozen just like 'em that we have in the graveyard," George Tobin pointed out. "Unknown, and unlamented."

The railroad having bypassed Shady Rest, their only connection with the outside world was the Shady Rest–to–Van Horn Stage-coach line. Tobin owned that stage line.

"Yes, well, that sort of brings us to the purpose of this meeting, doesn't it?" Hawkins said. "Did any of you read that article in the San Angelo newspaper last week?"

When no one spoke up, Hawkins pulled out the paper and read it to them. After he finished he looked back at the others.

"Deadliest town in America. Citizens, prisoners in their own homes," Hawkins said. "Is that the kind of reputation we want?"

"Of course not," Clinton answered. "But what is the solution? What can we do about it?"

"I have a suggestion as to what we can do about it," Hawkins said. "But the moment I make the suggestion, you people, and every-one in town, will think it is a self-serving suggestion."

"I know what you are going to say," Mil-ner said. "And you are right, it is what needs to be done. But you are also right, if you push closing down the other saloons, it will seem self-serving."

"It wouldn't be self-serving if I pushed for it," Annabelle said. "I think we should close those saloons, the dance halls, the gambling house, the prostitute cribs, and the two houses of prostitution. What do you think, Mayor?"

"I don't know that the city has any right to close them," Trout said. "They all have business licenses, and they pay their taxes on time. And where I might see closin' down Abby's Place, as far as Suzie's Dream House is concerned, well, the doc says she runs a clean house. He checks the girls regularly. Besides, Suzie doesn't allow any misbehaving in her house, not even drinking."

"What about the Chinaman?" Ponder asked.

"What about him?"

"He's runnin' a laundry. Does he have a business license?"

"He's using my license," Cook said. Earl Cook was the barber. "The building where he runs his laundry is right behind my barbershop, and I own it. That means my license is all he needs."

"Yeah, but a laundry isn't all he runs back there," Ponder said. "He's runnin' an opium den too."

"Yes," Mayor Trout said. "But at least the men who go back there to take the pipe just lie around without bothering anyone. There haven't been any killings in the opium dens."

"Mayor, when are we going to get another marshal?" Milner asked. "It's been some time now since Jarvis was killed, and we still don't have a marshal. You know, I know, and we all know, that Wash Prescott isn't up to the job. He's a pretty good deputy, but he's not a marshal."

"Nor does he want to be," Trout said. "But there is a young man who worked as a cowboy out at the Double R Ranch who has applied for the job. I talked to Mr. Richards about him. He said he's a good man."

"Who is it?" Hawkins asked. "I know just about all the cowboys."

"His name is Devry Pruitt."

"Richards is right, Pruitt is a good man. But he won't be a very effective marshal."

"Why do you say that, Gerald?" Tobin asked.

"Because he will be in way over his head," Hawkins said. "He's too young and too inexperienced to be able to handle the job."

"Yeah, well, Jarvis had been a deputy sheriff before. What good did his experience do him?" Dupree asked.

"I'm just telling you what I think," Hawkins said. "I don't believe young Pruitt will be able to handle the job."

"So what are you suggesting?" Trout asked. "You think we should just give up, do you?"

"No, I'm not suggesting that at all," Hawkins said. "But with only Wash Prescott to help him, I'm afraid we're just setting ourselves up to get another marshal killed."

CHAPTER FIVE

Big Rock, Colorado
When Matt Jensen stepped down from the train it was nearly midnight. Dark and cold, the little town of Big Rock, always a hotbed of activity during the day, was quiet and empty at this time of night.

Matt was here at the invitation of Smoke Jensen, and though he was expected tomorrow, he had taken advantage of an earlier train and a faster connection. Now he was alone on the depot platform and there was no one here to meet him. He watched as Spirit was off-loaded from the stock car, and he walked down to pat his horse on the neck.

"I know, I know," he said. "You're mad at me because you couldn't ride in the same car. But believe me, Spirit, you were a lot more comfortable than I was."

Behind him, the engineer blew his whistle twice, then opened his throttle to a thunderous expulsion of steam. The huge driver wheels spun on the track, sending out a shower of sparks until they gained traction; then with a series of jerks as the slack was taken up between the cars, the engine got on its way, puffing loudly as it did so.

As the train pulled out of the station, Matt watched the cars pass him by. Most of the windows were dark because at this hour, the passengers were trying to sleep. But the windows of the day cars were well lit, and here he could see the tired faces of passengers who were either unable or unwilling to pay for more comfortable accommodations. He smiled at the thought, because that was exactly how he had traveled, seeing no need to take a berth for only half a night.

"Matt Jensen," a friendly voice said. "It's good to see you back in Big Rock."

"Hello, Mr. Tinkham. I thought I'd visit with Smoke and Sally for a while."

"Well, I know they are going to enjoy your visit. Will you be riding out there tonight?"

"No, I thought I'd get a room for the rest of the night and go out there tomorrow."

"In that case, you'll be wantin' your horse looked after."

"Yes, if you don't mind."

"I don't mind at all," Anderson said. "It's always good to see you when you come to town. You just don't come often enough."

"I don't ever want to make a pest of myself."

"Believe me, you're never a pest, at least not to anyone that knows you. I hope you have a pleasant visit," he added as he led Spirit off.

Matt Jensen had been born Matthew Cavanaugh. He was ten years old when he killed his first man — one of the outlaws who had killed his parents and his sister. Orphaned, he soon wound up in the Soda Creek Home for Wayward Boys and Girls.

He escaped from the home a few years later, and was found in the mountains, half frozen to death. The man who found him was Smoke Jensen, and the legendary mountain man not only saved Matt's life, he raised him, and taught him how to ride, shoot, and track. But mostly, he taught Matt how to be a man, and a grateful Matt took Smoke Jensen's last name to honor his friend and mentor.

Then he used every skill Smoke taught him to track down, and bring to justice, the rest of the men who had killed his entire family. Since that time, Smoke and Sally Jensen had been Matt's family and, from time to time, he dropped in on them when he found it necessary to renew his soul.

59

Now, for no specific reason, felt like such a time.

"Ha!" Cal shouted. Another ringer!"

Matt was having a game of horseshoes with Cal and Pearlie.

"Let me see that horseshoe," Matt said. "I don't think that's a real horseshoe. I think it's a magnet."

"I knew it!" Pearlie said. "I knew it had to be somethin' like that for Cal to throw as many ringers as he does. He's been using magnets all this time."

"It's not magnet; it's magic," Cal said. He held his hand up and wiggled his fingers. "I've got magic in this hand, didn't you know that?"

Matt's toss landed on top of Cal's, and Pearlie laughed. "How about that, Cal? He just canceled you out."

"Yeah, well, his ringer don't count either," Cal said.

Inside the house Smoke had built, Sally was just finishing up dinner. Smoke was in the parlor, looking at a new stack of stereopticon photographs of Yellowstone National Park that Matt had brought as a gift to them. Matt had also brought a couple of new musical discs, and they were now playing

60

on the large mahogany, coiled spring-driven, disc-operated music box. The music it produced was full throated and vibrant, resonating throughout the room.

"Smoke," Sally said. "Would you like to call the boys?"

Smoke chuckled. "I don't think any of the three of them would appreciate being called boys," he said. "But they would appreciate being called to dinner."

Smoke put down the stereopticon, and stepped out onto the back porch to call in Matt, Pearlie, and Cal.

"Have you heard anything else about the man who killed your friends?" Smoke asked over dinner that evening. "What was his name? Mutt Crowley?"

"Yes, his name is Mutt Crowley, and no, it's been a year since he escaped, and I haven't heard another thing about him," Matt said. "And it still blisters my . . ." He paused and looked over at Sally. "Uh . . . blisters my you-know-what that he didn't hang for what he did."

"The word you are looking for is ass," Sally said easily. "Cal, would you pass the biscuits, please?"

"Yes, ma'am," Cal said with a smile.

"He'll turn up somewhere, Matt," Smoke

promised. "People like him don't have enough sense to stay out of trouble."

Monotony, Kansas
The sign at the edge of town read:

MONOTONY, KANSAS
Population 235
Gateway to the World

The gateway to the world referred to the fact that Monotony was a water stop on the Union Pacific Railroad. It was also a transfer point for funds being moved about by Wells Fargo, so that the small bank often had a great deal more money than anyone would suspect.

Today the bank had on deposit twelve thousand five hundred dollars, a temporary holding credit until the Wells Fargo stagecoaches would take varying amounts of money from the account to deliver to those banks that weren't on the railroad.

The greatest security in holding such funds lay in the secrecy of their operations. Any time there was to be a significant transfer of funds, only the shipper and receivers of the funds were aware of the transaction, though of course the railroad messenger also knew.

And it was the latter, the fact that the railroad messenger knew about the transfer of funds, that presented the fatal flaw in the operation. Because Dingus Perry, a railroad messenger, had recently sold the information for one hundred dollars. The purchasers of the information were the Crowley brothers, Prichard and Mutt, Mutt having joined his brother's gang shortly after Prichard helped him escape from prison.

Prichard and Mutt, along with four other men, Bill Carter, Lenny Fletcher, Dax Williams, and Titus Carmichael, rode into the little town of Monotony at just after nine o'clock in the morning. All six men were wearing long, tan dusters, though the dusters would not raise suspicion because such dusters were routinely worn against trail dust.

What was unusual was to see six men, total strangers, arrive in town at the same time. Monotony never had visitors except during those brief moments when the trains would stop to take on water, and the weary travelers at the windows would stare blankly at the lethargic scene before them.

"Titus, you stay down here at this end of the street," Prichard ordered. "When we leave, we'll be coming this way. I don't want to be surprised by having someone waiting down here to waylay us. Bill, you'll be holding the horses. Lenny, you and Dax will come into the bank with Mutt and me."

"You done told us all that a dozen times," Bill Carter said.

"And I'll tell you a dozen more times if that's what it takes," Prichard said. "When you undertake an operation like this, you must plan everything to perfection. You cannot afford to take any chances."

Titus dropped off as directed, while the remaining five men rode on down to a small brick building with a weathered sign identifying it as the Wells Fargo Bank of Monotony. There Prichard, Mutt, Lenny, and Dax dismounted, and handed the reins of their horses over to Bill. After looking up and down the street for a moment, Prichard nodded at the others, and the four men went into the bank. There were two men inside, a bank teller and a customer.

"Gentlemen, this is a robbery!" Prichard said in a low, and well-modulated voice. "You, sir," he said, pointing to the customer, "please step away from the counter."

"You," he said, as he handed a cloth bag to the teller. "I want you to put twelve thousand five hundred dollars in this sack."

"Twelve thousand five hundred dollars? Mister, maybe you didn't notice, but this is

64

a very small bank in a very small town. What makes you think we have that much money?"

"I don't think you have it, I know you have it," Prichard said. "It's the Wells Fargo transfer. Now fill up that bag as I instructed."

"Hey, Prichard, Mutt, there's someone ridin' up this way. What if he comes in?"

"Dax, you idiot! Don't use our names!" Mutt said, angrily. He turned back toward the teller. "Hurry it up."

The teller dropped several bound stacks of bills into the cloth bag, then handed it over to Prichard.

"All right, we got the money, let's go," Mutt said.

As Prichard and the others started toward the door, the teller suddenly pulled a shotgun out from under the window.

"He's got a gun!" Lenny shouted.

All four men turned their guns on the teller, and he went down under a barrage, unable to get off one shot.

"Son of a bitch! What did he do that for?" Mutt asked.

Prichard looked over at the lone customer. "I do hope you don't attempt anything like that. I assure you, it would be most disastrous for you."

"I don't even have a gun!" the customer shouted, holding his hands in the air.

From outside, the men heard the sound of gunfire and, rushing out of the bank, they saw that Bill was engaged with someone who was standing in the middle of the street. The man was wearing a badge.

"Shoot 'im, shoot 'im!" Mutt shouted, and again their guns roared, and the lawman went down.

Leaping into their saddles, the horses thundered out of town, the six robbers firing their pistols into the buildings on both sides of the street to discourage anyone from coming after them.

In Cates General Store, six-year-old Katie Holmes was standing next to her mother when a bullet from the gun of one of the fleeing bank robbers came through the front window. Katie fell to the floor with a bleeding chest wound.

"Katie!" her mother screamed in agonized sorrow.

Within moments, the six riders were clear of the town and were riding hard, having made their escape. The stunned town prepared to bury their dead.

BANK ROBBERY

Felons Take Thousands of Dollars

Culprits Said to Be Crowley Brothers

MONOTONY, KANSAS — On the fifteenth, the streets of the small railroad town of Monotony, Kansas, rang with gunfire as six men made good their escape. Behind them Oleg Simmons, the teller, Stewart Mason, the marshal, and Katie Holmes, a six-year-old girl, lay dead of gunshot wounds.

Eyewitnesses in the bank and on the street have identified two of the bank robbers as the Crowley brothers, Prichard and Mutt. The four others with them have not been identified. Prichard is the older of the two Crowley brothers and, unlike so many others who share his chosen profession, is a very well-educated man. He is sometimes referred to as "The Bandit Professor," and is known for his precise use of the English language.

Despite Prichard Crowley's education, grammatical skills, and trappings of a gentleman, he has proven himself to be a man who is totally devoid of any redemptive qualities. He has used the gun with deadly efficiency and is known to have killed at least three men prior to the recent bank robbery.

Mutt Crowley, the younger of the two brothers, was previously convicted and sentenced to be hanged by a court in Colorado. Shortly before the hanging was to take place, however, he escaped. It is now believed, though not known for a fact, that his escape was facilitated by his brother, Prichard.

Within a week of the robbery, wanted posters were issued.

WANTED
DEAD OR ALIVE
$5,000 DOLLAR REWARD
will be paid for
MUTT CROWLEY
5'4" tall, scar through left eyelid

Rewards were also offered for "anyone who it could be proved was with the Crowley brothers during the perpetration of the bank robbery." As none of the other perpetrators were known, they weren't named, and the reward for each of them was limited to fifteen hundred dollars. Though only the state could issue the wanted posters, the reward money was being offered by Wells Fargo. And, though the total reward money offered exceeded the amount of money stolen, it was the policy of Wells Fargo to offer large rewards for the capture of anyone who stole from them. This was done to discourage would-be robbers from targeting Wells Fargo and, for the most part, it was an effective ploy as Wells Fargo shipments were much less frequently robbed than other banks and money transfer agencies.

Initially, however, circulation of the reward posters was limited to within the borders of the state of Kansas.

When Prichard made the division of the money he and Mutt took two thousand five hundred dollars apiece, and he gave each of the other four men one thousand eight hundred and seventy-five dollars each.

"I think me 'n you should get three thousand dollars each, and let the others divide up what is left," Mutt suggested.

"No, as long as everything is kept on the up and up, we will forever have the loyalty of those who ride with us. And in this business, loyalty of the men who ride with you is the most valuable commodity."

Prichard tended to think and talk in a way that Mutt often found difficult to comprehend. That was because Mutt had spent five years in the state penitentiary at Canon City, Colorado, while Prichard had spent four years at the University of Colorado. When he graduated with a Bachelor of Arts degree, he took a job as an assistant professor of English in a small college in Wyoming.

It was there that Prichard had discovered the dark side of himself, a side that he could not control. He lured a pretty young freshman into his office one night, with the offer to provide private tutorship. There, he raped and murdered her; then he left her body on the side of a lake.

The murder of the young girl remained a mystery, and Prichard was never suspected. When the bodies of two more young women were found, the town became panicked at the thought of a crazed killer and despoiler of young women. And because the last two women were not college students, no connection was made that could lead anyone to suspect young, handsome Professor Prichard Crowley.

After only one year of teaching in the university, Prichard left the school and got a job in the Denver Loan and Trust bank. It was the "trust" part that did him in, because less than three months into the job, he decided to augment his salary by embezzling fifteen thousand dollars. From that moment on, Prichard was on the outlaw trail.

CHAPTER SIX

After he left Sugarloaf, Matt Jensen wandered around a bit until he found himself in West Texas. For days he had been riding through unremarkable country, but now the Guadalupe Mountains rose ahead of him, the purple mass coming up from the earth like islands rising from the sea.

With a carpet of grass and the dappled shade of live oak, cedar, and ash trees to keep him out of the sun's glare, Matt found the area to be more reminiscent of Colorado and Wyoming than Texas.

When he made camp that evening, a rabbit came out from under a mesquite bush, sniffed the air for a scent of danger, then began nibbling on some grass. Matt shot, skinned, cleaned, and then spitted the rabbit, cooking it over an open fire. He watched it brown as his stomach growled with hunger. The rabbit was barely cooked before he took it off the skewer and began eating it ravenously, not even waiting for it to cool.

At dawn the next day the notches of the hills before him were touched with the dove-gray of early morning. Shortly thereafter, a golden fire spread over the mountaintops, then filled the sky with light and color, waking all the creatures below. He heard the staccato hammering of a woodpecker, the yelping back and forth of coyotes, and the scream of a cougar. High overhead, a hawk was making lazy circles.

Matt rolled out of his blanket and began digging through his saddlebag of possibles for coffee, but found none. He would have enjoyed a biscuit, but he had no flour. He had no beans either, and was out of salt. The bacon had been used up a long time ago. It was now clear that he was going to have to go into town sometime in the next few days to replenish his supplies.

Shady Rest

Annabelle wasn't a member of the city council, but as a representative of the Merchants Association, she was able to sit in on the meetings, and she was present on the day Devry Pruitt was sworn in as the new town marshal.

"You have quite a job cut out for you, Marshal Pruitt," Mayor Trout said. "Conditions over on Plantation Row are practically out of hand now."

"Not practically out of hand, they are out of hand," Earl Cook said.

"The tactless side of me would say that Plantation Row has been very good for my business," Ponder said. "Though, since the last seven burials have been at the expense of the town, I have to say I'm not making that much out of it."

"Yes, paid for by the town," Mayor Trout said. "And that is beginning to be quite a problem. Our tax base is barely able to keep up with the expense of all these burials."

"Ah, there is a possible solution to our problem," George Tobin said.

"What?"

"Suppose we charge the businesses that are down in Plantation Row a special tax, a tax higher than we charge any other business in town? That will do two things. It will help pay the cost of all the burials, and it might even be so burdensome to them as to make them shut down."

"Can we do that?" Martin Peabody asked. "Charge them an extra tax, I mean."

"What about it, Mr. Dempster? You're the city attorney. Can we?" Mayor Trout asked.

"Well, we could charge an excise tax on the sale of liquor, gambling, and whoring,"

Dempster said. "To be honest, if it is challenged though, the state might not allow it, especially if it is applied only to Plantation Row, which it would have to be, otherwise Gerald Hawkins would have to pay it as well. And he hasn't really given us any trouble."

"He doesn't have whores in his place," Peabody said.

"No, but I do sell liquor, and while I didn't use to have gambling, I do now, ever since Emerson Culpepper arrived."

"Maybe we can find some way to exempt you from the excise tax," Milner suggested.

"I don't see how," Hawkins replied. "If you charge the people on Plantation Row an excise tax, Mr. Dempster is right, you're going to have to charge me as well."

"I have a suggestion," Dupree said. "We don't have a courthouse, and the few times we've had a trial, we've had to find a place to hold them. Suppose the city were to lease the Texas Star Saloon to serve as a courthouse when needed. And the lease payment will exactly equal the excise tax. That way, it will be a wash."

"What do you say, Mr. Hawkins?" Mayor Trout asked. "Would you be willing to rent your place to the city for special occasions?"

75

"I would be honored to do so," Hawkins replied.

"Then yes," Dempster said with a broad smile. He nodded enthusiastically. "Yes, that's the way we will handle it."

Shortly after the meeting of the city council, Jacob Bramley, in the far end of town, called a meeting of the other businessmen, and women, of Plantation Row. Fred Foster was there for the Crooked Branch; so was Red Gimlin from the Ace High. There was also a representative from the dance hall, and one from the gambling house. Abby Dolan of Abby's Place was there too. Abby weighed about two hundred and fifty pounds, and she sat there, smoking a cigar and fanning herself, her frizzy blond hair sticking out in all directions.

"What'd you call the meeting for, Jacob?" Foster wanted to know.

"I called this meeting to discuss the excise tax the city has placed on us."

"Yeah," Gimlin said. "What are we going to do about that?"

"There's not much we can do but pay it," Foster said.

"I think the time has come for us to organize," Bramley said.

"Organize what?" Gimlin asked.

"Organize ourselves. The town of Shady Rest has a city council, and it has a Merchants Association, but neither one of them meet our needs. And let's face it, this excise tax is just a start. You know damn well if they could find a way to close us down, they would."

"How are they going to do that? We have licenses, we pay municipal taxes. We are legal."

"About these excise taxes," Gimlin said. "I don't think that's anything to worry about. I don't think any of the merchants of the town will put up with having their taxes raised."

"They won't be getting their taxes raised," Bramley explained. "Just the businesses on Plantation Row."

"What? How can they do that? Abby asked.

"Because the new taxes will be applied only to the sale of liquor, to gambling, and to whoring. And that gets all of us."

"All right, what do you propose we do to stop them?"

"At the moment, I don't have any idea. That's why I called this meeting. I think that if we organized ourselves, maybe into something like the Plantation Row Citizens' Betterment Council, we might be able to come up with a way to fight it. But for now, the most important thing for us to do is to form the council."

"All right," Gimlin said. "I'm in."

"Me too," Foster said.

"Count me in as well," Abby said.

"Who's going to be the head of it?" Foster asked.

"Bramley thought of it, I say it should be him," Gimlin suggested.

"So do I," Abby put in quickly.

"All right, Bramley, you're the man," Foster said. "So, come up with something."

"I'll work on it. I'll have a suggestion next time we meet."

Mutt Crowley did not come to Shady Rest alone. Bill Carter and Lenny Fletcher had come with him. Since the bank robbery in Monotony, Kansas, they had spent their money on expensive food and liquor, expensive whores, and even more expensive games of chance. When they arrived in Shady Rest, they were down to just a couple hundred dollars each.

They were spending almost all their time in one saloon or another. At first, they split their time among three of the four saloons in town, generally avoiding the Texas Star. They had tried the Texas Star, but the problem, as far as Crowley, Fletcher, and Carter were concerned, was that the women were "bar girls" only. They would drink and provide company for the men, but they let it be known from the outset that they weren't prostitutes, and no amount of money any of the three men offered them would make them change their minds.

Mutt Crowley was well aware that he was a wanted man, so when he arrived in Shady Rest, he took the name of Dale Morgan. Bill Carter and Lenny Fletcher, who had not been identified for their parts in the Kansas bank robbery and murders, did not find it necessary to change their names.

The fact that the bar girls at the Texas Star weren't prostitutes wasn't the only reason the three men no longer frequented the Texas Star. They hadn't been barred from coming back, but none of the women, and very few of the patrons, would have anything to do with them. Now, they spent all their time on Plantation Row, and though they did occasionally visit the Crooked Branch and Ace High, the Pig Palace had become their saloon of choice.

Because they had been warned by Prichard to stay out of trouble, the three men did nothing to raise anyone's suspicions. However, the very fact that they did "nothing" is what did raise the suspicions of many.

"What the hell do them boys do?" Doomey asked. Doomey, who was a frequent patron of the Pig Palace, worked at the feed and seed store. "I mean, no matter when I come in here I see 'em in here, either drinkin', or playin' cards, or sportin' with one of the women. But I ain't never seen a one of 'em do the first lick of work. Where do they get their money?"

"I've seen men like them before," a cowboy named Seymour replied. "More'n likely they was workin' in one of the mines up in Nevada or California or some such place. Them mines pay real good money, and lots of folks just work hard, save up their money, then go spend it."

"Yeah, I reckon so," Doomey agreed. "I mean, it ain't like they're spendin' a whole lot. It just seems peculiar that they don't never do nothin' to earn what little bit of money they are spendin'."

"Well, it don't seem to bother Bramley none that they are here all the time," Doomey said.

Seymour chuckled. "Why should it? Hell, they're spendin' money with him, ain't they?"

Mayor Trout was not only a supporter of

Annabelle's right to belong to the Shady Rest Merchants Association, his wife was also one of Annabelle's best customers. The mayor planned to attend an upcoming political conference at the state capital in Austin, and that meant a formal ball. Despite the fact that she had a closet full of dresses and fancy gowns, Lillian Trout insisted that she had "nothing to wear," so she came to the Elite Shoppe to ask Annabelle if she could do something to alleviate her desperate, bereft situation.

"Why of course, Mrs. Trout, I'll do whatever I can for you. What seems to be the trouble?"

"I want you to sew for me the most beautiful gown you have ever made," she said. "Everyone in Austin is so snooty, I'm sure they think that anyone who doesn't live in Austin must wear dresses made of flour sacks."

"It will be the most beautiful," Annabelle promised. "And I can't think of anyone more beautiful to wear it."

Lillian Trout blushed under the compliment. "Cost is not a consideration," she said, and Annabelle smiled, because that was exactly the response she wanted her comment to elicit.

Annabelle O'Callahan was looked up to

81

by everyone in Shady Rest. In addition to being an excellent seamstress, she was also a very good businesswoman. She was so skilled and so at home in running a business that everyone who knew her was certain that she had a sound business background, perhaps in some family business. That was because everyone who knew her only thought they knew her. The truth was, they didn't know her at all, and the first mistake they made about her was thinking that they actually knew her name.

When she first arrived in Shady Rest to begin her business, she had introduced herself as Annabelle O'Callahan, but that was a deception. Her real name was Kathleen Murphy. She had taken the name Annabelle from Edgar Allan Poe's poem of the same name.

It was many and many a year ago,
In a kingdom by the sea,
That a maiden there lived whom you may
    know
By the name of ANNABEL LEE;
And this maiden she lived with no other
    thought
Than to love and be loved by me.

O'Callahan had been the name of a green

grocer in the Philadelphia neighborhood where her grandmother had lived.

Annabelle's (Kathleen's) mother had died when she was fourteen years old, and her father remarried. Less than six months after he remarried, her father was killed in a railroad accident and her stepmother, who "couldn't deal with a fifteen-year-old girl," sent her to Philadelphia to live with Mrs. Alice Grayson, her maternal grandmother.

The old lady was thrilled to have Kathleen live with her, because when her only daughter, Kathleen's mother, had died, Mrs. Grayson had thought she would be cut off from her grandchild forever. It turned out to be a wonderful experience. Her grandmother sent Kathleen to a finishing school, and introduced her to Philadelphia society. She also taught Kathleen how to sew, intending it to be an "acceptable" hobby for a woman of substance. Kathleen loved her grandmother and, more important, knew that her grandmother loved her.

Not once during the six years she was in Philadelphia did her stepmother ever come to visit her, though she did get frequent letters from her. Her stepmother lived in Kansas City, Kansas, and the letters were filled with the most wonderful descriptions of the hotel she had bought with the life insurance Kathleen's father had provided. The letters often included vignettes about some of her guests.

Then, in Kathleen's last few months of school, her grandmother died. Kathleen was heartsick over the loss of her grandmother, but she learned, to her surprise, that her grandmother had left everything to her. The total amount of money, after she sold the house, came to almost seven thousand dollars.

Kathleen returned to Kansas City, intending to live with her stepmother until she found a position and a place of her own. She had not yet told her stepmother of the inheritance, deciding she would surprise her.

But the surprise was Kathleen's, because when she got to Kansas City she learned that the hotel wasn't a hotel at all. It was a rather high-class brothel.

"You will be my prize attraction," her stepmother told her. "You are beautiful, and I know of at least five very important and very wealthy men who will get into a bidding war. Someone is going to pay a great deal of money for the opportunity to be the first one to . . ." The woman paused and flashed a twisted smile. "Deflower you."

"No! I won't do it!" Kathleen said. "What

would my father think about such a thing?"

"Don't be so high and mighty," her step-mother said. "How do you think I met your father?"

"I won't do it," Kathleen said. "Tomorrow, I will move out of the hotel, and we can each go our own way."

That night, without Kathleen's knowledge, her stepmother held the auction anyway, and sent the winner into Kathleen's room to "claim his right."

In the struggle that ensued, Kathleen hit the man with an andiron. Without stopping to see whether he was dead or alive, she got dressed quickly, then climbed out the window with only the dress she was wearing, and the seven thousand dollars in cash.

That was the night Kathleen Murphy "died," and Annabelle O'Callahan was born.

That was three years ago, and to date, Annabelle still didn't know if she had killed him or not. Not, in all that time, had she ever made any effort to reestablish contact with her stepmother. And why should she? As far as she knew, Annabelle O'Callahan had not one relative in the world.

CHAPTER SEVEN

Pecos, Texas

Prichard Crowley had gone first to San Francisco, where he spent heavily, staying in the bests hotels and dining in the finest restaurants. On the night that he'd planned to be his last night in San Francisco, he took a young, female violinist to dinner.

"My dear, your playing tonight was absolutely brilliant," Prichard said. "You played with . . . how can I express this? With seductive warmth and richness, not so much technically as interpretively, and with an introspective lyricism."

The young woman glowed under the compliments, and when Prichard reached across the table to take her hand, she offered no resistance.

At midnight, as Prichard waited for the train, he had a hard time controlling the excitement that still coursed through his body, remembering the thrill he'd felt as he took the young woman, then killed her. He'd left her body in the alley behind his hotel. He would be gone before the San Francisco police could find her, and it would go down as just another of San Francisco's unsolved murders.

After the bank robbery, the Crowley gang had left Kansas and gone to California where they'd spent nearly all their money; then they'd left California for Texas. Mutt decided to go to Shady Rest while Prichard chose Pecos, which wasn't too far away. Prichard and Mutt also took on assumed names — Mutt would call himself Dale Morgan, and Prichard would adopt the name Abe Conner. That way, they would be able to keep in touch with each other.

When Prichard Crowley rode into Pecos, Texas, he found it to be full of activity and, like ants at a picnic, cowboys were everywhere. He reined up in front of a saloon, but as he dismounted he didn't notice that a young cowboy was crossing the street right behind him. His dismount caused the cowboy to have to step away, and when he did, he stepped directly into a pile of horse dropping. There was a young woman who was crossing the street with him, and she managed to avoid it.

"Hey, mister, look what you just made me do!" the cowboy complained.

"You have my apologies, sir. It was unintentional," Prichard said.

"Yeah? Well your apology ain't good enough," the young cowboy said. He held his soiled boot out. "Get down there and clean it off."

The girl with the cowboy saw the danger in Prichard's eyes before the cowboy did, and she reacted to it by pulling on his arm. "Come on, Teddy, don't make such a stink over it. Let's go. I'll clean your boot for you. There's only a little on it anyway."

"No," Teddy said, obviously trying to make a show of it in front of the people who, having heard the agitation in Teddy's voice, had stopped to see what was going on. "This saddle tramp is the one who messed up my boot. He is the one who is going to clean it off."

Prichard made no reply. Instead, he tied his horse off at the hitching rail.

"Maybe you didn't hear me, mister. I'm talking to you."

Prichard stared directly at the young cowboy.

"Young man, you are beginning to grow tiresome. You would be well advised to take the young lady's advice and let this issue drop."

"You would like that, wouldn't you? You are a coward and you want me to just go away. Well, I'm not going away. I'm calling you out!" the young cowboy said, his voice cracking in anger.

"Are you now? Are you that anxious to die?" Prichard's voice, in direct contrast to that of the young cowboy's was exceptionally calm.

If the cowboy didn't sense the danger, the young woman with him did, and again, she reached out to put her hand on Teddy's arm. "No, wait, Teddy please!" the young girl pleaded, her voice now on the verge of panic. "Let it be."

"Young lady, if you and your young man will just walk away, this will all be over," Prichard said.

"Don't be talkin' to my sister. She ain't the one you got to worry about. I am."

"You mean the young lady is your sister?"

"Yes, not that it's any of your business."

"Evidently your sister is the only one in your family who has any sense," Prichard said. "You had better listen to her, sonny."

"Don't call me sonny, you son of a bitch!" Teddy reached down to put his hand on the butt of his pistol. "Now I'm going to give

89

you one last chance. I'm going to count to three. You either apologize and clean off my boot, or go for your gun. I don't care which."

"Teddy, no!" the young woman said, her words now on the verge of a scream.

"Lucy, you get on out of the way," Teddy said, waving her away.

"Teddy, please!"

"Miss Lucy, you'd better get on over here," one of the onlookers said. "It don't look to me like Teddy's goin' to back down."

"Teddy, I beg of you," Lucy said. Again she reached for him, but this time Teddy shrugged her off, then pushed her away. The man who had spoken took hold of her, and pulled her out of harm's way.

"What's it going to be, mister?" Teddy said to Prichard. "Are you going to clean off my boot? Or do I start counting?"

"I've already apologized, and I shall do so again," Prichard said. "But I've no intention of cleaning your boot. So if that is the only thing that can interrupt this *danse de la mort* you have initiated, then I suggest you start counting," Prichard said, calmly.

Teddy blinked a couple of times; then a small patina of sweat broke out across his upper lip. It was as if, until that moment, he had thought he could bluff his way through.

Now he realized that this man couldn't be bluffed. He knew, also, that he couldn't take him. But that realization had come too late. It was impossible for him to back out of it now, without spending the rest of his life in shame.

Teddy licked his lips a couple of times; then, with a voice that had none of the thunder or bluster it had had before, he began counting.

"One," he said. He paused, then said, "Two." After the word two, he paused for a long time, hoping, somehow, that the man would stop it. But the man continued to look at him with a cold, unblinking stare.

"Three," Teddy said, starting his draw even as he said the word.

Although Teddy had never been in a gunfight before, he was pretty fast with a gun, and had often practiced his fast draw. He also had the advantage in that he started his draw first, so that he actually had his gun out, and leveled before Prichard drew his. Realizing that he had won the draw, he smiled and hesitated. Surely, seeing that he was covered, the other man wouldn't continue with the fight.

But Teddy had underestimated Prichard's cold detachment. Where Teddy would hesitate before killing a man, Prichard had no

91

such compunction. Prichard pulled his gun and fired.

The bullet plunged into Teddy's chest, and his eyes opened in shock that such a thing could have actually happened to him. He dropped his gun, then fell back onto the boardwalk.

"Teddy!" Lucy shouted and, pulling away from the person who tried to hold her back, she rushed to her brother's side, reaching him just as he took his last, gasping breath.

"Miss, I'm very sorry about all this," Prichard said. "I want it well understood that I did all I could to avoid this fight."

"What's your name, mister?" The question was asked by the same man who had held Lucy back from the fight.

"The name is Conner," Prichard said. "Abe Conner."

Prichard put his pistol in his holster, then walked into the Silver Spur Saloon. The saloon had been practically emptied when everyone ran outside to see what the gunshot was about. Now they all went back inside to get a closer look at this man who had only today arrived in town, and had already shot and killed one of their citizens.

"I would like a whiskey, please," Prichard said, his words as devoid of any sense of excitement, fright, or remorse, as if he had just stepped in uneventfully.

The bartender, who had moved to the window to watch the action when all his customers left the saloon, served the whiskey without comment. A moment later a man wearing a badge came in and, seeing Prichard at the bar, walked over to him.

"I'm Sheriff Nelson," he said.

"It's very good to meet you, Sheriff Nelson. I'm Abe Conner. Won't you join me for a drink? Bartender?"

"No," Sheriff Nelson said, holding his hand out to stop the drink from being poured. "Mr. Conner, you just killed a man."

"Yes, I'm afraid I did. It was most unfortunate, but as I am sure that any of those who witnessed it will attest, I had no choice. I was literally forced into a kill-or-be-killed moment, despite repeated efforts on my part to defuse the situation."

"The stranger is right, Sheriff, I seen ever' thing," one of the saloon patrons said. "This here feller tried his damndest to keep it from happenin'. He even apologized to the Rogers boy."

"How about the rest of you?" Sheriff Nelson asked. "Did any of you see it?"

Nearly everyone else in the saloon testified as to having witnessed the shooting, and to a man, they all said that the gunfight had been forced by Teddy Rogers, and that Abe Conner was innocent of any wrongdoing.

Over the next several days, Prichard began to make himself at home in Pecos. He sent a wreath of flowers to the funeral of Teddy Rogers, and made a point of apologizing to Lucy.

"I want you to know how much I regret that the — disagreement that developed between your brother and me got so quickly out of hand."

Prichard's apparent contrition for what had happened to Teddy, his gentlemanly behavior, and his soft-spoken manner quickly won the respect of the townspeople. Within a couple of weeks after he arrived in town he was having his dinner when Sheriff Nelson of Pecos County came into the restaurant. Prichard saw the sheriff inquire at the counter, and he saw the clerk pointing toward him.

The sheriff was coming after him! What had happened? Had he gotten word from Kansas? Slowly, and without being observed, Prichard pulled his pistol from its holster and held it under the table. If the sheriff attempted to arrest him, Prichard would kill him.

The sheriff nodded at the clerk, then started toward Prichard's table. Prichard debated whether or not he should shoot the sheriff even before he reached the table. Slowly, quietly, he pulled the hammer back and turned the pistol slightly, so that it was aimed squarely at the sheriff.

The sheriff was smiling as he approached.

"Mr. Conner?"

That was good. He had called him Conner, and the smile appeared to be friendly rather than triumphant.

"Yes?"

"I would like to talk to you. Would you mind if I joined you?"

"What would be the subject of our conversation?" Prichard said. Then he added, "But please do have a seat."

Prichard managed to slip his pistol back into its holster without its presence being noticed.

"I've been watching you, Mr. Conner. And I've had others watching you as well."

"Oh?"

"Yes, I thought it best to see how the town was taking to you before I made the offer. I wanted to see if there was anyone holdin' it against you by you killin' Teddy Rogers. And, since there doesn't seem to be, I feel I can make the offer without any reservations."

"You are confusing me, Sheriff Nelson. What offer would that be?"

"I would like to appoint you to the position of deputy sheriff of Pecos County."

The offer completely shocked Prichard and he almost laughed out loud. Then, before giving away his reaction, he asked, "Why?"

"Well, sir, it's very obvious that you can handle a gun, Nearly the entire town saw your encounter with young Teddy Rogers."

Prichard shook his head. "I'm not proud of that, Sheriff. The boy pushed me into it — it actually reached the point of my life or his. I tried to dissuade him as witnesses will attest, and . . ."

Sheriff Nelson held out his hand.

"Please, Mr. Conner, there was absolutely nothing implied in that remark. I'm merely stating that as validation for extending the offer. I'm afraid the county can't pay much, but we can furnish you with a room in the back of the sheriff's office, and we have a contract with Kirby's Café to furnish you all of your meals."

Prichard's first reaction was to turn the offer down, but as he thought about it, he realized that having a position in the sheriff's office would put him on the inside. If any information, such as wanted circulars or physical descriptions, should come in to the sheriff's office, he would be well situated to take care of it.

Prichard chuckled.

"You are laughing, sir, but I am quite serious."

"I am laughing, Sheriff, because I never saw myself as a peace officer, but, yes, I think I will accept your offer. Maybe my serving as a deputy sheriff will go a long way in mitigating the unfortunate circumstances of my arrival."

Sheriff Nelson laughed out loud.

"I'll say this for you, Conner. You have one hell of a way of talking. I don't think I've ever heard anyone who wasn't a college professor, or something, talk the way you do. You're going to give the sheriff's office a lot of class. How about coming over to the office after you finish your meal, and I'll swear you in?"

"I'll be there," Prichard promised.

When Prichard showed up at the sheriff's office a short while later he saw several others there as well. Sheriff Nelson identified them as the mayor, the judge, and the city attorney. The judge administered the oath of office; then the others offered their congratulations.

Smiling, Prichard pinned on the star of his office. Then, after an introductory stroll around town, during which he met the businessmen of the city, he stopped by the telegraph office to send a message to his brother in Shady Rest.

TO DALE MORGAN
HAVE ACCEPTED POSITION AS
DEPUTY SHERIFF IN PECOS
COUNTY TEXAS STOP WILL EN-
DEAVOR TO DO MY BEST TO KEEP
THE PEACE STOP

ABE CONNER

The telegram sent, Prichard continued his introductory stroll through the town, opening doors for women, greeting the men, and being friendly with the children.

"The best thing ever to happen to us was getting Abe Conner as our deputy," Paul Peters, the banker, said.

"He is such a gentleman," Miss Margrabe, the schoolteacher told her friends. "And, so handsome," she added with a little self-conscious laugh.

"But, don't forget, he did kill young Teddy Rogers," Sally White said.

"Everyone, just everyone, says that he had

no choice, that he was forced into it," Miss Margrabe said. "They say that he has apologized to the Rogers family, and I just know he feels very bad about what happened."

"Why, Margaret, you sound as if you are setting your cap for him," Sally teased.

"So what if I am? He is an educated man. And while I don't want to sound snobbish, there are precious few eligible, educated men in Pecos."

"Have you forgotten the terms of your contract? You are a schoolteacher. You can't be married, nor even be seen with a man."

"I don't intend to be a schoolteacher forever," Margaret replied.

Sally laughed. "You are, aren't you? You are setting your cap for the new deputy sheriff."

"I'm sure he won't be a deputy sheriff forever. Anyone can see that he is much too intelligent for that."

CHAPTER EIGHT

Shady Rest

Crowley, Fletcher, and Carter were playing cards at the Pig Palace when a boy of about sixteen, wearing a Western Union cap, came into the saloon.

"Morgan? Mr. Dale Morgan? Is there someone here named Dale Morgan?" the boy called out.

Crowley was studying his hand, and made no reaction to the telegrapher's shout.

"Morgan? I have a telegram for someone named Dale Morgan."

"That's you," Fletcher said, poking Crowley.

"What's me?"

"That Western Union boy is callin' for Morgan. That's you, don't you remember?"

"Oh, yeah," Crowley said. He looked toward the door, just as the delivery boy was about to leave.

"Wait a minute, boy," he called. "I'm Morgan."

The telegraph delivery boy stopped, and turned back. "You got any proof of that, mister? I can't give out telegrams to just anyone."

"These two men know me. They'll tell you."

"Yeah," Fletcher said. "He's Morgan."

The boy came over to hand the piece of paper to Crowley; then he stood by the table for a moment.

"What are you standin' there for?" Crowley asked.

"Most of the time when I deliver a telegram, why, the person that gets it gives me a tip," the boy said.

"A what?"

"A tip." The boy was surprised to see that Crowley apparently didn't know what he was talking about.

"Don't you know what a tip is?"

"No, what is it?"

"It means you give me money for delivering the telegram to you."

"What for? I didn't ask for the telegram."

"It's just what folks do," the boy said, realizing that he was fighting a losing battle.

"Did whoever send this telegram to me pay for it?"

"Yes, sir, of course they did. It would not have been sent, otherwise."

"Then go away. You got your money."

The boy glared at Crowley for a moment, then left.

"Who sent you a telegram?" Carter asked.

"I don't reckon I'm goin' to know that until I open it."

Opening the telegram, Crowley read it; then he laughed out loud. "I'll be damned."

"What is it?"

Crowley showed the telegram to the other two.

"My brother's a lawman!" He laughed again. "Can you beat that?"

West Texas

It was midday when Matt approached the little town. Stopping on a ridge, he looked down at the town as he removed his canteen from the saddle pommel. The water was tepid and had a strong undertaste, but he had been sweating under the blows of the sun and knew that he needed to replace the fluid he had lost.

Matt was here simply because he had no particular place to be, other than the place he was. That meant he could, and should, go south in the winter, and north in the summer. So, why was he here in Texas in the summer, when he could have been in Montana?

He chuckled as he thought of the answer. He was here, because south was the way his horse had been headed when he left the last town.

Slapping his legs against the side of his horse he headed the animal down the long slope of the ridge, wondering what town this was.

A small sign just on the edge of town answered the question for him.

SHERWOOD
Population 103
STILL GROWING

The weathered board and faded letters of the sign indicated that it had been there for some time. Matt doubted that there were a hundred and three residents in the town today, and despite the optimistic tone of the sign, he would bet anything that the town was not growing.

False-fronted shanties lined each side of the street, straggling along for no more than fifty yards. Then, just as abruptly as the town started, it quit, and the prairie began again.

The buildings were weathered and leaning, and the painted signs on front of the edifices were worn and hard to read. An empty wagon, its wood baked white in the sun, was backed up to the general store, and the attached team of mules stood unmoving in front of it.

Matt dismounted in front of a saloon called the Watering Hole, and went inside. Shadows made the saloon seem cooler, but that was illusory. It was nearly as hot inside as out, and without the benefit of a breath of air it was even more stifling. The customers were sweating in their drinks and wiping their faces with bandanas.

As always when he entered a strange saloon, Matt checked the place out. To one unfamiliar with what he was doing, Matt's glance appeared to be little more than idle curiosity. But it was a studied surveillance that he'd learned long ago from his mentor, Smoke Jensen, and he could hear Smoke's voice now.

"Take a look around to see who is armed, and what kind of gun they're carrying," he said. "Look at how they're wearing their guns — you can tell a lot by that. Also check to see if there's anyone that you might know, but what's even more important than that, study the faces to see if anyone recognizes you. What do you read in their faces? Is it someone

who might want to settle some old score, real or imagined, for himself or a friend?"

As far as Matt could determine, there were only workers and cowboys here, all but two of them unarmed. The two who were armed were young men, and Matt was sure they were wearing their guns as much for show as anything. He would bet that they had never used them for anything but target practice, and probably not very successfully at that.

The bartender stood behind the bar. In front of him were two glasses in which some whiskey was remaining, and he poured the whiskey back into a bottle, corked it, and put the bottle on the shelf behind the bar. He wiped the glasses out with his stained apron, then set them among the unused glasses. Seeing Matt step up to the bar, the bartender moved down toward him.

"Whiskey," Matt said.

The barman reached for the bottle he had just poured the whiskey back into, but Matt pointed to an unopened bottle.

"That one.

"Mister, I ain't goin' to open a new bottle just for you," the bartender said.

Matt saw that there was a beer barrel sitting on a pair of sawhorses behind the bar.

"All right," he said. "I'll have a beer."

105

Shrugging, the saloonkeeper took down a mug and started toward the beer spigot.

"Wait a minute," Matt said. "Let me check that mug."

"You're kind of particular, ain't you?" the bartender asked, handing the mug to Matt.

Matt looked at it, took a deep sniff, then handed it back to him. "All right."

The bartender drew the mug of beer, then set it in front of Matt.

"Ain't seen you before," the bartender said. "Just come into town, did you?"

"I'm not in town," Matt said as he paid for the beer. "I'm just passing through. Thought I'd have a couple of drinks, eat some food that isn't trail-cooked, then be on my way."

"What brings you to this neck of the woods?" the barkeep asked.

"Nothing in particular," Matt said.

A man who was standing at the other end of the bar looked over toward Matt.

"I don't think you're goin' to like it here, mister. I think you're goin' to find that things here is just a little too quick for your kind. You'd best just keep on movin'." The comment was low and sneering.

Paying no attention to the comment, Matt lifted the beer to his lips. Taking a swallow, he wiped the foam from his mouth with the back of his hand.

"Is there a place to eat in this town?"

"There's Kate's Place just down the street. Nothin' fancy, but the food is good," the bartender said.

"Good is good," Matt said.

"Hey, mister, are you deef?" the man at the far end of bar asked. "I said you'd best just be movin' on."

Matt turned to look at him for the first time. He was a big man, well over six feet tall, with a dark, bushy beard. Matt figured that he weighed at least two hundred and fifty pounds.

"Mister, you seem to have something stuck in your craw," Matt said. "What would that be?"

"I don't like saddle bums," the bushy-bearded man said.

"Waters, you got no call to ride one of my customers like that," the bartender said. "He ain't done nothin' but buy a beer, which he paid for."

"I know his kind. I seen 'em before, back when I was workin' as a bum chaser for the T and P. Bummin' rides on the cars, they was. Hell, I've lost count of the number of 'em I've thrown off the cars between Shreveport and El Paso."

Matt picked up his beer and held it toward

Waters. "Here's to you, Mr. Waters, for keeping the railroad safe."

"I don't drink with no-'count bums like you," Waters said.

"I'm not sure I understand," Matt replied. "Is it that you don't drink with any no-account bums? Or is it that you don't drink with no-account bums like me?"

The others in the saloon laughed, and Waters, realizing that they were laughing at him, grew very angry. He pointed at Matt.

"I don't like you, mister," he said. "I don't like you at all."

"I guess that means you won't be asking me to the barn dance. And I was so looking forward to it."

Again, the others in the saloon laughed.

"Waters, you was sayin' things here is a little too quick for this fella. Looks to me like he's a little too quick for you," one of the bar patrons said.

Waters, his face flushed red with anger and embarrassment, charged toward Matt with a loud yell. Like a matador avoiding a charging bull, Matt stepped easily to one side. He pulled his pistol and brought it down hard on Waters's head as the big man rushed by, and Waters went down and out.

Matt put his pistol back in his holster, then picked up his beer. "Does Mr. Waters greet all your customers that way?"

"To tell the truth, mister, we don't get that many visitors in Sherwood. But Waters pretty much has the whole town buffaloed. I reckon he figured he needed to take you down, just to show everyone else that he was still the top rooster."

Finishing his beer, Matt put the glass down and slapped another nickel on the bar beside it. "I'll have another."

"No, sir," the bartender said, pushing the coin back.

Matt gave the bartender a questioning look, and the bartender smiled.

"This one is on me."

When Waters came to a minute later, he stood up slowly, then rubbed the bump on his head.

"Say, what happened to me?" he asked. "How come I was lyin' on the floor like that?"

"You must've gotten some bad whiskey," the bartender said.

"Bad whiskey?"

"Yes, you took a swallow, then started runnin'. You must've tripped and fell, 'cause next thing we saw, you was lyin' there on the floor."

"Bad whiskey?" Waters repeated.

"Yeah, but don't worry about it. I poured

the rest of that bottle out."

"How come I got a knot on top of my head?"

"You must've hit the foot rail when you fell."

"Yeah," Waters said, still rubbing his head. He started toward the door, walking unsteadily. "Yeah," he repeated. He had no idea why everyone in the saloon was laughing at him.

Half an hour later, when Matt tried to pay for his meal, Katie refused to take his money.

"No, sir," she said. "I heard what you did to Waters. The whole town has heard. It's worth the price of a meal, just to see him get his comeuppance."

"I appreciate it," Matt said.

As Matt rode on, he thought of the little town he had just come through, off the beaten track. Except for his run-in with Waters, the people had been nice. He hoped it would survive, but doubted that it would.[1]

1. Today, Sherwood is a genuine ghost town in Iron County, Texas. It served as the county seat until 1939, when it was supplanted by neighboring Mertzon.

CHAPTER NINE

Shady Rest

In order to satisfy the demands of the mayor's wife, Annabelle O'Callahan took an inventory of all the dress-making fabric she had on hand and realized that it was going to be necessary to go to Van Horn to buy new material. She didn't mind making the trip — she needed to restock some items anyway — so she would let the dress she was making for Mrs. Trout be both the excuse, and the financial basis of the trip.

Van Horn wasn't much larger than Shady Rest, but it was located on the Texas and Pacific Railroad, and because of that, it acted as a distribution point for goods and supplies that came in by rail from all over the country. Shady Rest was connected to Van Horn, indeed to the outside world, by the Van Horn and Shady Rest Stagecoach Line. There was only one coach, and it made a run to Van Horn on one day then returned the next day. Annabelle, as she had done many times before, put up a sign in the door of her shop, or shoppe, as she preferred to spell it.

Elite Shoppe closed for the day.
Gone to Van Horn for supplies —
will reopen in two days.

George Tobin operated the stagecoach line and handled the ticket sales and all the book work. He had four employees: two drivers and two shotgun guards. They alternated the trips, and on the day they weren't on the trip, they maintained the livestock and equipment at the home depot.

When Annabelle approached the depot she saw that the team was being connected. Dusty Reasoner was standing near the rear of the coach with one hand up on the boot.

"Good morning, Miss O'Callahan," Reasoner said as Annabelle passed by the coach. "Are you taking a trip with us today?"

"Yes, I have to buy some material. Are you our driver?"

"Yes, ma'am. I'm driving, Jim Richards will be riding shotgun. I'll try and give you folks a real smooth trip today."

"Good, I'll hold you to that," Annabelle replied with a smile.

"Hello, Miss O'Callahan," a young woman greeted when Annabelle went into the depot. The young woman was Mindy, one of the girls who worked at Suzie's Dream House. Suzie's Dream House was a house of prostitution, but, as Mayor Trout had said at the last Merchants Association meeting, Suzie ran a clean house, with the doctor checking the girls regularly. And there had never been any trouble at her place of business.

Annabelle recognized Mindy because she had made a couple of dresses for her.

"Hello, Mindy. Are you going to Van Horn this morning?"

"Yes, ma'am, I'm going to catch the train back east. My mama lives in St. Louis, and she's took sick. I need to go back and look after my two little sisters."

"Oh, well, I'm sorry. I hope your mother recovers soon."

"Yes, ma'am, me too. She don't know what I am. She thinks I'm working as a maid in a hotel. I don't know what she will think of me, when I tell her."

"Don't tell her," Annabelle said.

"But what if she finds out?"

"How likely do you think you are to run across someone from Shady Rest in St. Louis?" Annabelle asked.

Mindy smiled. "Not very likely, I don't reckon."

"Then she's not likely to find out. Sometimes, it's best to keep some things secret," Annabelle said, thinking of her own secret past.

Dusty Reasoner stepped into the depot. "If you two ladies will come climb aboard, we'll get on our way," he said.

Van Horn, Texas

That afternoon Annabelle was standing at the fabric table looking at the bolts of cloth thereon displayed.

"Hello, Annabelle. It's good to see you again," Glenda McVey, the owner's wife said. "What brings you this time?"

"I'm to make a new dress for the mayor's wife," Annabelle said. "And I want it to be something special."

"Well, let me help you. We just got in some new cotton sateen that is quite lovely," Glenda said. Over the next several minutes, Glenda helped Annabelle pick out six bolts of material, from white cotton, to green silk, to purple wool.

"Do you want your purchases shipped to you, Annabelle?" Glenda asked.

"No, thank you, I'll be going back on tomorrow's stagecoach. Could you have them taken to the depot so they can be loaded onto the coach?"

"Of course, I'll be happy to do that," the owner's wife said, satisfied that the transaction had been quite substantial.

Leaving the fabric shop, Annabelle wandered through the other shops, buying a hat at one, and a reticule at another, while checking out all the stores to see if she could get any ideas for her own.

Annabelle ate dinner alone that night, then turned in fairly early. The forty-mile trip from Van Horn to Shady Rest the next day would be tiring.

Pecos

Prichard had quickly become very popular as a deputy sheriff. He helped women with their packages, and when he arrested drunks, he did so without belligerence or unnecessary force. He broke up fights in saloons, protecting the smaller and weaker men from being bullied. He visited the Rogers Ranch to again express his regrets for what happened between him and Teddy Rogers. And though the pain of his loss was still keen, even the Rogers family was ready to forgive him.

Everywhere Sheriff Nelson went, he was

complimented for having hired Abe Conner.

"I recognized something about him as soon as I saw him," Sheriff Nelson said. "Maybe you ain't noticed the way he talks, but I have. That is an educated man. I wouldn't be surprised if he wasn't a doctor, or maybe a lawyer or something."

"If Deputy Conner is an educated man, what's he doin' workin' as a deputy?" Ray Kelly asked. Kelly owned the feed and seed store.

"I'm goin' to ask him some day," Sheriff Nelson said. "I don't figure now's the time to do it — too early, I'd say. But more'n likely we're goin' to find out that somethin' tragic happened, like maybe a wife dyin' or somethin' like that, to cause him to turn his back on his profession."

The mystery of Prichard's past, rather than arousing suspicion, merely enhanced his status in the eyes of the citizens of Pecos. More than one single woman and widow of the community began to look at him as potential husband material.

Van Horn

Braxton Barlow walked down the dark street from the depot toward the town. The Railroad Bar was the most substantial-

116

looking saloon in a row of saloons, but there was a drunk passed out on the steps in front of the place and Braxton had to step over him in order to go inside.

Because the chimneys of all the lanterns were soot-covered, what light there was, was dingy and filtered through drifting smoke. The place smelled of cheap whiskey, stale beer, and sour tobacco. There was a long bar on the left, with dirty towels hanging on hooks about every five feet along its front. A large mirror was behind the bar, but like everything else about the saloon, it was so dirty that Braxton could scarcely see any images in it, and what he could see was distorted by imperfections in the glass.

Over against the back wall, near the foot of the stairs, a cigar-scarred, beer-stained upright piano was being played by a bald-headed musician. At a table next to the piano he saw his two older brothers, Ben and Burt. It was Ben who had come up with the idea of holding up a stagecoach.

"It's a lot easier than robbin' a bank," Ben told them. "Once you rob a bank, you still got to get away, and that means ridin' right down the middle of the street so's that damn near ever' one in town can take a shot at you. But whenever you hold up a stage-coach, you're already out in the country.

It's as easy as takin' candy from a baby, 'n all you got to do after you get the money is just ride off."

Ben was the oldest of the three Barlow brothers, Burt was in the middle, and Brax was the youngest. When Ben suggested they hold up the stagecoach to Shady Rest, it wasn't hard to talk his two brothers into going along with it.

"How much money will the stagecoach be carrying?" Burt asked.

"I don't know," Ben admitted. "But they always carry some money, deliverin' it back and forth between banks, and such. And if nothin' else, the passengers will be carryin' some money, 'cause there don't nobody travel anywhere without takin' some money with them. It'll be as easy as takin' candy offen' a baby."

"You know what I'm goin' to do when we get the money?" Brax asked.

"What?"

"I'm goin' down into Mexico and I'm goin' to buy me the best-lookin' whore I can find. No, no, make that the two best-lookin' whores I can find. One for the daytime and one for the night. And I'm goin' to get me some whiskey. . . ."

"Tequila," Burt said.

"What?"

"If you're down in Mexico, you won't be gettin' no whiskey, you'll be getting' tequila."

"All right, tequila, what do I care? I'm goin' to get tequila, then I ain't goin' to do nothin' but lay with the whores and drink tequila 'til the money runs out."

Ben laughed. "What you should do is get a pretty daytime whore, and an ugly night-time whore. The ugly whores don't cost as much."

"Why do I want a ugly whore? Iffen I got the money, I want me a pretty whore."

"Hell, at nighttime, ugly is as good as pretty. You can't see 'em in the dark anyway," Ben said.

Burt laughed. "He's right. No sense spendin' money on a pretty whore at night."

"When are we goin' to hold up the stage-coach?" Brax asked.

"Tomorrow mornin'," Ben said. "The coach will leave at about eight, so I figure if we leave around six in the mornin', we'll be in place to waylay it when it comes by."

"Yeah. Good idea," Burt said.

"Six o'clock? That's awful early, ain't it?" Brax complained. "You really think it'll take us that long to get to wherever it is we're goin' to be to do the robbin'?"

"I want plenty of time to find the right

119

place," Ben said.

"I agree with Ben," Burt said. "Six o'clock ain't too early to make sure the job gets done right."

"Good, I'm glad that's settled," Ben said. "So, you boys be ready to go when I call for you in the mornin'."

CHAPTER TEN

Pecos
"Abe, we got a new batch of wanted posters in yesterday afternoon, and I'd like you to take care of 'em."

"Take care of them in what respect?"

"Well, like we might get a poster that says somethin' like, 'John Calhoun is wanted,' only John Calhoun has already been caught, or killed. So if that's the case, you just tear up the poster and throw it away."

"How will I know the status of the subjects?"

"What?"

"How will I know if 'John Calhoun' has been killed or captured?"

"Oh, that's easy. Along with the posters, there will also be an update on the status of previous posters. If you get a notice that a poster is being recalled, you can take it down. I also have a list in my desk drawer of previous withdrawals, so check them all against that list, just in case you get a duplicate. The posters that are good, you can put up on the wall here, then later go down to put them at the post office."

"All right, that doesn't sound too difficult."

"I know this might be borin' work for you, bein' as how smart you are and all. But it's generally the job that the junior deputy does, and since you've been a deputy for the shortest time, it's goin' to be your job."

"I'll be glad to do it, Sheriff, and I shall do so without complaint."

Sheriff Nelson smiled.

"You're a good man," he said. "I'm going to take a stroll around town. I'll back in a while."

"Take your time, Sheriff," Prichard said as he started through the posters. "I'll be here when you get back."

The third and fourth wanted posters were for Mutt and Prichard Crowley, offering rewards of five thousand dollars for each of them. There were also dodgers out for Bill Carter, Lenny Fletcher, Dax Williams, and Titus Carmichael, offering fifteen hundred dollars. That surprised him, because he didn't know they had even been identified.

Prichard smiled as he tore the flyers into small pieces. This was exactly why he'd taken the job. It took him about forty-five minutes to go through all the posters and to make the updates. He had just finished when one of the jail prisoners called out from the cell area behind the office.

"Hey, Sheriff."

Prichard, who was drinking coffee, stepped back into the cell area. The prisoner who had called had been brought in the night before for public drunkenness, having been found passed out on the street. He was sitting up on the edge of the bunk, and he ran his hands through a shock of unruly hair.

"Something I can do for you?" Prichard asked, as he took a swallow of his coffee.

"You are the new deputy, ain't you?" the prisoner asked.

"I am."

"I could use a cup of coffee. You'll find my cup in the bottom right-hand drawer of the sheriff's desk. I take it black."

"You have your own cup here? You must be a regular."

"I expect to be issued a deputy's badge any day now," the prisoner answered sarcastically.

Prichard went to the sheriff's desk, opened the drawer, and found the prisoner's cup. Painted on the side of the cup was CE BLAN-

"So, you are a lawyer," Prichard said as he handed Blanton the cup.

"When I'm sober," Blanton replied.

"As a lawyer and an educated man, Mr. Blanton, I'm sure you realize that whiskey is the devil's brew. It defies reason, creates misery, dethrones men from the pinnacles of righteousness, and casts them into the bottomless pit of degradation, shame, and despair."

"So say you, sir. But I see it as the oil of conversation, the philosophic wine, the elixir of life, the ale that is consumed when good fellows get together, that puts a song in their hearts and the warm glow of contentment in their eyes."

Prichard heard laughter behind him and, turning, saw that Sheriff Nelson had just come in.

"Both of you are so full of it, you're a perfect match for each other," Sheriff Nelson said.

Van Horn

The next morning, Dusty Reasoner, the driver, and Jim Richards, the shotgun guard, were standing alongside the coach as four passengers for Shady Rest came out of the stage depot to board. Dusty, in his late sixties, was the older of the two men. His hair and beard were gray, and he still walked with a limp from a wound he had sustained at Shiloh. Jim was in his early forties and bald, though as he was seldom seen without a hat, only those who knew him well were aware of the fact. He had just rolled himself a cigarette and was smoking as the passengers approached the stagecoach.

Annabelle was the first one out, and Dusty touched his hand to his hat.

"Good mornin', Miss O'Callahan. Going back with us, I see. I hope you had a good visit to Van Horn."

"Good morning, Mr. Reasoner. Yes, my visit was quite productive," she replied as she climbed into the coach.

The second passenger was Gerald Hawkins, the owner of the Texas Star in Shady Rest. Hawkins was five feet seven inches tall and weighed just over a hundred and fifty pounds, which was about average for the cavalryman he had once been. His black hair was slicked down and parted in the middle. He had a closely trimmed moustache, and he wore a jacket, a vest, and a string tie.

"Dusty, you old horse thief, see if you can avoid hitting every pothole between here and Shady Rest," Hawkins said.

"Ha. I plan to find new potholes that ain't never been hit yet, just for you," Dusty replied. It was a standard bit of repartee between the two men, and it was exchanged without rancor.

The third passenger was Elwood Crocker. Crocker owned a small ranch just outside of town, and he dressed the part in denim trousers and a white shirt.

"Miss O'Callahan, you're going back to Shady Rest? Heck, I was hoping you were plannin' on moving to Van Horn," Crocker said. "If you was to do so, why, that sure would save me a lot of money."

Crocker's wife, Julia, was one of Annabelle's customers, and he made a joke about spending enough money in her shop to pay for Annabelle's ticket.

"Now, Mr. Crocker, are you going to tell me that you don't think Julia is just beautiful in the gowns I make for her?"

Crocker smiled self-consciously. "No, ma'am, I can't say that, so I reckon you've got me there," he said. "I always did think Julia was a pretty thing, but I have to admit that some of those dresses you make for her make her that much prettier."

"Just some of them?" Annabelle teased.

Crocker laughed. "All of 'em."

The fourth passenger was Percy McCall,

a notions drummer who called frequently upon Annabelle. Like Hawkins, McCall wore a suit, in keeping with his profession, and like Hawkins, McCall was a relatively small man, though he didn't have the wiry strength and toughness of Hawkins.

"Why, Mr. McCall, you could show me your wares while we are in the coach, and you wouldn't even have to call on me at my store," Annabelle said.

"No, ma'am, I want to call on you at your store. If we're there, you are likely to think of something you need that you will forget if we do business in the coach."

"Ha!" Hawkins said. "There you go, Miss O'Callahan. You aren't the only one with a sales pitch, are you?"

"You folks all settled in down there?" Dusty called back to his passengers.

"We're all ready, Dusty," Hawkins called back. "Let's get this show on the road."

"Heeyah!" Dusty's shout out to his team could be heard all up and down Austin Street.

They left Van Horn at eight o'clock in the morning for what would be a six-hour journey, and soon, Annabelle began passing the time by making sketches of the dresses she intended to make.

"I don't know how you can draw like that with all the bouncing around we're doing," McCall said.

"It's easy enough," Annabelle said. "I just draw when we're not bouncing."

"Please tell me you aren't drawing up more dresses to sell to my wife," Crocker teased.

"Not at all," Annabelle replied with friendly smile. "These are designs for Mrs. Trout."

"Ha!" Hawkins said. "Good for you! The more money that pompous ass of a mayor spends, the better I like it."

"I like it too. I especially like it when he spends the money with me," Annabelle said, and the others in the coach laughed.

"What were you doing in Van Horn, Mr. Crocker?" Hawkins asked.

"I've ordered me a seed Hereford bull from Fort Worth," Crocker said. "I was just makin' arrangements with the railroad to have him shipped here."

"He must be some kind of bull for you to go to all that trouble."

"Yes, sir, he is. He's in a direct line from Anxiety Four," Crocker said proudly.

"Anxiety Four?" Annabelle said with little chuckle. "That seems an odd name for a bull."

"Yes, ma'am, that might be, but he's the most famous Hereford bull there ever was."

The coach hit a hole hard enough to jar everyone inside.

"You folks all right down there?" Dusty shouted.

Hawkins stuck his head out the window and called up. "I see you found one for us."

Dusty laughed. "I do what I can," he said. "Heeaaah!" he shouted, snapping the whip over the head of the team to keep them in a trot.

It had been two weeks now since Matt Jensen had left Sherwood, the last town he had visited, and he was tired. It wasn't just a tiredness from several weeks of being on the road. It was a tired-to-the-bone weariness from a life lived always on the move, and even though it was a life that he chose, there were times, like this, when he could almost envy Smoke Jensen, with his ranch, wife, house, and bed to sleep in at night.

Right now he especially envied him the bed.

Matt stood in the stirrups just to give his butt a break. Then, seeing a clear, swiftly running stream, he headed toward it, and stopped to let his horse, Spirit, have a drink, while he filled his canteen. The water tasted good, but a beer would have been better.

Texas was not only a big state; it was a state with a lot of nothing in it, with vast distances between the towns, especially in the wide open spaces of West Texas. If he would, somehow, come across a town in this godforsaken wilderness, the first thing he would do, even before replenishing his possibles, would be to have a beer.

"Yeah, Spirit, what do you think of that?" he asked. "I say a cool beer, a hot meal, a hot bath, and a real bed. And don't you even think of waking me up 'til my birthday. But don't worry, I'll be taking care of you as well. I'm going to get you your own stall, some oats, and I wouldn't doubt but there might be a young filly there to turn your eye. But don't be taken in by her sweet talk, you have to be very careful of that," he added with a chuckle.

Matt was alone so much that he often talked to his horse just to hear a human voice, even if it was his own. And he figured that talking to Spirit was better than talking to himself. Refreshed, Matt remounted, then continued his ride.

Not more than a mile from Matt at that very moment, the Shady Rest Stagecoach was continuing its run from Van Horn to Shady Rest.

The three Barlow brothers, Ben, Burt, and Brax, were waiting in a little thicket of trees alongside the road where the coach would pass.

"How much longer?" Burt asked.

"I don't know," Ben answered. "Fifteen minutes, half an hour maybe."

"I wish it would come on. This just waitin' aroun' for it is makin' me nervous," Burt said.

"There ain't no call for you to be gettin' nervous. I tol' you, there ain't nothin' to it. When the coach gets close, we'll just jump out in front of it and stop 'em."

"What if they don't stop?" Brax asked.

"Then we'll shoot 'em," Ben answered easily.

"I gotta take a piss," Brax said.

"Well, if you're goin' to do it, do it now and do it fast, 'cause I can see the stagecoach comin'," Ben said.

"Where?" Burt asked.

"Look down that way."

Looking south, Burt saw a cloud of dust far down the road. Then, less than a minute later, emerging from the dust, he could see the coach itself. And now they could hear it as well, the hoofbeats of the horses, the rumble of the rolling wheels, and the squeaking sound of the coach rocking back and forth on the through-braces.

"Brax, Burt, you boys ready?"

"Yeah," Brax said as he buttoned his trousers. "I'm ready."

"When it gets close enough, we'll jump out in front of it," Ben instructed. He pulled a hood down over his head and positioned it so the two holes lined up with his eyes. Brax and Burt did the same thing.

CHAPTER ELEVEN

Dusty Reasoner and Jim Richards were upon the box seat of the stage. Dusty was handling the ribbons, but Jim was just sitting there, his shot gun propped up against the corner of the curved foot rest in front of them.

Jim carved off a piece of chewing tobacco and offered some to Dusty. Dusty accepted it, and Jim carved off another piece for himself.

"You know, I can't quite get a handle on Miss O'Callahan," Jim said.

"What do you mean?"

"Well, I mean, how come she ain't married? She's old enough, and she's sure pretty enough."

Dusty chuckled. "Thinkin' of askin' her, are you, Jim?"

"Who me? Heck no. That little ol' filly is way too smart for me. I mean, the way she runs that business and all."

"Well, you just answered your own question," Dusty said. "The reason she ain't married is 'cause, most likely, she's smarter'n just about any man in town. And most men don't like bein' married to a woman that's smarter'n they are."

Jim spit out a wad before he replied. "I reckon you're right," he said. "I once know'd a woman, a lot smarter'n me."

Dusty waited for him to finish the comment, but he added nothing to it.

"A woman smarter than you?"

"Yeah."

Dusty laughed. "I don't even have to ask who it was."

"What do you mean?"

"You figure it out."

"What the hell, Dusty, lookie there!" Jim shouted.

Just ahead of the coach, three mounted and masked men suddenly rode out into the road in front of them. All three were holding pistols, and the pistols were aimed at the coach. One of the mounted men held out his free hand.

"Stop the coach!" he shouted.

"Whoa!" Dusty called to his team, hauling back on the reins and putting his foot on the wheel brake.

"Damn!" Jim yelled, raising his shotgun.

Before he could come back on the two hammers, one of the men fired, and Jim felt a hammer blow to his shoulder. The impact of the bullet caused him to drop his shotgun.

"I'm sorry, Dusty," he said, his voice strained.

"Just take it easy," Dusty replied, reaching over to touch his friend. "We don't want to give 'em any more reason to shoot."

"Don't try anything like that again," one of the masked road agents said.

"What do you want?" Dusty asked.

"What do you think I want? I want you to throw your money box down," the road agent said. So far, he was the only one of the three men who had spoken.

"Are you crazy, mister?" Dusty called down to him. "I don't know what you think we're carryin', but we ain't got no money box. This here is the Van Horn and Shady Rest Stage. We don't hardly ever carry no money. The onliest thing we're carryin' now is a pouch of letters."

"All right, throw the pouch down," one of the other men said, speaking for the first time.

"I'll throw the pouch down if you say so, but do you really want to do that? You start messin' with the mail, and it becomes a federal offense," Dusty said. "And like as not there ain't goin' to be nothin' in there but just personal letters anyhow."

Inside the coach Percy McCall looked at the other three, his face reflecting his fear.

"Oh my, what is happening?" he asked.

"Sounds like the coach is bein' held up," Crocker said.

Hawkins leaned over to look through the window.

"Yes, there are three of them."

Crocker pulled his pistol, but Hawkins reached over to put his hand on the gun.

"Better not do it, Mr. Crocker. Like I said, there's three of them. You'll only wind up getting yourself shot," Hawkins said.

"Mr. Hawkins is right," Annabelle said.

"I don't like sittin' here, doing nothin'."

"Mr. Crocker, a man named Shakespeare once said that discretion is the better part of valor," Annabelle said.

"What does that mean?" Crocker asked.

"That means put the damn gun away," Hawkins said.

"Please do," McCall said. "I think our best bet would be to do nothing that might make them angry."

"All right," Crocker said as he slipped his pistol back into its holster. "But I tell you the truth, I don't like sittin' here like some frog just waitin' to be gigged."

Ben sighed. This wasn't going the way he had planned. He had hoped, he had thought, there would be a money shipment, at least one of a few hundred dollars.

"All right, don't throw the mail pouch down," Ben said. "We'll just take whatever money your passengers have on 'em."

Ben dismounted and approached the coach, holding his pistol at the ready.

"You folks inside there, come on out now. Climb down!"

When nobody emerged from the coach, Ben fired twice into the air. "I said, climb down out of there!" he shouted. "And I ain't askin' again. You better do what I told you, or else the next time I shoot, I'll start shootin' right into the coach."

The door opened and Hawkins was the first one out. He turned back toward the door.

"What are you doin', tryin' to go back inside?" Ben asked.

"One of the passengers is a lady," Hawkins said. "I'm helping her down."

"Yeah? Well, be quick about it. I don't plan to stand out here all day."

After Annabelle stepped down, she was

joined by the two remaining passengers.

From the moment Matt heard the gunshots, he urged Spirit into a gallop, racing to the sound. Cresting a rise, he saw a stagecoach stopped on the road. It didn't take but one quick observation to determine what was going on.

The passengers were outside the coach, three men and a woman, and all of them were holding their hands in the air. The driver and shotgun guard were still upon the box, but the shotgun guard was holding his hand over a shoulder wound, grimacing in pain. There were three masked men; two of them were mounted, while the third was dismounted and facing the passengers. All three of the men were holding guns.

Matt snaked his rifle from the saddle sheath, dismounted, and aimed at the one who was on the ground.

"You men, throw down your guns!" Matt shouted.

"What the hell?" one of the three men shouted, his words muffled by the mask.

Two of the armed men turned their guns toward Matt and fired. One of the bullets took Matt's hat off.

Matt returned fire, and the robber on the ground went down.

One of the two mounted robbers, the one who had fired at him the first time, fired again, but already Matt was on the move, and the shot missed. Matt fired a second time, and he didn't miss. The robber fell from his saddle. The third would-be robber, who had not fired at all, put spurs to his horse and galloped off. The two other horses, their saddles now empty, galloped off with him.

Matt put his rifle away, remounted, then urged Spirit into a brisk trot to close the distance between the top of the hill and the coach.

"Mister," the driver said. "I don't know who you are, but am I glad to see you. You just saved our bacon."

Looking up toward the box, Matt saw the shotgun guard holding his hand over the wound in his shoulder. He could see that the man's shirtsleeve was soaked with blood.

"How badly hurt are you?" Matt asked the shotgun guard.

"If you want to know how bad it hurts, it hurts like hell," the guard said. "But the bullet hit me in the shoulder, so I don't reckon it hit any of my vitals."

"You folks climb back in, and we'll get started into town," the driver said to the passengers.

"Before you get started we'd better see to the guard's wound," Matt suggested. "No sense in letting him bleed to death. We need to put a bandage on that."

The guard didn't respond, but his face was already pale from loss of blood.

"I've got some cloth in the boot you could use as a bandage," one of the passengers, a pretty redhead, said.

Her luggage was pulled from the boot of the coach, and a swath of cotton was removed. Climbing up onto the stage, Matt made a compression bandage which he put over the wound; then he held it in place by looping the guard's belt around it.

"Now, Jim, once we get into town, don't you go hoppin' down without no thought whatever," the driver said. "What with no belt on, why, you're liable to drop your pants right there in front of the whole town."

The driver chuckled, and Matt was glad to see that Jim smiled as well, showing that he still had his wits about him.

As Matt was tending to the shotgun guard, Crocker, Hawkins, and McCall pulled the hoods off the two dead, would be stagecoach robbers.

"Dusty, none of us know these galoots,"

Crocker said. "Have you ever seen either of them?"

Dusty looked down at them. "Can't say that I have," he replied.

"Well, there it is, I can't positively say I've never seen either of them," Hawkins said. "I get so many people coming through the saloon that after a while, they all start looking alike to me. But if I have seen them before, I sure don't remember them."

"All right, this should hold him until we get him to a doctor," Matt said as he finished bandaging Jim. "Where are you headed?"

"To Shady Rest. It's about ten more miles. Tell the truth, mister, with Jim shot up like he is, I'd appreciate it if you would ride along with us," the driver said.

"I'm not going to leave you," Matt said.

"Thanks," the driver said. "It'll be a comfort havin' you along."

"Do they have a place where I can get a cold beer in Shady Rest? And maybe a place to get a hot meal, and rent a room?"

"Mister, my name is Gerald Hawkins, and I own the Texas Star Saloon," one of the passengers said. "I don't know how much you can drink in one day, but seeing as you're going to be kind enough to ride along with us like the driver asked, then I personally guarantee you that for the rest of this day, you can drink free at my place. And as far as the meal and room is concerned, why there's places in town that can accommodate you."

"I'm much obliged, Mr. Hawkins," Matt said.

"No, sir, we are the ones who are obliged," the very pretty, young, red-haired woman said.

"All right, folks, now that Jim's patched up, if you'll all get back in the coach, we'll be on our way," Dusty said.

"What about these two?" Crocker asked, pointing to the two dead men who were lying on the road, one facedown, one faceup. "We can't just leave 'em lyin' here, can we?"

"Why not? They won't mind," the driver said.

"It just don't seem right," Crocker said.

"Don't worry about it. Ponder will send someone out after 'em," the driver said. "The county will give him thirty dollars apiece to bury 'em. That's twice what the town pays him, so it'll make it worth his time to hire someone to come out here in a wagon to pick 'em up. Now, you folks climb on back in. I need to get Jim here to a doctor, and get you folks home."

"Home, yeah, that sounds good to me,"

Crocker said. He held the door open until Annabelle got in, then he and the other two men climbed in behind her.

Hopping down from the coach, Matt remounted, then nodded toward the driver. The driver called out, "Heeaah!" snapped his whip, and the six-horse team started forward at a trot.

Brax Barlow had ridden off at a gallop as soon as the shooting started.

Then, after waiting about half an hour, he rode back to take a look around. The coach was gone, but his two brothers were still lying there, dead in the road.

"You sons of bitches didn't even bother to pick 'em up," he said aloud, conveniently excusing himself for abandoning them when the gun battle had broken out.

For a moment he wondered what should be done about them. Should he bury them? Should he try to take them somewhere? Where would he take them, and how would he explain the bullet wounds?

"Hell, Ben, Burt, it's your own damn fault," he said. "What did you start shootin' for?"

Brax ran his hand through his hair in exasperated frustration. "Like takin' candy from a baby, you said. Well, it weren't no such thing, and now you're lyin' here, dead."

That's right, he thought. They were dead, so it really didn't matter what he did with them. The best thing he could do for them, he figured, would be to kill the son of a bitch who'd killed them.

He had no idea who that was, but he was pretty sure he could find out if he went on in to Shady Rest. And, because he had been wearing a mask, and had never been to Shady Rest before, he was sure that he could go without fear of being recognized.

"All right, Ben, Burt, this is what I'm goin' to do. I'm goin' to find out who the son of a bitch is who done this to you, and when I find 'im, I'm goin' to kill 'im. That's the least I can do for you. Oh, an', Burt, seein' as you ain't goin' to be usin' 'em no more, I aim to take your boots. That is, if it's all the same to you."

Brax took Burt's boots, and, going through his brothers' pockets, found a total of thirteen dollars and seventy-five cents in cash. He also took both their pistols, figuring he could get maybe ten or fifteen apiece for them.

CHAPTER TWELVE

Shady Rest

When Mutt Crowley awakened that morning, he looked over at the woman who was lying in bed with him. The cover was turned down to her waist and he could see the blue veins of her bulbous breasts. She had a disfiguring scar on her cheek from an altercation with a drunken customer, and as she slept, her lips were fluttering and dribbling spittle.

Mutt wasn't exactly sure as to how he had wound up with this woman. He didn't know whether he had been too drunk or too horny when he came up to her room last night, but in either case, he was having a severe case of buyer's remorse this morning.

It had not been like this, right after the money split. While he'd still had money he'd been able to buy the best-looking whores in the highest-class whorehouses in places like

Denver, Flagstaff, and San Antonio. It wasn't until he reached Shady Rest that he'd realized he was going to have to be a little more conservative with his spending habits.

He had given a passing thought to killing either Fletcher or Carter, or both of them, and taking what money they had . . . but they had been even more spendthrift than he had, and had started out with less, so he actually had more money than either of them. And, being on the run as he was, it was probably good to have them around, people he knew and could trust.

Mutt had a terrible need to urinate, and he got out of bed and looked around for the chamber pot.

"Damn, where the hell is it?" he muttered.

The pressure was building to the point that he couldn't waste anymore time looking for it. Then, he saw the vase and wash basin. He walked over to them, and he took the vase down and, holding it in position, began to relieve himself.

When he finished, he put the vase back on the chest, then looked back at the woman and smiled over what he had just done. Hell, he thought, someone that ugly, what would it matter if she washed in piss? It couldn't make her look any uglier.

Mutt put on his clothes, then sat on the edge of the bed to begin pulling on his boots. When he did, it woke the woman. She lifted her arms, and put her hands behind her head. Dark tufts of hair were under her arms. She smiled at Mutt, and he saw that she was missing two teeth.

Damn, how could he have missed all that last night?

"Uhmm, good morning honey," she said. "Did you have a good time last night?"

"I don't even remember last night," Mutt said.

"Well, for another three dollars, I'll refresh your memory," the woman offered, laughing at her own joke.

"No thanks. I'm s'posed to meet my pards for breakfast."

"All right, if you say so. But just remember, I'm here anytime you want me."

Mutt went downstairs into the saloon to see if he could find Carter and Fletcher. He saw them sitting at one of the tables, drinking beer and eating boiled eggs and pickled pigs' feet for breakfast. The saloon kept boiled eggs and pickled pigs feet in big jars sitting on the bar.

Mutt ordered a beer, then stuck his hand down into the vinegar to fish out a couple of the pigs' feet. He joined Carter and

147

Fletcher at the table, then began chewing through the tough skin.

"I seen that you got yourself a woman last night. How did she look this morning?" Fletcher asked.

"What do you mean, how did she look?"

Fletcher laughed. "Well, last night you was carryin' on somethin' fierce 'bout how pretty she was."

"I was?"

"Yeah, you was. Wasn't he, Carter?"

Carter laughed. "Yep. You said she was one of the prettiest whores you'd ever seen."

"Damn. How drunk was I?"

"You was so damn drunk that you wouldn't listen to either one of us," Carter said. "We tried to tell you that she was so ugly she'd make a train take five miles of dirt road. But you told us to mind our own business."

"Yeah, well, that might be a pretty good idea right now, too," Crowley said. "If you want to know the truth, she was uglier than a toad, but I don't want to talk about it, so you two just mind your own business. Damn, when I had money, I had only the best-lookin' whores money could buy, nothin' like that ugly old hag I woke up with this morning. I tell you what, I'm goin' to find me a poker game today an' get some money back. I don't like livin' without money."

"Yeah, well, truth to tell, I done seen all the whores that's workin' the Pig Palace, the Crooked Branch, the Ace High, and even over at Abby's Place. And they ain't any one of 'em that's much better lookin' than the one you wound up with. And yours wasn't no worse than the ones me or Carter had," Fletcher said. "They ain't a whore in this whole town who could look into a mirror without breakin' it, an' that's a fact."

"They say they's some good-lookin' whores over at Suzie's Dream House. And some pretty good-lookin' women over at the Texas Star too," Carter said.

"Yeah, well, the ones at the Dream House wants too much money. And the women at the Texas Star ain't whores. Besides which, none of them will have anything to do with me, even if I do have money," Crowley said. "I don't know what makes 'em so damn snooty. Hell, they ain't exactly what you call high society. Anyway, that's why I don't spend much time over there."

"You're goin' to have to go over there if you want to get into a card game. That is, a card game where you can make a little money, 'cause the only games over here, even across the street in the gamblin' house,

149

are penny ante games. The real money game is over at the Texas Star," Carter said.

"Yeah, that's what I've heard too," Fletcher added. "They got a game goin' on there, near 'bout all the time. They say they's a gamblin' man there who's just real good."

"What do you mean, real good?"

"I mean he makes his livin' playin' cards. And you can't make a livin' playin' cards unless you win a lot more'n you lose."

"Yeah? Well, he ain't played me yet, has he?" Crowley said, confidently.

"You're that good, are you?"

"When I was inside I made friends with a professional gambler, and he taught me some tricks."

"You try any trick, you're liable to get yourself shot," Carter said.

"I ain't talkin' about cheatin' tricks, I'm talkin' about smart playin' tricks. But one thing is, you gotta have enough money to be able to play without runnin' scared all the time. And most all my money's gone now. Tell you what, you two boys loan me fifty dollars apiece."

"What? Damn, I ain't got but just a little over a hunnert dollars now," Carter said.

"An' I don't even have a hunnert dollars," Fletcher said.

"You wouldn't either one of you have that money if it wasn't for me 'n my brother. You loan me fifty dollars each, I'll also put up fifty dollars, and that way I'll have enough to play with. And we'll split my winnin's, three ways."

"You're pretty sure you're goin' to win, huh?" Carter asked.

"I'm damn sure I'm goin' to win."

Carter pulled out the money. "All right, come on, Lenny, let's pony up. Who knows, maybe he will win pretty big. I'd like to have a little spendin' money again."

Fletcher pulled out his money as well, and Crowley smiled, then started toward the Texas Star.

"What do you think, Bill? You think he'll really win anything?" Fletcher asked.

"I don't know, but we may as well try. Hell, the only other thing we'd do with it is spend it on liquor and ugly whores anyway. And this way, we at least have a chance of gettin' some money back."

The professional card player who was practicing his profession at the Texas Star was Emerson Culpepper. Culpepper was the quintessential Southern gentleman who was always well turned out, not only in the clothes he wore, but in his personal hygiene, the way he kept his hair and moustache neatly trimmed.

Emerson was the youngest son of Endicott Culpepper, a former congressman from Alabama who had once been considered as a replacement for Rufus King, Franklin Pierce's vice president who died after only one month in office. Because King had been from Alabama and Culpepper was also from Alabama, the congressmen from the northern states stopped it, and in protest, Pierce went for the rest of his entire first term without a vice president.

Then, when Alabama seceded from the union, Endicott Culpepper resigned his seat in Congress and raised a regiment in the Confederate Army. Because he had raised and equipped the regiment, which he called Culpepper's Legion, he was appointed colonel in command.

Emerson had been too young for the war, but his two older brothers were just of the right age. They served as lieutenants in Culpepper's Legion, and were both killed during the Battle of Spanish Fort. Emerson's mother died of a broken heart, and Emerson's father, who returned home from the war a man who was broken in body and spirit, became an alcoholic.

When the Culpepper Plantation, once the

largest in Coffee County, and one of the most productive in the entire state, was lost to delinquent taxes, Endicott Culpepper ended his own life.

Emerson Culpepper's personal future looked bleak until he discovered that his phenomenal memory and mathematical acumen could be used to great advantage in card games. He was able to remember cards played, and he could determine, quickly and with amazing accuracy, the odds of the appearance of needed cards. Putting that skill to use, Culpepper became a professional gambler. Since doing so, he had made a very good living at the poker tables.

Culpepper never cheated; his skill was such that cheating wasn't necessary. However, his success in cards often brought about charges of cheating, and he found it necessary from time to time to relocate from one place to another before he completely wore out his welcome. That was how he had arrived in Shady Rest six weeks earlier, and had, with the permission of Gerald Hawkins set up his operation in the Texas Star.

Culpepper secured Hawkins's permission in the same way he'd secured the permission of all previous saloons where he had worked, by offering them 10 percent of the table. Everyone who played cards with him was made aware that when they cashed in their chips, the house would keep 10 percent. And, there were enough repeat players who had seen that the chips set aside did indeed go to the house, that anyone who suggested that Hawkins was keeping the money for himself was quickly disabused of their mistaken notion.

It had been a relatively slow morning; indeed at the moment there were only two other players in the game when Mutt Crowley stepped up to his table.

"I want to play some poker," Crowley said.

"We have an open seat," Culpepper invited him.

Crowley sat down, then took out a stack of bills and put them on the table in front.

"What's your name?" Culpepper asked.

"Mu . . . uh . . . Morgan. Dale Morgan."

"Mr. Morgan, you may notice that there is no cash on the table. We play with chips," Culpepper said. "You can get them from the bartender.

"All right, keep this seat open," Crowley replied as he went over to the bar to buy some poker chips. When he returned, he put one hundred and fifty dollars worth of chips out on the table in front of him. Nobody else was showing more than forty dollars.

"What the hell, mister?" one of the other players said. "Are you plannin' on buyin' the pots?"

"What if I am?" Crowley asked.

"I would recommend that you don't try to do that," Culpepper said. "You can't buy what the cards don't win."

"Let's quit the gabbing and get on with the game," Crowley said with a growl.

"Very well. Gentlemen, new player, new deck," Culpepper said. He picked up a box, broke the seal, then dumped the cards onto the table. They were clean, stiff, and shining. He pulled out the joker, then began shuffling the deck. The stiff, new pasteboards clicked sharply. His hands moved swiftly, folding the cards in and out until it felt right. He shoved the deck across the table.

"You are the newest player. Would you like to cut?" he asked Crowley.

Crowley cut the deck, then pushed them back.

"The game is five-card stud," Culpepper said as he looked directly at Crowley.

"Fine," Crowley answered.

Crowley won five dollars on the first hand, and within a few hands was ahead by a little over twenty dollars. He smiled broadly as he raked in his last winning hand.

When Culpepper dealt the next hand, Crowley opened the bet with twenty-five dollars.

"Why don't we play for some real money?" he asked.

"I'm afraid that's a little too rich for my blood," one of the other players said.

"Too rich for me, too, but if you don't mind, I plan to sit here and watch until the bettin' comes back down to where I can afford to get back into the game."

CHAPTER THIRTEEN

As the game was going on in the Texas Star Saloon, Matt Jensen, riding ahead of the stagecoach, got his first glimpse of Shady Rest. Located in the shadow of El Capitan Mountain, the little town rose in front of him, at first barely distinguishable from among the hillocks and clumps of sage brush. As he got closer though, he could make out the town, a row of false-fronted buildings on either side of a north-and-south-running street. The tallest structure was the church steeple at the far end of the street. As soon as they passed by the sign welcoming them to Shady Rest, Dusty, the stagecoach driver, whipped the team into a trot so that the coach rolled rapidly down the street, a rooster tail of dust billowing up behind the two oversized rear wheels.

"We was held up! We was held up!" the driver started shouting as the coach rolled quickly down the main street of the town.

"We was held up! Jim's been shot! Get the doc! Jim's been shot!"

The stagecoach office was right in the middle of town, on the west side of the street. There, the driver stopped the coach and the following cloud of dust that had been thrown up by hooves and wheels now rolled back over them. It enveloped the coach for a long moment, and caused the passengers inside to cough and wave their hands in an attempt to brush the dust away.

It was the normal routine of several of the citizens of the town to meet the coach, as the town was not served by the railroad and the stagecoach was their principal connection to the outside world. But the number of people standing in front of the stage depot now was considerably larger than normal, the gawkers drawn not only by the arrival of the coach, but also by the driver's shouts of a holdup.

"Couple of you fellas, help me get Jim down," the driver said, and two of the younger men climbed up onto the coach to begin taking the guard down. Jim gasped in pain as they grabbed him.

"Take it easy with him," Dusty ordered.

"Sorry," one of the two young men said, and they exercised a bit more care in their handling of him.

"How much money did they get, Dusty?" one of the men in the gathering crowd asked.

"Ha!" Dusty said. "That's the beauty of it. They didn't get nothin' a' tall. Fact is, they's two of 'em needin' Ponder's services right now, seein' as they are a' lyin' dead out in the road 'bout ten miles back."

"I thought you said you was robbed."

"There were three men who attempted to rob us," Annabelle said. She looked over toward Matt, who was still sitting his saddle, and flashed him a big smile. "But this brave gentleman broke it up."

By now two more men came up to join the others. Both men were wearing stars, and one was much older than the other.

"Who was it, Dusty? Do you know?" the younger of the two men asked.

"I don't have 'ny idea at all, Marshal," Dusty replied. "Even when we took the masks off the two that was kilt, there didn't none of us recognize 'em. So we just skedaddled on out of there on account of Jim here bein' shot like he was."

"How bad is Jim hurt?" the marshal asked.

"I ain't dead yet," Jim called out to them. "Ya'll quit talkin' 'bout me like I'm done gone."

"I don't know what made 'em decide to

rob us in the first place. Hell, we wasn't carryin' no money at all, 'ceptin' maybe what the passengers might have had."

"Did Jim shoot the robbers?" the marshal asked.

"No, it was that fella right there," Dusty said, pointing to Matt.

By now Matt had dismounted and was tying Spirit off at the hitching rail. As he did so, the younger of the two star-packers, the one who had been talking to Dusty, came over to talk to Matt.

"My name is Pruitt. Devry Pruitt. I'm the marshal here."

Matt was a little surprised that it was the younger of the two men who was the marshal. The older man stood back, showing a degree of nonchalance as he leaned against one of the supporting posts of the front overhang.

"The driver says you killed two of the robbers?"

"Yes."

"You mind givin' your name?"

"It's Jensen. Matt Jensen."

"Jensen?" Matt heard one of the men in the crowd say. "Did that fella say his name is Jensen? Damn, what's he doin' this far south?"

Marshal Pruitt heard the comment as

well, and he turned toward the man who had spoken. "Grojean, do you know this man?" With a nod of his head, he indicated that he was talking about Matt.

"I don't know him, but I sure know of him. I can't believe you ain't never heard of him, Marshal. Why, folks say he's 'bout the best with a gun there is."

"Is that so? Would you be what they call a gunfighter, Mr. Jensen?" Marshal Pruitt asked, his face showing a concerned suspicion.

"I guess that would all depend upon your definition of a gunfighter," Matt replied. "I don't sell my guns, and I've never shot a man who wasn't trying to shoot me."

"That's right, Marshal," Grojean said. "Leastwise, that's the only way I've always heard it said. I mean, yeah, they say he's a good gunfighter, but there ain't never been no one who's said that he's gone bad with his guns."

"The two men you encountered today," Marshal Pruitt said. "Did they shoot first?"

"They did."

"This gentleman is telling you the truth, Marshal," Percy McCall, the drummer, said. "Mr. Jensen got the drop on the robbers and he even offered them the opportunity to give up, but they turned their weapons on him instead. And before Mr. Jensen came to our rescue, the three robbers were getting very threatening. I fear that if they had not been satisfied with what they got, they may well have taken it out on us. I don't mind telling you, I, for one, was very glad to see Mr. Jensen come along, arriving like the U.S. Cavalry, you might say."

"Well, Jensen, I suppose it is good that you came along when you did. Will you be in town for a while? I mean, in case I have any questions later."

"I plan to be in town for a day or two, or at least until I am able to build up my supply of possibles," Matt said. "But for now, as soon as I take care of my horse, I plan to get a drink, a bath, a hotel room, and something to eat, in that order."

"Mr. Jensen, you don't have to worry none about your horse," Dusty said. "I mean, in as far as boardin' him is concerned. Why, you can leave your horse with the coach horses. We'll take good care of him . . . fresh hay, his own stall. And there won't be no charge at all. I'm sure once Mr. Tobin hears what you done for his stagecoach company, why, he'll be more'n glad to take care of your horse."

"I know that Spirit is as tired as I am, so if you would, Dusty, give him some oats tonight. I'll be glad to pay for it."

"Oats he'll have, and anything else he wants. And that won't cost you nothin' neither. Like I said, the stagecoach company will be more than happy to pick up the tab."

"That's very nice of you."

" 'Least we can do, seein' as what you done for us."

Matt saw Jim, the shotgun guard, sitting on the porch of the stage depot, leaning back against the front wall. Someone — Matt assumed it was the doctor — was tending him. Matt walked over to him.

"How are you feeling, Jim?" he asked.

"Oh, tolerable, I reckon," Jim answered. His voice was rather thin, but stable. "And I thank you for patchin' me up like you done."

"Are you the one that put the bandage on Mr. Richards?" the doctor asked.

"Yes."

"Well, young man, you did just the right thing, applying a compression bandage like that. You probably saved his life by keeping him from bleeding to death. Do you have medical training?"

"Not exactly," Matt replied.

"What do you mean, not exactly?"

"I learned doctoring from a man named Smoke Jensen, and he learned it from an old mountain man called Preacher."

163

"Well, I learned in medical school that someone who treats a wound or an illness with experience and common sense can be as effective as a college-trained doctor. And that is exactly what you did. You have my congratulations, sir, on a job well done."

"And you have my thanks," Jim added.

"My pleasure," Matt replied.

"Mr. Jensen," Hawkins said, coming over to the depot porch to join Matt, the doctor, and the wounded stagecoach driver. "Do you still want that beer?"

"Oh, yes, I absolutely want that beer. The thirst hasn't gone away," Matt replied.

"Then come with me, I'll show you some of the town as we walk down to my place."

"All right."

"Mr. Jensen?" Annabelle said.

Matt looked over toward the pretty redhead who had been the only female passenger on the stage. "Yes, ma'am?"

"Mr. Jensen, my name is Annabelle O'Callahan, and if you will allow me, I would be delighted to buy dinner for you this evening. I feel that would be the least I can do for you, after what you did for us."

"Why, Miss O'Callahan, I would love to have dinner with you, but I wouldn't feel right having a woman pay for it."

"Nonsense, I insist upon it. Shall I see

you this evening?"

"Yes, ma'am, and you have my appreciation for your generous offer," Matt said.

"You are very welcome. But don't you dare say ma'am to me again. I'm not your schoolteacher," Annabelle scolded. Her scolding, however, was ameliorated by a broad and very pretty smile.

Matt and Hawkins continued on down the street, with Hawkins pointing out the town. "That first building there, just on the edge of town, is Rafferty's Grocery Store. Next comes Clinton's Drugstore. Over there on the other side of the street is a leather goods shop, it's run by Mark Worley, next is McGill's feed and seed store, then Dupree's Emporium," Hawkins said as they passed each of the buildings. "You mentioned that you wanted a hotel room. This is the Milner Hotel. I would tell you that it is the best hotel in town, which it is, but it's also the only hotel in town," he added with a chuckle. "And don't worry about the livery being right across the street. When the wind's right, you don't smell anything at all."

"It might sound crazy, but I like the smell of horses," Matt said. "There's something very comforting about them."

"I know what you mean," Hawkins said.

"I may not look like it now, being as I own a saloon, but I was once a member of the United States Cavalry. I rode with General George Crook when we were chasing Geronimo all over hell's half acre. Oh, and you'll most likely be takin' your supper here, at Moe's. It's the . . ."

"Best in town?" Matt asked.

Hawkins chuckled. "Yes, and the only one in town."

"Then it'll be a pleasure to have a drink at the best saloon in town," Matt said. "I'm assuming it is the only one in town."

"You assume incorrectly, sir," Hawkins said, holding up his finger. "On one thing you are right, though, the Texas Star is the best in town, but there are three other saloons, the Pig Palace, the Crooked Branch, and the Ace High, down on Plantation Row."

"Plantation Row?"

Hawkins chuckled. "Yeah, they are actually down on First Street. Plantation Row is the locals' attempt at a little humor."

"I take it they aren't stellar establishments."

"You got that right. Seems someone is killed down on Plantation Row just about every other day. The biggest one, and probably the worst one, is the Pig Palace, owned by Jake Bramley. He waters his whiskey."

"He does?"

Hawkins looked around to see if anyone was close enough to overhear him. "Well, truth is, I don't know if he waters it or not. But that's what I tell everyone." He laughed out loud.

"Don't worry, Mr. Hawkins, your secret is safe with me," Matt replied with a chuckle.

"And this, sir, is my place, the Texas Star," he said as they reached the front of the building.

Pushing through the front door of the Texas Star, Matt saw that it could have been any saloon, in any town he had ever visited. Saloons like this, with the wide plank boards of the floor, the long, polished bar with the brass foot rail at the bottom, the piano at the back, the scattering of tables, and the saloon girls, garish in their makeup, were part of Matt's existence. This all defined his past, and he could no more deny it than he could deny his own history. As was his custom, he made a quick perusal of the saloon before he moved on in. There were three men standing at the bar, six tables with two to four men at each of the tables. At two of the tables there was a woman standing nearby, bantering with the men. There was a card game under way at the one of the tables and Matt could see the faces of three of the men. The fourth man had his back to Matt so that he couldn't see his face — but there was something about him, about the way he was sitting, that caused Matt's look to linger.

CHAPTER FOURTEEN

Braxton Barlow tied his horse off in front of the pawnshop that was on First Street next door to the Crooked Branch Saloon. When he walked into the shop carrying a gun in each hand, he was met by a man wielding a double-barreled shotgun.

"Hold it right there, mister!" the man with the shotgun said.

"What?" Brax said, startled to have the shotgun pointed at him. Then he realized why. "Wait, wait, these here guns ain't loaded! I come to pawn 'em, is all."

"Then take them by the barrels and lay them on the counter."

Brax did as instructed and when he did so, the shopkeeper put the shotgun down, and dragged both the pistols across the counter toward him. Picking them up one at a time, he ascertained that both were empty, then put them back down.

"I'll give you five dollars apiece for them,"

the pawnbroker said.

"Five dollars? Look here, I happen to know that these pistols cost twenty-five dollars when they was new."

"They ain't new now."

"But they still shoot as good as when they was new."

"Where did you get 'em?"

"What difference does it make where I got 'em? The point is, I got 'em, and now I'm tryin' to sell 'em to you."

"How do I know you didn't steal 'em?"

"I didn't steal 'em."

"Five dollars," the pawnbroker said again. "Take it or leave it."

"All right, all right, I'll take five dollars apiece for 'em."

The pawnbroker opened a little box, took out two five-dollar bills, and passed them across the counter to Brax. "It's been good doin' business with you," he said.

With a growl of disgust over how little money he got for the two pistols, Brax stuck the bills down in his pocket. He was closest to the Crooked Branch, but the Pig Palace was a bigger saloon, and he heard a woman's laughter coming from it, so he crossed the street, then pushed through the batwing doors to go inside.

■ ■ ■ ■

A quarter of a mile away, in the Texas Star, Matt managed to dismiss the little, niggling feeling he had about the fourth card player, and he followed Hawkins up to the bar.

Hawkins walked around behind the bar, then spoke to the bartender. "I will personally serve this gentleman, Johnny."

"Yes, sir," the bartender replied.

Hawkins drew Matt a beer, then set the golden mug in front of him, high with a foaming head.

Matt lifted the mug, blew away some of the foaming head, then took a long, satisfying drink before he set it back down, now half empty.

"That was good," he said.

"You drank that beer like you haven't had one in a while."

Matt thought back to Sherwood. Two weeks since he'd last had a beer, but it seemed more like a month of Sundays.

"It's been a dry day or two," he said.

"Let me freshen that for you," Hawkins offered.

"Thanks."

It took but a moment to put a new head on the beer in front of Matt.

To the casual observer it might appear that Matt was so relaxed as to be off guard. A closer examination, however, would show that his eyes were constantly flicking about, monitoring the room, tone and tint, for any danger . . . a kinesthesis developed from years of exposure to danger.

"This man, Pruitt," Matt said. "He seems a mite green yet to be a marshal. He must be pretty good to hold the job as young as he is."

"It isn't a matter of being good, as much as it is a matter of him being willing to take on the job," Hawkins said. "It hasn't been all that easy for us to find marshals."

"Why are you having trouble filling the position and keeping them on? Aren't you paying enough?"

"Oh, we're paying about as much as any town within a hundred miles of here. That's not the problem," Hawkins said, drawing a beer for himself.

"Well, if it's not a matter of paying them enough, what is the problem you have with keeping them on the job?"

"It's not a matter of keeping them on the job. It's a matter of keeping them alive," Hawkins said, speaking in a matter-of-fact voice as he took a swallow of his beer.

At that moment Marshal Pruitt came into

the saloon and, seeing Matt standing at the bar, smiled and started toward him.

"Mr. Jensen, I've interviewed the driver, the shotgun guard, and the passengers of the coach, and they are all singing your praises."

"Let me hasten to add my voice to the choir," Hawkins said. "I know for a fact that he saved me two hundred dollars, for that's the amount I had on my person at the time the coach was stopped. And I don't doubt but that he may have saved my life as well."

"I also learned a little about you," Marshal Pruitt said. "But you are a little off your range down here, aren't you? From what I've heard, you're from Colorado."

"To be honest, Marshal, I don't know as I could say I'm from anywhere," Matt said. "Though I have spent quite some time in Colorado. I was partly raised there, by a man named Smoke Jensen."

"Well, Mr. Jensen, on behalf of the good people of Shady Rest, I'd like to welcome you to our little town. Gerald, give Mr. Jensen a drink on me."

"Ha!" Hawkins said. "You picked a good day to be generous, Marshal. I've already told him that everything he drinks today is on me."

Matt held up his beer. "I appreciate it,

Marshal, but this is about my limit. I generally drink one for thirst and one for taste, and this is the one for taste."

"At least let me pay for one of them," Marshal Pruitt said, putting a nickel on the bar.

At that moment the conversation was interrupted by the crashing sound of a breaking bottle.

"You cheating son of a bitch!" a man shouted angrily.

Looking toward the disturbance, Matt saw a man standing over a table, holding a broken whiskey bottle. It was the man whose back had been to him when he first came into the bar, and he still couldn't see his face. He could see the other man though, and there were streaks of blood streaming down from a wound on his scalp, though the bleeding didn't appear to be too severe.

The injured man took out a handkerchief and held it to his head.

The two other players in the game had backed away from the table so quickly that their own chairs were on the floor, having been knocked over by their rapid withdrawal.

"By God, nobody cheats me and gets away with it," the man holding the bottle said.

Matt tensed. There was something damn

174

familiar about the belligerent man's voice.

"He wasn't cheating you, Morgan," one of the other players said.

Morgan? Matt didn't know anyone named Morgan.

"The hell he wasn't. It's been over an hour since I won my last hand."

"I don't have to cheat to beat you, Morgan," the bleeding man said. This man was dressed differently from everyone else in the room. He was wearing a white shirt with a black bolo tie and red garters around his sleeves. "You bet wildly without having the cards to back you up. You aren't aware of the cards that are already on the table, you have no concept of the law of averages. Simply put, Morgan, you have no business gambling, because you don't know how to play cards."

"The hell you say. I can play cards as good as anyone, and I say you're cheatin' me! I'm callin' you out on it!"

"Is the fancy dude a cheat?" Matt asked Hawkins.

"No, that's Emerson Culpepper. He's a professional gambler, and he is very good. I get ten percent of the table, plus he draws in a lot of players, some who come from neighboring towns just to try their luck with him. And of course, when they come to play

175

cards, they also buy drinks."

"Who's the loudmouth?"

"That unpleasant gentleman goes by the name of Morgan. I don't know if that is his first or his last name. He spends most of his time down on Plantation Row, which is fine by me. None of my girls will even go around him anymore, and he once tried to cheat my bartender, Johnny, out of some money, claiming to have paid for a drink with a five-dollar bill, when it was only a dollar. All things equal, I'd just as soon not have his business."

"You say his name is Morgan. Do you know that for a fact?" Matt asked. "I mean, have you known him for a long time?"

"No, I haven't. He's only been here a month or so," Hawkins said. "Morgan is the name he goes by. Why do you ask?"

By now, Matt knew who the man was.

"Marshal, does the name Mutt Crowley mean anything to you?" Matt asked.

"No, not particularly," Pruitt replied. "Should it?"

"Mutt Crowley and his partner killed a rancher and his wife a little over a year ago. The last time I saw him he was in jail in Trinidad, Colorado, waiting for the hangman's noose."

"Sounds like a pretty unpleasant fellow,"

Pruitt said. "Why do you ask about him?"

"Less than an hour before he was scheduled to hang, he managed to escape jail. I've not seen nor heard from him since then, but that's him, over there, arguing with the gambler."

"How sure are you that this is the same man?"

"I'm one hundred percent sure. I told you he was in jail in Trinidad? I'm the one who put him there. This is the first time I've seen him since then. I'd appreciate it, if you would appoint me as your deputy so I could finish the job I started."

Crowley continued his rant.

"I'm going to put a bullet right through that fancy shirt of yours, you cheating son of a bitch," Crowley said in a cold and harsh voice.

"Mr. Morgan, as I'm sure you can see, I am not armed," Culpepper said, his voice remained calm, and unhurried. He smiled, nervously. "I have found that not being armed manages to defuse most arguments." He removed his bloody handkerchief from the wound on his head and looked at it. "Broken whiskey bottles notwithstanding," he added.

"It only means that you are a coward," Crowley said. "You better get healed pretty damn quick, 'cause I aim to shoot your guts out."

"I appreciate your offer," Pruitt said to Matt. "But being as I'm the marshal, I'd better handle the job myself."

Pruitt drew his pistol, then turned toward Crowley. "Crowley, you are under arrest," he said.

Upon hearing his name spoken, Crowley stopped, then turned toward the marshal.

"What did you call me?"

"I called you Crowley. That is your name, isn't it? Mutt Crowley?"

"I don't know what you're talking about. You've got me confused with someone else," Crowley said.

"Have I? Well, I'll tell you what. Why don't you come with me on down to the office? I'll send out a few telegrams, and if you're not Crowley, we can get the situation resolved pretty quickly."

"Why don't you mind your own business?" Crowley said.

"I just heard you threaten Mr. Culpepper. And whether your name is Morgan or Crowley, that threat alone is enough for me to put you under arrest. But this gentleman is willing to swear that you are Mutt Crowley, and that you are wanted for murder," Pruitt said. "And, seeing as I'm the marshal in this town, I believe that makes it my business."

Crowley looked over at Matt, noticing him for the first time. "Jensen!" he said in an angry bark. "What the hell are you doing down here?"

Matt took a swallow of his beer. "So we meet again, Crowley."

"I — I don't know what you are talking about," Crowley said. He looked at Pruitt, and pointed toward Matt. "This man is lyin'. I've never met him before in my life. And I'm not Mutt Crowley."

"What do you mean you never met him?" Marshal Pruitt asked. "You just called him by name."

"That don't mean nothin'. He's famous. Ain't you ever heard of him?"

"I think you had better come with me, Mr. Crowley," Marshal Pruitt said, making a motion toward the front door with his drawn pistol.

Crowley turned toward him with a humorless smile. "Well now, Mr. Town Marshal, I gave you your opportunity to mind your own business, but it seems like you've just invited yourself to this party."

"Indeed I have," Pruitt replied. "Now, unbuckle your gun belt and let it fall to the floor."

Crowley moved his hand toward his gun belt, slowly and deliberately, and as he did so, Pruitt looked over toward Culpepper, who was still bleeding from his scalp wound.

"Mr. Culpepper, are you badly hurt? Do you need to see the doctor?"

The young marshal's expressed concern for Culpepper's well-being was a fatal mistake, because when he took his eyes off Crowley that gave Crowley the opening he needed. Crowley drew his gun and fired before Pruitt could react. With a look of shocked surprise on his face, the young marshal dropped his pistol, took a couple of staggering steps backward, then fell.

Matt had seen this same scene many times before, and he could tell by the lax look on the marshal's face, as well as the sightless stare of his open eyes, that Pruitt was dead.

"All of you seen that, didn't you?" Crowley called to the others, all the while holding a smoking gun in his hand. "You all seen that he drawed his gun first. He made a mistake, is all. I ain't this man Crowley that he was talkin' about. My name is Morgan."

"You are lying, Crowley," Matt said. He put his beer down and faced Crowley. "Your name is Mutt Crowley, and you are a thieving, murdering, lying son of a bitch. Marshal Pruitt told you to unbuckle your gun belt, which, as a lawman, he had every right to do. What you just did is commit another murder."

"Oh yeah? Well, what business is this of yours, anyway?"

"I just don't like to see my work undone," Matt said. "If you recall, I'm the one that got you put in prison the last time, and I'm the one that's going to do it again."

"You're goin' to put me in prison, are you?" Crowley said. He laughed a short, sarcastic laugh. "I don't think so."

"I'm either going to put you in prison, or I'm going to kill you," Matt said. "Which will it be, Crowley? You can make the choice."

"Jensen, you ain't got no sense at all, have you? Maybe you ain't noticed it, but there's two of us here, and only one of us is holdin' a gun." Crowley held his pistol up. "And as you can see, you ain't the one holdin' the gun."

"Mr. Hawkins, would you kindly send someone for the deputy?" Matt said.

"Mr. Jensen, I hate to say this, but Deputy Prescott isn't up to handling something like this."

"Oh, don't worry about that, Mr. Hawkins. It won't be a problem. By the time the deputy gets here, it will all be over," Matt said easily. "Crowley will either surrender without resistance, or I'll kill him, right here, and right now."

"The hell you say!" Crowley shouted, lifting his pistol. Even though he was holding his pistol in his hand, he was unable to bring his pistol to bear before Matt drew and fired twice, the two shots coming so close together that they sounded like a single shot.

"How the hell . . . ?" Crowley said, his voice strained. He clasped his hands over his wound and looked down at them as blood oozed through his spread fingers. He looked up again. "How the . . . ?"

Crowley fell to the floor, his head on the foot of Marshal Pruitt, the man he had just killed.

CHAPTER FIFTEEN

It wasn't necessary for Hawkins to send someone for the deputy marshal because he was just down the street when he heard the shooting, and he hurried to the saloon.

"Here's Deputy Prescott now," Hawkins said.

This was the same man Matt had seen leaning against the support post back at the stage depot. He was small and wiry, with a scraggly white beard and unkempt hair. He took one look at the two bodies on the floor, then, turning his head, started a well-aimed squid of tobacco toward a brass spittoon. It hit the spittoon with a dull thud.

"I'll be damned," Deputy Prescott said. "It looks like we done had us another marshal get hisself kilt. At least this time he kilt the man that kilt him."

"No, I'm afraid not," Hawkins said. "Crowley killed Marshal Pruitt. Then Crowley was killed by Matt Jensen here. The

183

same man who thwarted the coach robbery."

"Crowley? Who's Crowley?"

"That man," Hawkins said, pointing to one of the bodies.

"I thought his name was Morgan."

"He was just calling himself Morgan. It turns out that his real name was Mutt Crowley."

"How do you know that was his real name?"

"Because I knew him," Matt said.

"You knew him, and you kilt one of your own friends?" Prescott asked, looking at Matt.

"Believe me, he was no friend."

"Damn," Prescott said. "You've had a busy day, ain't you, Mr. Jensen? How many men have you kilt today? Three?"

"It has been a bit more active than a normal day," Matt agreed.

"Mr. Jensen, I owe you my thanks," Culpepper said. "You saved my life."

"No," Matt said. He pointed to the body of the young marshal. "It was Marshal Pruitt who stepped in and saved your life," Matt said.

"Yes, I suppose it was," Culpepper said. Culpepper looked down toward the dead marshal. "He didn't last any longer than the others, but you can't say the young man was lacking in grit."

"Well, Wash, looks like that makes you the marshal," Hawkins said. He smiled. "Has a nice ring to it, doesn't it? Marshal Wash Prescott?"

"It don't have no ring to it at all, on account of I ain't goin' to be the marshal," Prescott said resolutely.

"Where's your sense of civic duty?" Hawkins asked.

"I'm servin' as the deputy. That's all the civic duty I want. You can just go find yourself someone else to get hisself kilt, 'cause I ain't goin' to do it." Prescott looked over at Matt. "You want a marshal, then why don't you get the city council to hire this fella? Hell, he's been here less than one full day and he's done kilt three people."

"May I remind you, Wash, that all three people needed killing?" Hawkins said. "And I can personally attest to that, as I was a witness to all three incidents."

"Don't get me wrong," Deputy Prescott said. "I ain' sayin' they didn't need killin'." He pointed toward Mutt's body. "If that scar-faced son of a bitch kilt the marshal, then he sure as hell needed killin'. I was just commentin', that's all. I mean, when you think about it, we're goin' to need a

185

marshal that ain't all that easy to kill, and seems to me like Jensen here fits the bill."

"Yes," Hawkins said, reacting then to the deputy's suggestion. He looked over toward Matt. "What about it, Mr. Jensen? Would you be interested in bein' our town marshal? I know that the mayor would appoint you in a heartbeat."

"I appreciate the offer," Matt said. "But no, I don't think I would be interested."

"That's too bad," Hawkins said. He looked back at Deputy Prescott. "That leaves you, Wash."

"No, it don't, 'cause I ain't a' goin' to do it."

"Marshal Pruitt's been kilt!" someone said, coming into the Pig Palace with the news.

"Are you sure?" Jacob Bramley asked.

"Yeah, I'm sure. I was there, and I seen it with my own eyes."

"Damn! Another marshal kilt?" one of drinkers at the bar said. "That's how many? Four?"

"Yeah, four in as many months," Bramley said.

"Man, you couldn't pay me enough to be a marshal in this town."

"Doomey, did you say you were there?

Who shot the marshal?" Jacob Bramley asked.

"Morgan shot 'im," Doomey said.

"Morgan? You mean the fella that's been hangin' around here so much?" Bramley asked.

"Yeah, only his name warn't Morgan. It was Crowley, but it ain't nothin' now, seein' as he's dead."

"Wait a minute, are you saying it was Morgan who was killed? I thought you just said that he was the one who killed the marshal," Durbin asked.

"Crowley," Doomey said.

"Who is Crowley?"

"Morgan."

"What?"

"Turns out Morgan's real name was Crowley. Crowley kilt the marshal, then he got hisself kilt."

"So Morgan, or Crowley, whatever his name is, is dead?"

"Yep, him too," Doomey said.

Lenny Fletcher was sitting over in the corner of the saloon and he looked up when he heard Doomey say that Crowley had been killed. At the moment, Bill Carter was with Lila, one of the whores. They had made a deal with her that she would give them a little off of her normal price if they would both buy her services. Carter won the coin toss as to who would be first.

Doomey looked over toward Fletcher. "Crowley was your friend, wasn't he? Yours and Carter's. I've seen the three of you together all the time."

"I, uh, wouldn't call him a friend exactly," Fletcher said. "I mean I never met either one of them boys until I come here."

"So you're saying you didn't know that his real name was Crowley?"

"I ain't never heard of nobody named Crowley."

"Doomey, who says that Morgan's real name was Crowley?" Bramley asked.

"The man that kilt him."

"Now you're getting me all confused," one of the other bar patrons said.

"Hell, Howard, there ain't nothin' confusin' about it. It's like I said. Crowley kilt the marshal, then he got kilt his ownself."

"Will you for crying out loud tell us who killed Crowley?" Bramley asked in exasperation.

"Matt Jensen shot 'im. You know, the same fella that saved the stagecoach and kilt two of the robbers? And here's the thing, Morgan already had his gun out whenever Jensen drawed his own gun and shot 'im."

"So, Morgan is dead?" one of the bar girls asked.

"Not Morgan, Crowley," Doomey said.

"Whatever his name is, you're sure he's dead?"

"I'll say. He's deader'n shit."

"Good," the woman said.

"Why do you say good? Hell, you just spent the night with him last night, didn't you?" Bramley asked.

"Yeah, and you'll never guess what the son of a bitch did with my water vase."

"What?"

"He . . . well, never mind, it doesn't matter now. Morgan's dead, and I sure as hell ain't goin' to cry about it."

"Crowley," Doomey repeated.

"Matt Jensen kilt him, huh? Matt Jensen is a famous man, did you know that? There's been books wrote about him they say, though I ain't never read one of 'em," Howard said.

"Hell, Howard, you can't even read, so how would you read a book about him?" one of the other customers teased.

"That's what I'm talkin' about. I ain't never read nothin' about him."

Those within earshot laughed.

Lenny Fletcher wasn't the only one listening with interest to the conversation. Brax Barlow, who hadn't been in the saloon long enough to drink his first beer, was standing at the far end of the bar also listening. But his interest was less in Crowley than it was in the man who they said had killed Crowley. When it was mentioned that the one who'd killed Crowley was the same one who had killed the two stagecoach robbers, he began following the conversation with more interest.

"This man, Matt Jensen," Brax said. "Are you sure he's the one that saved the stagecoach?"

"He's the one all right. They say he kilt two of the robbers, and sent the other 'n a' skedaddlin'."

"I'd like to meet him," Brax said.

"What for?" Doomey asked.

"I'd like to shake his hand. I mean, a good citizen like that, who wouldn't want to shake his hand?"

"Well, More'n likely, you'll find him down at the Texas Star. Leastwise, that's where he was when I left over there, and that warn't more 'n a couple minutes ago."

"Where is the Texas Star?"

"It's up at the other end of town, on Railroad Street," Doomey told him. "You can't miss it. It's the only saloon over on

Railroad Street."

"You won't like the drinks down there, though," Bramley called to him as he started toward the door. "Hawkins tells his bartender to water 'em."

Carter was sweating, and grunting, and thrusting against the woman who lay beneath him. She was totally inert, neither resisting nor reacting to him.

"Why don't you help a bit?" Carter asked.

"You're not paying me enough for that," Lila replied.

Carter was beginning to wonder if he would even be able to finish, when he heard a loud knock on the door.

"Bill! Bill, it's me!"

Carter stopped in mid thrust. If there was anything he didn't need now, it was to be interrupted.

"Uhmm, honey, that was good," Lila said in a matter-of-fact voice. "Are you finished now?"

"What?" Carter replied, loudly and angrily.

"Bill! Bill, come to the door!"

"I told you I would come get you!" Carter yelled. "Can't you wait your turn?"

"That ain't it. It's somethin' else. Somethin' important," Fletcher yelled through the door.

"Honey, iffen you're finished, get offen me so's I can get myself cleaned up for your friend."

"I'm not . . ." Carter started; then, realizing that he had lost all interest, he sighed and rolled off her. "Never mind," he said.

Fletcher continued to bang on the door.

"Open the door for my friend," Carter said.

"I'm naked, honey. I don't have any clothes on," Lila said.

"What the hell does that matter? He's goin' to see you naked in a few minutes anyway."

Carter got up; then he looked back at Lila and pointed at her. "All right, I'll answer the door, but you stay there in bed 'til I tell you you can get up." He walked over to the door and jerked it open. "What do you want?" he asked. Then, realizing that he was standing naked in the doorway, he stepped back. "Come on in," he said.

"It's Crowley," Fletcher said as he stepped on into the room.

"You mean Morgan?"

"No, I mean Crowley. Ever' one knows about him now, since he's been kilt."

"Kilt? Wait a minute. Are you sayin' Crowley's been kilt?"

"Yes."

"Who kilt him?"

"Matt Jensen."

"Jensen? Son of a bitch, that's the one Crowley told us about, ain't it? The one that put him jail when they was goin' to hang him? What the hell is he doin' way down here? Are you sure it was Matt Jensen that kilt him?"

"I'm sure, all right. Seems some men tried to hold up a stagecoach today, and Jensen kilt two of 'em, an' run a third one off."

"Yeah, well, Crowley said he was a corker. So, Crowley got hisself kilt, did he? Why did you come bangin' on the door, disturbin' me? What does him gettin' hisself kilt have to do with us?"

"Think about it," Fletcher said. "Now that ever' one knows who Crowley was, that means that, more'n likely they're goin' to know about the bank robbery, and the killin's up in Kansas. And, they'll know we've been runnin' with him, and they'll start puttin' two and two together."

"Shhh," Carter said. He glanced over at Lila, but it appeared that she either had not heard or hadn't put anything together.

"I don't think she heard nothin'."

"Nevertheless, I think we should get out of here," Carter said.

193

"Not yet," Fletcher said. He grabbed himself and looked over toward the whore, then smiled. "I ain't had my time yet."

"And I ain't finished with my time," Carter said. "It was just goin' good when you come up and started bangin' on the door. You're just goin' to have to wait."

"Why do I have to wait?" Fletcher asked with a bawdy smile. "We're sharin' her anyway, ain't we?"

CHAPTER SIXTEEN

After leaving the Texas Star, Matt Jensen walked down to the stagecoach depot, where he was warmly greeted by Dusty Reasoner. Reasoner was talking to another man, average sized, bald except for a ringlet of gray hair that passed around his head just above his ears.

"Mr. Jensen, good to see you again. Mr. Tobin, this is Matt Jensen. He's the fella I was tellin' you about."

"Mr. Tobin," Matt said.

"Dusty told me what you did for us today, and you have my thanks," Tobin said.

"There wasn't much to it. I just happened to be there at the right time."

"Yes, but a lot of people, even if they had been there, would have been too frightened to get involved. You got involved, and for that, I thank you."

Matt knew that Tobin's comment about a lot of people not getting involved was right, but he didn't address it.

"I heard you just had another — let us call it an adventure," Tobin said. "Word is we just lost another marshal, and that you killed the man who killed the marshal."

"Yes," Matt replied without elaboration. He wasn't really surprised at how fast the news traveled. He had been in small towns before and was well aware of the effectiveness of word of mouth.

"Well, that's some consolation. I'm sure you've already heard that we've had three marshals killed before this one. At least, this time the killer didn't get away with it."

"I hope you're not leavin' us so quick," Dusty said. "Did you come to get your horse, or just to check on him? 'Cause if all you want to do is check on him, you can step back there and have a look. You'll see that he's getting along just fine."

"Thanks, but actually I have come for my saddlebags. I'm going to take a much needed bath, and I'll be needing a change of clothes."

"Ahh, no problem. I brought your tack in. It's right over there in the corner."

"Thanks," Matt said.

Matt slung his saddlebags over his shoulder, then, with a nod of good-bye, walked down to the Model Barbershop, where a

196

sign in front proudly proclaimed:

HAIR CUTS – SHAVES – BATHS
SHOES AND BOOTS SHINED

A small bell on the door rang as he pushed it open, and a man wearing a long white coat came from the back.

"Yes, sir?"

"I'd like a bath."

"Yes, sir, I'll get the hot water for you."

"I didn't notice, is there a laundry in town?"

The barber smiled. "You came to the right place. Fu Kwan has a place in the alley, just behind the barbershop, and he does a real bang-up job."

"It's getting pretty late. Is he still open?"

"Chinamen don't never sleep. Didn't you know that?"

Matt chuckled. "I didn't know that. That must be a piece of knowledge that escaped me."

When Brax Barlow reached the Texas Star, he saw a wagon parked out front. There was a body in the wagon, covered by a shroud, with only the feet sticking out. Going inside the saloon, he saw another body lying on the floor, with a few people looking down at it. He stepped up to the bar.

"I saw a body in a wagon out front, and now this one. Which one is Mutt Crowley?"

"This one is," the bartender said. "The fella in the wagon out front is our town marshal. That is, he was our town marshal. Now he's dead. Crowley kilt him, then Crowley got hisself kilt."

"Who kilt Crowley?"

The bartender smiled. "None other than Matt Jensen. I reckon you've heard of Matt Jensen, ain't you?"

"Is he the one who kilt the two men out on the road?"

"You mean the two outlaws that was tryin' to hold up the stage? Yep, he's the one."

"Where is he now? This Matt Jensen fella, I mean?"

"More than likely he's down at the barbershop, getting himself a bath," Hawkins said.

Brax felt a bit of apprehension over the new man who'd joined the conversation. He recognized him as one of stagecoach passengers, and he was concerned that, despite the hood he'd worn, this man might recognize him.

"He's goin' to be having dinner with Miss Annabelle O'Callahan. Now, if you were you going to be having dinner with a pretty woman like that, wouldn't you want to get all gussied up?" Hawkins asked.

Brax breathed a bit easier. It was obvious that he had not been recognized.

"Damn," one of the other customers said. "Wait a minute! You mean to say that Annabelle O'Callahan is havin' dinner someone that just come into town today? She ain't never had dinner with no other man in town, as far as I can recollect."

"Maybe she just has better taste than to have anything to do with anyone in town," Hawkins teased.

Brax turned to leave.

"Wait a minute," Hawkins called, and Brax froze in his tracks. Had he been recognized?

"Do you know Jensen? Do you want to leave a message for him?"

Brax breathed easier. "No, I don't know him. I've just heard a lot about him is all, and I thought I'd like to meet him."

"Well, I haven't known him all that long," Hawkins said. "And I know he's famous and all, but he strikes me as a man who doesn't like to be fawned over. So I would remember that, if I were you."

"Yeah, thanks," Brax said. "I reckon I'll just take a look at him from some distance, just so that someday I can tell folks I've seen him." Brax hurried on out the door.

"That was sort of a strange fella," the bartender said after Brax was gone.

"Yes, he was," Hawkins agreed.

"Hey, Gerald," one of the patrons called. "How long does this stinky son of a bitch have to lie on the floor in here?"

"Ponder promised to come back for him as soon as he got the marshal's body delivered," Hawkins said.

"What about his chips? They're still on the table."

"I don't know, what do you think we should do with his chips, Mr. Culpepper?"

"Looks to me like there's enough to buy a round of drinks," Culpepper replied, and the others let out a cheer as they rushed toward the bar.

Matt was, at this very moment, sitting in the bathtub in the back of the Model Barbershop. He had finished his bath, but he had stayed in the tub until the hot water began to cool, remaining there because it was relaxing to a body that was sore from several days of being in the saddle as well as sleeping on the ground.

He was just about to get out of the tub when he heard someone speaking very loudly from outside.

"Sir, you can't go in there! I told you, the

bathing room is occupied!" Matt recognized the barber's voice.

"Get the hell out of my way, or I'll shoot you too!" a gruff voice replied.

Quickly, Matt stepped out of the tub, then moved over into the corner, where he pulled his pistol from the holster.

The door to the bathing room was pushed open and a man stepped inside.

"You son of a bitch, I'm goin' to kill you!" the man shouted. Pointing his pistol toward the bathtub, he began blazing away, the gunshots unbelievably loud in the little room. The bullets splashed into the water of the vacated bath tub. The intruder fired until the hammer began to fall repeatedly on chambers that were no longer charged.

"Where the hell are you, you son of a bitch?" the intruder shouted as, frustrated, he continued to pull the trigger, getting nothing in return but empty metallic clicks.

"I'm over here," Matt said casually, speaking from the corner.

"What?"

"Barber?" Matt called. "Would you get the deputy, please?"

Tentatively, the barber looked into the room and saw Matt, standing naked in the corner, holding his pistol on the intruder.

He smiled when he saw that the danger was passed.

"Yes, sir, Mr. Jensen, I'll get him right away," the barber said.

Doing a balancing act, and passing his gun from hand to hand, Matt pulled on a pair of pants.

"You want to tell me why you were trying to kill me?" Matt asked.

"You mean you don't know?"

"How am I supposed to know? I never saw you before one minute ago when you barged in here shooting. What's your name?"

"The name is Barlow. Braxton Barlow."

"Why were trying to kill me, Braxton Barlow?"

"Them two men you kilt out on the road today was my brothers," Barlow said.

"Were you with them?"

"No, I — uh — I wouldn't just ride off and leave my brothers like that."

"Who said anything about anyone riding off?"

"Nobody, uh, I mean, I heard people talking."

"I see. Well, Barlow, when you go into the business of stagecoach robbing, you have to be prepared to take the consequences. And more times than not, those consequences could mean getting yourself killed."

■ ■ ■ ■

Wash Prescott had just left the mayor's office, and was walking down the street with his hands thrust down in his pockets, and his eyes looking at the ground. When he'd agreed to take on the job of deputy there were some who had told him he was crazy for taking the job, that he was too old. They were right about his age, because he was fifty-eight years old, and that was too old to be an active lawman.

But that was the thing. Prescott was not an active lawman, not in the sense that he would ever actually be involved in confronting an outlaw. Those who wondered why he had taken the job simply hadn't figured out Prescott's reasoning. First of all, there was no real physical labor, nothing that required him to do heavy lifting, or shoveling, or swinging an ax or a pick or a hammer.

Physically, the job was pretty easy, because most of the time all he did was stay in the marshal's office and keep an eye on the jail inmates. And although Shady Rest was beginning to get a reputation for lawlessness, especially with four marshals killed in four months, not one of the serious lawbreakers had been caught.

That meant that the only inmates who were in jail were there for minor infractions, such as public drunkenness, or vagrancy. Hell, Prescott even passed the time by playing cards with them. And truth to tell, though nobody in town knew it, Prescott had had his own experience with jail when, as a much younger man, he had served five years for armed robbery in the Ohio State Penitentiary.

As it turned out, that five years, occurring as it had during the Civil War, had kept him from going into the Army and, perhaps, being killed. And if he hadn't turned his life around he could well be in jail today, but he considered one incarceration enough. He appreciated being on the good side of the law, and the badge not only paid for his drinking, it also kept him out of trouble.

What he didn't like was the fact that, for the time being at least, he was the only law in Shady Rest. After the discussion with Gerald Hawkins, who had been pushing hard for him to take on the responsibility of being the marshal, Prescott felt it necessary to visit with Mayor Trout. He wanted Trout to know that since Marshal Pruitt had gotten killed, it would be incumbent upon the mayor and the members of the city council to appoint a new marshal. He also told the mayor that he had no intention of taking Pruitt's place.

"Now, Wash, you have been the only stabilizing influence in our town," Mayor Trout said. "You've been a deputy for nearly two years now, and every marshal we have had has spoken very highly of you. It seems to me like the most logical thing you could do would be to assume the position of marshal. And how about this? I'll have the city council approve a new salary for you. You'll be making more than any marshal this town has ever had."

"What good is more money if I'm dead?" Prescott asked. "I'm satisfied with being the deputy."

"Well, if you think about it, you are the titular marshal now, you just aren't being paid for it."

"I'm the what? What does titties have to do with bein' a marshal?"

Trout laughed. "Never mind. What I'm saying is, with young Devry Pruitt dead, you are the acting marshal."

"I'm not tryin' to get out of that. I'll be an acting marshal for you, but only until you can get a real marshal."

Prescott was still replaying the conversation in his mind, and was in front of Dupree's Emporium Store when he heard the sound of gunshots.

Hearing gunshots in Shady Rest wasn't unusual, in fact he heard them so often that he could almost tell by the sound whether the shots were being fired in anger, or drunken exuberance. But what made these shots unusual was that they seemed to coming from the barbershop.

The barbershop? What were gunshots doing coming from the barbershop? The saloon, yes, but not from the barbershop.

Prescott saw Earl Cook, the barber, hurrying toward him.

"Deputy Prescott, come quick!" Cook said.

Prescott held back. "What is it, Cook? You ain't plannin' on gettin' me into no gunfight now, are you? I'm just the deputy, remember."

"No, no, it ain't nothin' like that. Mr. Jensen, he's already got the fella captured."

"What fella are you talkin' about?"

"The fella that tried to kill 'im, that's the fella I'm talkin' about," Cook said.

"You ain't makin' no sense at all."

"You don't have to be worryin' about nothin'. All you have to do is put the fella in jail. Like I said, Jensen has him captured, and he isn't even armed."

"All right, all right, hold your horses. I

didn't say I wasn't comin'."

Matt wasn't able to put on any more clothes than his pants, because he had to keep an eye on Brax Barlow. Then, after a couple more minutes, during which neither he nor Barlow said a word, he heard someone from the front of the shop.

"Hello?" The call was tentative and hesitant.

"We're back here," Matt replied.

"Is everything all right?" It was the deputy marshal's voice, and he called into the room without making a physical appearance.

"If you mean am I still holding him prisoner, the answer is yes. Come get him now, so I can get dressed."

The deputy stepped into the room with his gun drawn. "Who have you got?" he asked.

"He says his name is Barlow. He and his brothers were the ones who tried to hold up the coach today."

"Is that a fact?" Prescott said. "Well, Mr. Barlow, I reckon you just chose the wrong town to mess with. Come on, let's go."

Prescott waved his pistol to signal Barlow to follow him.

"I'll be down later to sign a statement for you, if you want," Matt said.

207

"What kind of statement? What do you mean?" Prescott said.

"Won't you need a statement as to how he came in here and tried to kill me?" Matt asked.

"Oh, yeah. I guess so. You can come down anytime."

Matt finished dressing, then walked out front to pay Cook for his bath.

"Oh, there won't be any charge," Cook said with a wide smile. "I'll more'n get my money's worth by telling people that Matt Jensen had a shoot-out right here in my shop."

CHAPTER SEVENTEEN

"You know we're goin' to have to take care of Jensen, don't you?" Carter said to Fletcher when they were alone.

"What do you mean, take care of him?"

"You know what I mean. We're goin' to have to kill him. If he found Crowley, then he'll find us."

"But from what Doomey said, he wasn't lookin' for Crowley, he just happened to find him."

"Which means he could just happen to find us, if we don't do somethin' about it."

"I don't know about you, but I don't have any hankerin' to go up ag'in Jensen, even if it is two to one. You heard what Doomey said. Crowley already had his gun out, but Jensen kilt him anyway."

"Who said anything about goin' up against him? I said we were goin' to have to kill him — I didn't say nothin' about doin' it fair. This ain't no contest. It's just us against him, only I don't plan to give him a chance."

"How do you plan to do it?"

"We'll shoot the son of a bitch from ambush. He won't even see it comin'."

"Yeah," Fletcher said. "Yeah, if we're goin' to kill 'im, that would be the best way to do it. When?"

"The sooner the better."

Annabelle O'Callahan stood back and looked at the way the dress was hanging. Lillian Trout, wife of the mayor, was wearing the dress Annabelle had made for her, a slate-gray velvet walking suit, trimmed in red cashmere frieze.

"Oh, this is absolutely the most beautiful thing I have ever seen," Mrs. Trout said. "Annabelle, my dear, you are a treasure. Please don't ever leave Shady Rest. Why, the ladies would be absolutely bereft."

"I have no plans to go anywhere," Annabelle said. She glanced toward the clock. "Oh, except for dinner tonight, and I must hurry and get dressed. Do you mind if I leave you to find your own way out?"

"No, of course not, I don't mind at all, my dear," Mrs. Trout said. "But what is it about dinner that has you so eager?"

"I'm having dinner with Matt Jensen."

"Matt Jensen?" Mrs. Trout replied with a

curious expression on her face. "Who is Matt Jensen? Has he recently arrived in town? I don't believe I have met him."

"He is the one who stopped the stagecoach robbery today," Annabelle said.

"Oh, yes, I heard about that. So, you are having dinner with the hero, are you? Well, you must tell me all about it."

"It's just a dinner, there's nothing to it. It's my way of saying thank you. You see, I was carrying more money with me than I normally would, because I had been on a buying trip for material. And if the robbers had gotten away with it, it would have been a devastating loss."

"Yes, well, speaking for my husband, the mayor, please give him the thanks of the entire town," Mrs. Trout said.

"I shall."

The sun slipped down below El Capitan, and while it was not yet dark, the shadows had begun to lengthen by the time Matt left the barbershop and walked down the street to the Milner Hotel. The floor of the lobby in the Milner was of wide, unvarnished planks of wood, though much of it was covered with a patterned carpet of rose and gray. There was a leather sofa and several comfortable chairs scattered about. A large fireplace was at one end of the lobby, though as it was summer, no fire was burning. Matt walked across the lobby to the front desk.

"Yes, sir, may I help you?" the desk clerk asked with a welcoming and practiced smile.

"I would like a room," Matt said. "Preferably one at the front of the building, with a window view that looks down onto the street."

"I think we can accommodate you, mister . . ."

"Jensen. Matt Jensen."

The smile broadened. "Jensen? Yes, I've heard your name mentioned many times today. You are the one who saved the stagecoach, aren't you?"

"I was there. I don't know that you would say I saved it," Matt replied. Although he had spent a lifetime as the recipient of accolades, he still wasn't comfortable with them.

"Well, Mr. Jensen, I will give you a room in front of the hotel that looks right down onto the street. And if you want to know the truth, it's also the finest room in the hotel. I heard what you've done for the town, so there's nothing too good for you, Mr. Jensen."

"Thank you."

Matt took the key, then climbed the stairs to his room. He looked down the long, narrow hallway, which was flanked on both sides by closed doors. A couple of wall-mounted gas lamps hissed quietly, and emitted an orange light that lit the way. Behind the stairway Matt saw a small alcove that was dark, except for the dim splash of light that did little to illuminate it. At the front of the building, there was a cross hallway, making a T, and those were the rooms that looked out onto the street.

Before Matt went to his room he walked down to the opposite end of the hall to check on the window there. Examining it, he could see that the window overlooked the alley behind the hotel.

Opening the window, Matt leaned out and looked in both directions to see if there was a way this window could provide entry into the hotel without someone having to come through the front lobby. There didn't appear to be any access to the hotel through that window, short of climbing up a straight brick wall, and that was good. Matt had learned long ago, both from his mentor, Smoke Jensen, and from life experiences, to always err on the side of caution. As he stood there looking down, he saw a cat poised on the top of a fence, its tail moving back and forth slowly as he stared down at a rat. The rat, nibbling on a piece of bread, was totally unaware of the cat's presence, and his own imminent mortality.

Satisfied that the rear window offered no danger, he walked down to check out the room he had just been assigned. He had stayed in rooms that were larger, and much plusher, but this room was adequate. He would certainly be more comfortable here than he was on the frequent nights he spent out on the trail.

Now Matt checked out the front window. From here he had a good view of the main street. It was scarred with wagon ruts and dotted with horse droppings. The stagecoach depot was halfway down the street and he saw that the same coach he had escorted in today, now without horses, sat hulking and empty, awaiting the morrow when it would make a return trip to Van Horn. Right across the street from the hotel, as Hawkins had pointed out earlier in the day, was the livery stable.

Below him now, and next door to the hotel, was the Texas Star Saloon, and because the Texas Star was on the same side of the street as the hotel, he couldn't actually see it from his window. He was able to discern its presence though, by the bright splash of light the saloon threw into the street. He could also hear laughter and piano music.

That was for him. After he had his supper, he would go back to the Texas Star and see if Culpepper had returned to the game. Culpepper had left the game to have the doctor tend to the cut on his head, but, from what Matt had seen, the cut didn't seem serious enough to keep him away. Matt enjoyed poker, which was one of his few vices.

Wait a minute, he thought. He was having dinner with the woman from the stagecoach tonight. It might not be convenient for him to leave the dinner table early, just so he could have a game of poker. He might have to give up the game of poker, but spending the evening with a beautiful woman — and she was a beautiful woman — could have its own rewards.

He smiled at the thought of it.

Annabelle O'Callahan was having her own flights of fancy. She was thinking about the dinner she would be having with Matt Jensen, and she realized that, despite her age, experience, and a self-made life of success, she had never actually had an engagement with a man before. Oh, she had had dinners with men, sometimes even with one man, but in every previous case the dinners had been working dinners. Not once, on any occasion, had she ever forgotten that.

But this dinner tonight was different. She had invited him, ostensibly to "thank him" for what he had done in saving the stage-coach. But the truth was, she wanted to have dinner with him. She wanted to know what it was like to engage a man in conversation that wasn't related to business in one way or another.

Annabelle was different from almost any other woman she knew. She depended on no one but herself, and this left her out of the mainstream of life. Her best friends were books, her only adventures were in her mind, and her stimulation was her work

Her apartment was on the second floor over her shop, and she laid out a change of clothes — her usual working outfit, a gray wool flannel skirt and a white muslin blouse. But before she changed clothes, she stopped to consider her wardrobe. That was very good for business meetings, but this wasn't a business meeting. She wanted to look more feminine tonight.

Now, why would she want to look more feminine tonight over any other night? she wondered. But even as she wondered, she knew the answer. She just didn't want to articulate the answer, either in word or thought.

Annabelle chose a gold dress that clung to her figure, and she spent extra time with her long red hair, securing it in the back with a yellow ribbon, forcing some ringlets to fall casually in front of her ears. When she looked in the mirror she hardly recognized herself. She was very pleased with her appearance.

It had grown dark enough in the lobby for lanterns to be lit, and the hotel clerk went over to the wall where the anchor point of the chandelier suspension rope was. Releasing the rope, he began turning the pulley crank, until the great lobby chandelier was lowered enough to allow the clerk to light the fixtures. When Bill Carter stepped through the front door, the clerk was so engaged, standing on a small stool and holding a lighted taper to each lantern wick.

"I'll be right with you, sir," the clerk said as he continued with his task.

Carter walked over to the front desk and looked around to see if he could find the registration book, but didn't see it.

With the chandelier lit, the hotel clerk stepped back over to the wall and turned the pulley crank so that the rope lifted it back to the ceiling. That done, he secured the rope, then came over to the desk.

"Yes, sir, now how may I help you?" the hotel clerk asked.

"I'm looking for Emmett Barnes," Carter said. "What room is he in?"

"Emmett Barnes? I don't believe I remember such a person checking in."

"He's here. I know he is, 'cause I'm s'posed to meet him, right here at this hotel."

"I will check, but I'm sure I don't remember seeing that name."

"Don't tell me he ain't here."

The clerk examined the registration book, then shook his head. "No, sir, it is just as I thought. We have nobody by the name of Barnes who is registered at this hotel."

"This is the only hotel in town, ain't it?"

"Yes, sir, it is. But I assure you, there is nobody by the name of Emmett Barnes registered here."

"You're lyin'. Let me look at your registration book, I'll find 'im myself."

"All right, look for yourself," the clerk said, turning the book around. "I have no reason to be lying to you, sir, and as you will see, there is no such person here."

Carter looked through the book until he

found the name he was looking for; then he pushed the book back.

"You're right, he isn't here."

"Of course, I'm right," the hotel clerk said, indignantly.

Carter started toward the door.

"Sir," the hotel clerk said. "Would you like to leave a message in the event Mr. Barnes checks in?"

"In case who checks in?"

"Mr. Barnes."

"No, why would I want to leave him a message?"

"Well, I don't know why, sir. You were the one who was looking for him."

"Oh, yeah, yeah, I was, wasn't I? No, no message."

"Very good, sir," the clerk replied, thinking the entire conversation was rather odd.

Chapter Eighteen

"You see the second window from the left?" Carter asked Fletcher a few minutes later. "I'm talkin' about the one on the top floor," he added.

"Yeah, I see it."

"That's Jensen's room." Carter looked up and down the street; then he smiled. "Damn!" he said.

"What is it?"

"Hell, this is goin' to be easy. All we got to do is climb up in the loft of the livery stable. It's right across the street, and from there we'll have a prefect view of the hotel."

"What good will that do?"

"Well, think about it, Lenny," Carter said. "If we are up there in the loft with rifles, he's goin' to come stand in the window sometime. They don't nobody take a hotel room without lookin' through the window out onto the town. And soon as he does that all we got to do is pull the trigger. He'll be dead before he knows what hit him."

Fletcher smiled. "Yeah," he said. "Yeah, I like that."

The two men went into the livery.

"Just a minute," someone called from the back of the livery. "I'll be right with you."

With nobody up front to see them, Fletcher and Carter climbed the ladder quickly and silently. A moment later they were both lying on their stomachs in the hay at the loft window. They had a perfect view of Matt Jensen's room.

"All right, now what can I . . ." the stable man started to say as he came back to the front. He stopped when he didn't see anyone. "Hello?" he called. He scratched his head, shrugged his shoulders, then went back to whatever had been occupying his time at the rear of the barn.

Very quietly, the two men jacked rounds into the chambers of their Winchesters, then waited.

Deciding she was as ready as she was going to get, Annabelle left her apartment and strolled down the boardwalk to the hotel, which was but three buildings north of her shop on Railroad Avenue.

When she stepped into the lobby a couple of minutes later, the hotel clerk was surprised to see her.

"Miss O'Callahan? What are you doing here?" he asked.

"Hello, Michael. I'm having dinner with Mr. Jensen tonight. I assume he is one of your hotel guests?"

"Oh, he is indeed," Michael said with a broad smile. "He is on the second floor, room two-oh-one. Would you like me to run up and summon him for you?"

"No, if it is all right with you, I'll go up myself." She smiled. "That is, if you don't think it would be too scandalous."

"Miss O'Callahan, your reputation is such that I don't think it would be possible for you to do anything scandalous," Michael said. "Go right on up."

"Thank you."

Bathed, shaved, and in clean clothes, Matt Jensen bore little resemblance to the trail-worn and dirt-covered traveler who had ridden into town today. It had grown dark outside and the first thing Matt had done after checking into his hotel room was light the lantern. He had just turned it up when there was a knock at the door.

Taking no chances, Matt stepped up to the wall just beside the door, then, reaching out, turned the knob and jerked the door

222

open. A woman who was just about to knock on the door a second time, lost her balance because of the sudden opening of the door and she had to step into the room very quickly in order to stay erect.

"Hello," Matt said.

Because Annabelle had stumbled into the room, she hadn't seen Matt, who was now behind her. At the sound of his voice she turned toward him with a smile, but the smile left her face when she saw that he was holding a gun.

"Oh!" she said, startled by the sight of the pistol in his hand.

"I'm sorry," Matt said. "I didn't expect a woman at my door." He put the pistol back into his holster.

Annabelle suddenly realized she was staring. Earlier, she had thought that he was handsome in a rugged and unsophisticated way. But the man she saw standing before her now was an exceptionally handsome man who would be at home in any setting in Philadelphia. She actually had to take a second look before she could satisfy herself that this really was the same man.

"Mr. Jensen?" she asked. Then, realizing that she may have sounded somewhat awestruck by him, she added to her comment. "Do you so often expect brigands that you must answer your door while armed?"

"Well, to tell the truth, it's just a habit that I've developed over time. I always figure that it's better to be safe than sorry," Matt replied. "And, to tell the truth, I didn't expect you to come calling for me."

"Was I mistaken? We did have a dinner engagement for this evening, did we not?"

"Yes, ma'am, I'm happy to say that we do. Only I figured I would probably just meet you there."

"Meet me where? We hadn't made any plans beyond just having dinner."

"I had supposed that I would meet you at the restaurant."

"Which restaurant?"

"Which one? Mr. Hawkins led me to believe that there is only one restaurant in town."

Annabelle laughed, the laughter reminding Matt of a bubbling stream. "Mr. Hawkins is talking about Moe's Café, no doubt. And he is correct when he says that Moe's is the only restaurant in town." She held up a finger to make a point. "But we aren't going to Moe's Café. Shady Rest has a Merchants Association Club that is surprisingly urbane for a town this size. It has a wonderful chef, and they serve dinners that are far superior to anything Moe's can put on the table. If it is all right with you, that's where I thought we would eat tonight. It is a private club, but, as a merchant, I belong. You shall be my guest for the evening."

The woman who was now standing in Matt's hotel room was not only beautiful; she exhibited the innocence of that breed of woman that Matt often saw, but never touched. She belonged to what he referred to as *the other life.* The other life consisted of hardworking, honest men who ranched or farmed, who drove wagons or stagecoaches, who clerked in stores, and worked in offices. It also consisted of the women and children who were there in support of those same hardworking, honest men.

Matt's referring to theirs as the other life was not a derisive sobriquet. On the contrary, they were people he admired, respected, and envied. For nearly his entire life, Matt had lived in a world that was parallel to, but not a part of, the other life. Had he not been orphaned at an early age, had things not been so drastically changed by events over which he had no control . . . he might have been one of those people, and a woman such as Annabelle might be his own. But the world in which Matt now lived was one of transience and a surprising amount of violence. And the women of this

225

life of transience and violence were nothing like the woman who had identified herself as Annabelle O'Callahan.

"Shall we go, Mr. Jensen? Or are you just going to stand there and look at me as if I were on display?" Annabelle asked, an easy smile playing at the corners of her mouth.

"Can you blame me? I'm enjoying the display," Matt replied, matching her smile. "But give me just a moment to put out the lantern before we leave, would you? I don't like leaving a lit lantern in an empty room."

"That's probably a good idea," Annabelle agreed.

Matt walked over to the window and reached down toward the lantern. Bending down just as he did proved to be a fortuitous move, for out of the corner of his eye he saw a sudden flash of light from the livery stable just across the street. He knew he was seeing a muzzle flash, even before he heard the gun report, and he was already pulling away from the window at the precise instant a bullet crashed through the glass of the window and slammed into the wall on the opposite side of the room.

Annabelle screamed and, quickly, Matt moved across the room to grab her and pull her to the floor with him as there was another shot on the heels of the first.

"Oh!" Annabelle said. "What is it? What is happening?" She tried to stand, but Matt held her down.

"No!" he commanded. "Stay down."

"Who is shooting at us?"

"They aren't shooting at us, they are shooting at me," Matt said. "You just happen to be with me."

Slithering across the room on his stomach, Matt rose up and extinguished the lantern. Then, without the backlight, he raised his head up just far enough to stare into the darkness across the street. He was certain that the muzzle flash had come from the loft of the livery stable, but he was equally certain that whoever it was had left when they realized they hadn't hit him, and no longer had a target.

"Damn, we missed!" Carter said.

Fletcher raised his rifle to his shoulder, but Carter pushed it down. "No sense in shooting now, he's put the light out. We'd just be shooting in the dark."

"What do we do now?"

"We go back to the Pig Palace."

"Don't you think we ought to maybe get out of town? We just shot into a hotel room tryin' to kill somebody," Fletcher said.

From the other side of town, they heard a

couple of gunshots.

"Did you hear that?" Carter asked. "Hell, someone shoots a gun off in this town just about ever' fifteen minutes. What's a couple of more gunshots?"

"Yeah, I reckon you're right," Fletcher said. Fletcher started toward the ladder to go back down.

"Wait, let's make certain the livery man's not down there," Carter said. He walked over to the edge of the loft, then looked down. Not until the coast was clear did he signal for Fletcher. Going back down, they managed to exit the stable by the back way without being seen.

By the time they returned to the Pig Palace, it was filled with noise, piano music, and laughter. Carter and Fletcher stepped up to the bar and ordered a beer each, then they found a place back in the corner.

"You two still sittin' back there?" Doomey asked. "Damn, you been there all night. Don't you ever do anythin' but sit around?"

"Sittin' around is hard work, and you get so tired doin' it, that you can't hardly do nothin' else but sit," Carter said, and Doomey laughed.

"Damn," Fletcher said, quietly. "There don't anybody even know we was gone."

"Yeah, don't say nothin' else," Carter said.

"Let's keep it, that way."

From his hotel room, Matt continued to stare out into the darkness, but he saw no activity of any kind, and decided that, without the glowing lantern providing a target, his assailant, or assailants, had probably left by now. Feeling confident enough to stand up, he looked at the two panes of glass that had been shot out.

"Oh my," Annabelle said from her position on the floor. "I just know that I'm getting my dress all wrinkled."

Matt chuckled. "If the worst thing is that you're getting your dress wrinkled, then I guess you're in good shape," he said.

"Yes, I suppose that's right."

"I guess I won't have to raise the window tonight," he said with a little chuckle. "I'm getting plenty of air now. Shall we go to dinner?"

"What?" Annabelle asked. "Someone tries to kill you, and all you can say is, 'shall we go to dinner?'"

"I'm hungry," Matt replied. "Besides, that's no different from you worrying about getting your dress wrinkled."

He held his hand down toward her to help her up. But she hesitated.

"It's all right. It's safe now," Matt said.

"Whoever it was, they're gone."

"How do you know they're gone?"

"Because when I stood in the window they didn't take another shot at me."

"That seems a rather foolish way to test your theory," Annabelle said.

"But effective," Matt said. He was still holding his hand down toward her, and she took it, then got to her feet. Matt led her out into the hallway, which was illuminated by low-burning, wall-mounted, and quietly hissing gas lanterns.

When they reached the lobby of the hotel, the clerk was standing at the front door looking out onto the dark street.

"Mr. Jensen, Miss O'Callahan, did you hear the shooting from outside?" the clerk asked.

Annabelle started to respond, but, with a look, Matt stopped her.

"Yes, I thought I heard something," Matt said. "Oh, by the way, just for your information, there are a couple of broken panes in the window to my room."

"I will tell Mr. Milner about it tomorrow," the clerk said. "Enjoy your dinner."

Matt nodded, then held the door open for Annabelle.

"Good night, Michael," Annabelle said as they stepped outside.

CHAPTER NINETEEN

The Merchants Association Club was actually on the top floor of Dupree's Emporium. When they stepped inside, Matt was quite surprised. He had certainly been in places that were as elegant, or even more elegant before. But he didn't expect such a place in Shady Rest.

Inside the club, the hardwood floor glistened under a very large Axminster carpet. The carpet was lawn green with wine-colored nine-point starbursts in attractive patterns throughout. The walls were paneled with rich cherry, with carved camphor wood insets, and the chairs around the white linen-covered tables were elegantly upholstered in a green and wine bargello needlework tapestry.

"What do you think of our club?" Annabelle asked.

"I'm impressed."

"The decent citizens of the town need

something like this," Annabelle said. "Sometimes I fear our town is defined by those terrible places down on First Street."

"First Street?"

Annabelle chuckled. "You've probably already heard it referred to as Plantation Row."

"Yes," Matt agreed with a smile.

A well-dressed waiter approached the table.

"Would you trust me to order for us?" Annabelle asked.

"I would appreciate it if you did order for us. After all, I presume you know the club, and the chef."

"*Bon soir, Marcel. Nous aurons le roti de boeuf, pommes de terre cuites, les asperges, et une bonne bourgogne, s'il vous plait.*"

"*Tres bonne, Mademoiselle O'Callahan,*" Marcel answered.

"Now, I really am impressed," Matt said. "What did you order?"

Annabelle chuckled. "I'm showing off. I studied French in school — not Spanish, mind you, but French. So where do I wind up? In Texas, where many speak Spanish, while Marcel and I may be the only two people within a hundred miles in any direction who speak French. So we always take advantage of that when we can. I ordered roast beef, baked potato, asparagus, and a good red wine."

"And to think that last night I had rabbit," Matt said.

Annabelle laughed out loud. "Rabbit?"

"Without salt," Matt added.

As they were waiting for the meal to be delivered, they were approached by a middle-aged woman who was dressed all in black, and wearing a black lace veil. When she reached the table, Matt stood.

"Please," the woman said, holding out her hand. "Be seated, young man. I just want to say a few words to Miss O'Callahan."

"Mr. Jensen, this is Mrs. Pruitt," Annabelle said. "She is — was Marshal Pruitt's mother."

"Oh," Matt said. "You have my sincerest condolences, ma'am."

"Thank you," Mrs. Pruitt said. "And, Miss O'Callahan, I want to thank you so much for this mourning dress. What a wonderful and caring thing for you to do. And I want you to know that I will pay for it as soon as I can save the money."

"No, please, no," Annabelle said, reaching out to put her hand lightly on the woman's arm. "The dress is yours for no charge. I am only sorry that the occasion arose that required such a dress."

233

Mrs. Pruitt smiled, a wan smile. "Well, I must go. I'm not a member of the club, but the maitre d' graciously let me in to speak with you."

"Won't you stay, as my guest?" Annabelle invited.

"Thank you, but no, I must get back home. Mr. Pruitt and I have been receiving callers all day, as you can imagine. And I must be there with him to help welcome them. But, again, I thank you."

Although Mrs. Pruitt had excused Matt from standing, he remained on his feet until the grieving woman left the dining room.

"Sometimes I think the people of Shady Rest think of the many killings that go on here as little more than a stain on the reputation of our town. They don't go beyond that, to think about the human part of it, the mothers, wives, and loved ones who are left behind," Annabelle said.

Matt just nodded. He made no verbal answer because he couldn't. His life was such that he often encountered life-and-death, kill-or-be-killed situations, and he couldn't afford such thoughts. In order to survive in his world, it was absolutely necessary that he develop a degree of detachment. Nonetheless, he could feel a sense of respect and admiration for Annabelle's sensitivity.

When the meal was delivered, Matt savored every bite, storing it away to be remembered at some future point when, on the trail, he would be eating jerky and drinking tepid water.

Then, just as they were finishing their meal, they were approached by Deputy Prescott. Prescott nodded his greeting toward Annabelle, then turned to Matt.

"Mr. Jensen, when do you expect to leave town?" he asked.

"Why do you ask? Are you running me out?"

"No, sir, nothin' like that," Deputy Prescott said. "Nothin' like that at all. It's just that, I'm wonderin' if you are goin' to be stayin' around long enough to collect the reward."

"Reward? Oh, yes, for Mutt Crowley. Five hundred dollars from Las Animas County in Colorado, I believe, for escaping jail. Sure, I'll wait around for it."

"No, sir, I don't know anything about that reward," Deputy Prescott said. "The reward I'm talkin' about ain't from Las Animas County, it's from Wells Fargo."

"Wells Fargo? Why would Wells Fargo be

paying a reward for someone who escaped from jail?"

"That ain't what they're payin' the reward for. And the reward ain't for five hundred dollars, neither. It's for five thousand dollars."

"Five thousand?" Matt said, pleasantly surprised by the amount.

"Yes, sir, five thousand dollars. Seems Mr. Crowley and his gang stole twelve thousand five hundred dollars from a bank in Kansas, and they also kilt some people up there. I'll contact the county sheriff tomorrow and have him send off for the reward. That is, if you're a' plannin' on stayin' aroun' town long enough to collect it.

"Oh, I'll be here, all right," Matt said.

Deputy Prescott chuckled. "I sort of thought you might be."

After dinner, Matt walked Annabelle back to her apartment.

"Thank you very much for the great dinner," he said. "But I do hope you will let me repay you. Though I guess dinner at Moe's is about the best I can do."

"Why, Mr. Jensen," Annabelle replied with a broad smile. "Don't you know that the best ingredient for any dinner is the company you share? I not only would be delighted to have dinner at Moe's with you, it is something that I positively expect."

After Matt left, Annabelle stepped up to the front window of her upstairs bedroom and, pulling the shade aside, watched him as he walked back to the hotel. She had never given serious consideration to settling down with any man, and she could enumerate a dozen or more reasons why. Principal among those reasons was the fact that she had no wish to give up her independence and any man would insist that she do so.

It wasn't something she had to think about in Shady Rest anyway. There had never been any single men in town that she found interesting enough to even consider giving up her freedom. Until Matt Jensen. She was glad he was not a permanent resident of Shady Rest, nor did it appear that he would soon become one.

She watched him until he turned into the front door of the hotel; then she left the window, undressed, and went to bed. Alone. That was funny, she thought as she lay in bed, staring up into the darkness. She had been going to bed alone for her entire life, but never, until this very moment, had she thought about it that way.

As Matt returned to the hotel, he thought of Annabelle. He found her a most fascinating woman. She was a little like a drop of morning dew. Seen from one angle, a dewdrop can turn a sunbeam into a brilliant burst of blue light. Tilt the eye just so, and the drop of dew turns into a splash of crimson, a flash of gold, or any one of the colors of the rainbow.

This woman was like that. At first, he'd admired her cheekiness, though he'd thought she might be just a little too forward. Of course, he was also aware of her beauty. Then tonight, he'd learned that she was a woman of great sensitivities. What a brilliant spectrum of color to come from just one woman.

Matt's chosen lifestyle was such that there really was no room for a woman, though he certainly wasn't without experience. A banker's daughter in Cheyenne once thought she could make him settle down — a soiled dove in the Territories knew that she couldn't, but she took what he offered. There had been, from time to time, women along the way, like mile posts on a journey. Was Annabelle O'Callahan such a woman? It was too early to tell.

When Matt went to bed in his hotel room that night, he hung his holster from the headboard of the bedstead so he could get to the gun easily if he had to. He had no idea who it was that had taken a shot at him tonight, but if they tried again, he wanted to be ready for them.

The next morning a series of loud popping noises woke Matt from the soundest sleep he had enjoyed in several days. Startled, he sat straight up in bed, slipped his pistol from the holster which hung from the bedpost, then got to his feet, ready for any intrusion.

There was another series of loud pops, followed by the high peal of a woman's laughter, then the sound of a brass band.

Matt moved over to the window and pulled the curtain to one side as he looked down on the street. The street was full of men and women, and Matt decided he would go down to have breakfast and see what was going on.

Fifteen minutes later, Matt was in Moe's Café, eating a sandwich of bacon, egg, and biscuit, when Deputy Prescott came into the café and, seeing Matt, came over to visit him.

"I haven't been keeping up with the date," Matt said. "Is it the Fourth of July?"

Prescott laughed. "The Fourth of July? No, what makes you think that?"

"Then why all the fireworks?"

"Ha!" Prescott replied. "You're the cause of the fireworks."

"Deputy, I don't have the slightest idea what you are talking about. How am I the cause of your celebration?"

"I take it you haven't gone down to look at the display in front of Ponder's shop yet," Prescott said.

"No."

"Go take a look, Mr. Jensen. Then you'll see what all the celebratin' is about."

Finishing his biscuit, Matt walked down toward the Ponder's Mortuary. There were several people, men, women and children, standing around, looking at what was displayed there. Just as Matt approached, a pan of phosphorous powder flashed, the result of a photographer taking a picture. He wondered what the picture was of, but when he picked his way through the gathered crowd, he saw the subject of the photography. Mutt Crowley's body, his skin now a pale blue-white, had been tied to a board and propped up against the front of Ponder's place of business. Crowley's right eye was shut, but the left eye, the one with the scar-disfigured eyelid, was open, and opaque. Many of the more daring children would occasionally get close enough to touch the cold, clammy skin.

"The county sheriff has asked that a picture be taken of the body, so as to prove that Mutt Crowley has actually been kilt," Prescott explained. "He said without the proof, he can't rightly tell the Wells Fargo folks that they need to pay the reward."

"Look, that's him!" someone shouted, noticing Matt for the first time.

"It's Matt Jensen!"

"Three cheers for Matt Jensen!" someone else called. "Hip, hip . . ."

"Hooray!"

"Hip, hip . . ."

"Hooray!"

"Hip, hip . . ."

"Hooray!"

Matt held up his hand to silence them, then noticed, for the first time, a hand-lettered sign.

**HERE IS THE BODY OF
MUTT CROWLEY
KILLED BY
MATT JENSEN
JUST AFTER CROWLEY MURDERED
MARSHAL DEVRY PRUITT**

"I still don't understand why all the celebration," Matt said.

"It's simple," Prescott said. "Pruitt is the

241

fourth marshal we've had kilt in the last four months. The man who kilt the marshal was kilt himself, and there he is." Prescott pointed to Mutt Crowley's body. "And you're the one that done it."

CHAPTER TWENTY

Pecos

Prichard Crowley was asleep in the sheriff's office when someone awakened him.

"What the hell?" he said, sitting up in the cot. "Who is it? What do you want?"

"You the sheriff?" a voice asked from the dark.

"I'm the deputy."

"Sheriff or deputy, it don't matter none. You'll do just as good."

"I'll do just as *good* as what?" he asked. He emphasized the incorrect grammar, though he knew that the person wouldn't catch it.

"For me to turn in the body for bounty."

Prichard walked over to the desk, lit the lantern, then turned it up. In the lantern's glow he saw the bounty hunter. About five feet nine, the bounty hunter had a hook nose and an upturned chin that looked almost as if they wanted to join. His cheeks were sunken and his eyes were dark beads under dark eyebrows. He was wearing a stained hat.

"Who have you got?" Prichard asked.

The bounty hunter pulled a folded and wrinkled wanted poster from his pocket, and spread it out on the desk by the lantern.

WANTED
By the State of Texas
for MURDER
BARRY HOLDER
$2,500
DEAD OR ALIVE

"I've got this here feller throwed belly down over his horse outside," the bounty hunter said. "All I need from you is a receipt sayin' yeah, this is him. Then you can put in for my reward."

"How do you know the man you have is Holder?"

"Hell, it's easy. He got part of his ear bit off last time he was in prison. And he's missin' two fingers on his left hand," the bounty hunter said.

That was what Prichard wanted to hear. Because he was in charge of posting all the wanted posters, he was aware not only of who Holder was, but of his physical description.

"What's your name?" Prichard asked.

"The name is Franken. Harry Franken. There prob'ly ain't nobody 'round here ever heard of me. I mostly stay 'round San Antone, but I got word that Holder was over here and, sure enough, when I come over here, I found 'im. He was hidin' out in a cabin, no more'n five miles from here."

"So this was the first place you came?" Prichard asked. "What I mean is, nobody else has seen the body?"

"No, why would I go anywhere else? I told you, I found him in a cabin, not more'n five miles west of here, down in a draw, it was. Why, you could damn near ride right by it, and miss it. But I know'd what I was lookin' for, you see, and I found it. So what I done is, I took my rifle and laid nearby is some rocks. Where I was, was no more'n fifty yards away from the front door. I waited 'til he come out to take a piss." Franken laughed. "Then, while he was standin' there takin' 'im a piss, why, I shot 'im." Franken laughed again. "Don't you know he was some surprised, gettin' shot right while he was takin' a piss?"

"I will have to validate your claim," Prichard said.

"You'll have to what?"

"I'll have to see him," Prichard said.

"Oh, well, sure, if that's all. Like I said, I've got him throwed over his horse. Come on outside, and I'll show 'im to you."

Franken started toward the door, and Prichard followed along behind. Franken stopped, and looked back. "Won't you be needin' the lantern?"

"Why? I can determine if part of his ear and two fingers are missing without a lantern."

Franken chuckled. "Yeah, I reckon you can at that."

As the two men started through the door, Prichard, who was following behind, reached over to pick up a piece of wire that was left over from having suspended from the picture rail a photograph of John Ireland, governor of Texas.

The two men stepped out into the dark night, made even darker by the fact that there was no moon. There were also no streetlamps near the sheriff's office.

"I don't know," Franken said. "It's pretty dark. You sure you'll be able to see enough?"

"I'm sure."

There were two horses tied in front of the sheriff's office. One of them had a body draped over the saddle, and the other was empty.

"Grab him by the hair and lift his head up," Prichard said.

"All right," Franken replied. He grabbed Holder's head by the hair and lifted it up. "It was his left ear that was bit off, and if you look here you can see what I'm tal . . . arrrrrrghhh!"

Prichard looped the wire around Franken's neck, then tightened it. Franken struggled, and reached up to try and grab the wire, but by now it was not only strangling him, it was cutting into his neck.

"This is called a garrote," Prichard said quietly. "You may be interested in knowing that it was used primarily as a means of execution by the Spanish."

Franken continued to make barely audible gurgling sounds.

"But it is also an excellent weapon for killing quietly, and without too much blood," Prichard continued, as if conducting a class.

Franken's body stretched out in a spasmodic death shudder, and his tongue protruded from his mouth. Within less than a minute he grew limp, and even in the dim light Prichard could see that his face was now discolored and contorted. His tongue was forced out of his mouth.

Prichard removed the wire, and let Franken's body fall to the ground. Then, he looked around to make certain no one had seen what just happened. It was a needless precaution because it was two o'clock in the morning, it was pitch dark, and the nearest house was at least one hundred yards away. He was absolutely positive he hadn't been seen.

Prichard draped Franken over his own horse and tied him securely. Then he saddled his horse and led the two horses, both bearing bodies, out of town.

When Prichard had first come to Pecos he'd seen a deep crevice in a nearby draw about eight miles northwest of the town. The crevice was narrow, and several hundred feet deep. Prichard rode up to the edge of the crevice, removed Franken's body from the back of the horse, and dropped it down into the crevice. He took off the saddle and dropped it down into the crevice as well. After that he gave Franken's horse a whack on the rump and sent it galloping off. That done, he started back to town with Holder's body draped across the dead outlaw's horse.

It was well after daylight when Prichard returned, and Sheriff Nelson was waiting for him.

"Where've you been?" Sheriff Nelson asked.

"Didn't you get my note?"

"What note?"

"Well, as you are aware, since you are the one who assigned the task to me, I've been processing wanted posters. Because of that I've come across considerable information about many of the wanted men and, last night, I saw Barry Holder coming into town. I challenged him, and he turned and galloped off. It took me a couple of minutes to get saddled, so I left you a note to tell you where . . . oh, no wait. That was dumb of me. I wrote the note, but I forgot to leave it."

He pulled the note out of his pocket.

"Anyway, you can read the note. It says that I am going in pursuit of Mr. Holder." Prichard smiled, broadly. "Which I did, and I've got him. He's draped across his horse, and now the state of Texas owes me twenty-five hundred dollars."

Sheriff Nelson chuckled. "Conner, you need to slow down a little. At the rate you're going, you could wind up having my job after the next election."

"Not to worry, Sheriff. I have no intention of standing for sheriff. I am perfectly content to be your deputy."

"I've said it before. You're a good man."

Shady Rest

"It ain't right," Bill Carter said. "It ain't right at all to have Mutt's body hung up there like a side of beef for ever' one to come by and gawk at."

"It would be all right if Jensen was standin' up there alongside him, dead as Mutt is," Lenny Fletcher said. "We shouldn't a' shot at him last night. We should a' waited till we had a better shot than to try 'n shoot him through the hotel window at night."

"They's only one thing wrong with that idea," Carter said. "Iffen we'd a' had a better shot at him, that means he would a' got a shot at us. You want to go up ag'in him, do you?"

"No, I don't."

After the unexpected celebration, and the unsolicited and unwanted congratulations, Matt felt the need to get out of town for a while, so he took Spirit out for a ride, just to give him some exercise.

About an hour's ride out of town, Matt came across a clear lake. The surface of the lake, as smooth as a mirror, reflected the nearby complex assemblage of thorny and deciduous plants, a blue sky with a few

250

white puffs of clouds, as well as the serrated peaks of the Guadalupe Mountains. Matt dismounted and led Spirit down to the water's edge. The horse lowered his head into the water and took a long drink.

"Yeah, I know," Matt said. "It's nicer to be out here than to be cooped up in a stall somewhere, isn't it? Truth is, I like it out here better than I do in town also."

Matt picked up a rock and threw it out into the lake. It made a splash, and a hawk came swooping down to investigate.

"Funny thing is, when we're on the trail, I get to thinking about how nice a real bed would be, and maybe a meal at a restaurant, and a few beers, and I want to get into to town. Then, when I'm in town, it seems like things start closing in on me, and I want to get out on the trail again."

Fifty yards away a doe came out of the woods, stood for a long moment, then looked back to signal her fawn. Doe and fawn came down to the water's edge to drink.

"Tell me, Spirit, how does that deer know I'm not going to shoot her? You know she saw me here."

Spirit whickered.

Matt chuckled. "I know, I know, you've told me before. You're a horse, and you

251

can't talk." Matt swung back into the saddle. "But I'll say this for you. You're a damn good listener."

Pecos

Prichard was sitting behind the desk in the sheriff's office when a pretty, blond-haired woman came in. She was carrying a package.

"Yes, ma'am, may I be of assistance?" Prichard asked, standing to greet the woman.

"Deputy, I don't know if you remember me — we spoke briefly the other day. I'm Margaret Margrabe."

"Oh, indeed I do remember you, Miss Margrabe. You are the schoolteacher."

"Yes, I'm flattered that you remember."

"How could I not remember someone as lovely as you?"

Margaret blushed, then reached up self-consciously to adjust her already perfectly coiffed hair.

"I — that is, some friends and I — wanted to welcome you to our fair city. Especially as you have taken on the dangerous responsibility of the role of deputy sheriff. So we — that is, I, on their behalf — made a batch of cookies for you. I know that it is probably foolish and perhaps even juvenile, but I

— that is, we — just wanted to express our appreciation."

"Ah, oatmeal cookies," Prichard said as she opened the package for him.

"I hope you like them. Some people, I suppose, think of oats only as food for horses."

Prichard took a bite of one of the cookies, then smacked his lips in appreciation. "It is said of the oat, Miss Margrabe, that it is a grain which in England is generally given to horses, but in Scotland supports the people. But the Scots say that England is noted for the excellence of her horses, while Scotland is known for the excellence of her men."

Margaret clapped her hands together, and laughed out loud. "Oh, what a delightful tidbit," she said.

"Yes, I perceived that you were of the intelligence and education to enjoy something like that," Prichard said.

"Oh, Deputy Conner . . ."

"Couldn't you call me Abe?"

"I, I wouldn't want to be so forward as to presume," Margaret said.

"There is no presumption if the invitation is offered . . . Margaret."

"Very well, I shall be happy to call you Abe. You know, Abe, it has been very difficult for me to make . . . gentlemen friends in Pecos."

"Oh, now, that is difficult to believe. You are an exceptionally beautiful woman, well mannered, educated, and intelligent."

"Yes, and there is the rub. I do hope that you not take this as being conceited, though I confess that it may sound so. The truth is, Abe, I find it difficult to relate to men who are . . ." Margaret stopped in midsentence.

"Intellectually inferior?" Prichard asked, suggesting a finish to her statement.

"Oh, dear, you must think me quite the snob."

"On the contrary, Margaret. I understand perfectly, for I have had the same difficulty in establishing any type of relationship with a woman. I bore quickly of their talk of quilting, and cooking, and babies, and such. I find myself longing for a discussion that will satisfy my intellectual curiosity."

"Oh, we *are* alike!" Margaret said. "I knew it!"

"I would appreciate the opportunity to call on you, sometime."

"Yes!" Margaret said; then, quickly, the smile left her face. "Oh, no," she said. "I'm afraid that can't be."

"Why is that?"

"My contract with the school board. Not only must I remain single, I cannot be seen

254

publicly with a man."

"Then, as Romeo and Juliet were forced to keep their love a secret, so too shall we keep our friendship a secret," Prichard said.

Margaret started toward the door, then turned and held her hand out toward Prichard. *"Good night, good night! Parting is such sweet sorrow, that I shall say good night 'til it be morrow."*

Prichard smiled, then held his hand out toward her as he replied. *"Sleep dwell upon thine eyes, peace in thy breast. Would I were sleep and peace, so sweet to rest."*

Margaret, with a self-conscious smile, let herself out.

Prichard ate another cookie after she left, then chuckled. "Methinks this bird is prime for the plucking," he said, laughing at the double entendre.

CHAPTER TWENTY-ONE

Shady Rest

Because Matt had to wait for the money to arrive, he wound up spending more time in Shady Rest than he had originally intended. He occupied his time by taking rides in the adjacent countryside, and visiting with new-found friends in the Texas Star. On this particular afternoon he was in the Texas Star Saloon, playing cards with Emerson Culpepper.

"Since you probably saved my life a few days ago, I shall go easy on you," Culpepper said as he dealt the hands to the table.

"No, don't do that," Matt said. "I enjoy playing cards with a professional. There is always room to learn."

Culpepper smiled. "All right, Mr. Jensen, I'll do what I can to instruct you."

During the poker game, Mayor Trout was conducting a meeting of the city council.

And even though Annabelle O'Callahan wasn't a member of the city council, she was present for the meeting as a "representative of the merchants of Shady Rest." Deputy Prescott wasn't a member of the city council either, but he was there as well.

"As you can clearly see, it seems to me like you would be the perfect one to elevate to the position of town marshal," Mayor Trout said to Prescott. "I mean, you are the deputy, after all. And you have been the deputy for some time now and that provides some needed continuity. That means nobody knows the position better than you."

"I know the position well enough to know I wouldn't be worth a damn as the marshal," Prescott said. Then, toward Annabelle, he added, "Pardon my language, ma'am."

"But if you think about it, the pay will more than double what you're drawing now," Dupree said.

"What do I need more money for?" Prescott asked. "I've got a free place to sleep right there in the jail. The city pays Moe to furnish my meals free. The onliest thing I need money for is a few beers, and maybe a whiskey now 'n then. The money I make deputyin' pays me enough so I can do that without no problem. If I got more money, I'd just drink more, and next thing you know I'd turn into a drunk. Now, you sure don't want that."

"No, most assuredly, we would not want that," Rafferty, the grocer, said.

"Besides which," Deputy Prescott continued, "mayhaps you ain't noticed, but all the marshals we been hirin' seem to have a habit of gettin' themselves kilt."

"We are all very aware of that, Deputy," Roy Clinton said.

"Yeah, well, I don't aim to be the fifth marshal to get kilt in this town."

"We have to do something," Annabelle said. "Last month three more families moved away because they said that Shady Rest wasn't a safe place to raise their kids. It seems that every brigand and rapscallion in the entire state has come to town at one time or another, just to make mischief."

"I've got an idea, if the council will go along with it," Deputy Prescott said.

"What is the idea?" Mayor Trout asked.

"Supposin' we was to ask Matt Jensen to be our town marshal? Why, just hearin' the name of who the marshal is would be enough to scare off anyone who was thinkin' about comin' here to raise trouble."

"What do you mean, just hearing the name?" Clinton asked. "What's so particular about the name Matt Jensen?" Clinton, who owned the apothecary, had recently relocated to Shady Rest from Atlanta, Georgia.

"I can't believe you ain't never heard of Matt Jensen," Prescott said. "Why, he's about the best person with a gun there is. And he's famous, too, 'cause folks has wrote books about him."

"Do you think we could get him to stay around town long enough to be our marshal?" Mayor Trout asked. "From what I've heard of Jensen, he tends to move around a lot."

"Oh, he'll stay here for a little while, anyway," Prescott said. "He's got a reward comin' for shootin' Mutt Crowley."

"Enough to keep him here?" Milner asked.

"Five thousand dollars," Prescott said.

Milner whistled softly. "That should keep him here for a while, anyway."

"Where does that reward come from?" Mayor Trout asked.

"It comes from Wells Fargo," Prescott said. "They had one of their employees kilt when the Crowley gang robbed a bank in Kansas."

"What if the reward were to be delayed for a while? He'd have to wait here for it, wouldn't he?"

"What makes you think the reward will be delayed?" Dupree asked. "I've done business with Wells Fargo. They've always been on the up and up."

"Who has to authorize the payment?" Moe Woodward asked.

"Well, sir, Wells Fargo will release the money, but it'll actually be the county sheriff who will have to authorize it to be paid," Prescott said.

"Well, there you go," Mayor Trout said with a conspiratorial smile. "All we have to do is convince the sheriff to hold up on the payment for a while."

"How are we goin' to do that?" Prescott asked. "There's no doubt in my mind but that the fella that was kilt was Mutt Crowley. There was plenty of folks who saw that Jensen is the one who kilt him. And I've got the dodger on Crowley that says there is a five-thousand-dollar reward for him. Now, you tell me how the sheriff can be convinced to delay the payment."

"We can hold it up while we hold a hearing to determine the circumstances of death," Mayor Trout said.

"Are you wantin' to know how he died? It was two bullet holes in his heart!" Prescott said loudly and with obvious irritation. "Hell, the son of a bitch was propped up down there Ponder's for half the day. If you wanted to know how he died, all you would have had to do would be just go down there and take look at him! If you wanted to, you could've stuck your finger in the bullet holes!"

"There will be no hearing to determine the circumstances of death," Dempster said. "As the city prosecutor, I have already submitted a report to the circuit judge that no such hearing is necessary."

"Besides," Annabelle said, "if Mr. Jensen has truly earned the reward, as everyone has stated, it would not be ethical to withhold the payment for any reason."

"All right, all right, you folks win," Trout said, holding up his hands. "It was just a suggestion, is all. But that leaves us right where we started. At the moment, we are a city without any effective law enforcement."

The mayor's pronouncement was punctuated by the sound of a gunshot coming from Plantation Row.

"And as you can readily see," the mayor continued, using his thumb to point in the direction from which the gunshot had come, "we are badly in need of someone."

Pecos

Margaret Margrabe had been reading, and she was just about to put out the lantern when someone knocked, lightly, on the back

261

door of her tiny one-room house. Surprised, and even a little frightened that someone would knock on her door this late at night, and the back door at that, she moved, hesitantly to it.

"Who is it?" she called out.

"Margaret, it's me, Abe Conner."

"Is something wrong?"

"No, I just thought I would like to call on you, if you would be so good as to grant me a few moments of your time."

"But I'm already in my nightgown," Margaret replied.

From just on the other side of the door, Prichard recited, softly, sonorously, lines from an Elizabeth Barrett Browning poem.

"Love me Sweet, with all thou art,
Feeling, thinking, seeing;
Love me in the lightest part."

"Oh, how delightful!" Margaret said. Then she responded in kind.

"Yes, I answered you last night;
No, this morning, Sir, I say.
Colors seen by candlelight,
Will not look the same by day."

Margaret opened the door to let him in.

"I came to your back door so no one would see me, and think ill of you," Prichard said.

"That was so thoughtful of you," Margaret said, touching her hair.

Seventy-five feet down the alley from Margaret's back door, Charley Keith was sitting on the back stoop of a closed store. He was holding a whiskey bottle in his hand. The bottle, which was nearly one-third full, contained the last dregs of discarded bottles he had gathered from all over town. He'd emptied into it assorted whiskies, wines, and even some beer. He had turned the bottle up to take a drink of this unlikely cocktail just as he saw a man go into the back door of the teacher's house.

"Well now," he said. "Looks to me like the teacher has got her a secret boyfriend. Shhhh," he said, putting his fingers to his lips. "It's a secret, so I can't be talkin' out loud about it."

Laughing quietly, he turned the bottle up for another drink.

Prichard had just finished with the newest batch of posters when Sheriff Nelson came into the office the next morning. There was a look of shock and dismay on his face, and

263

he shook his head.

"Who would do something like that?" he asked. "What kind of inhumane monster could do that?"

"What are you talking about, Sheriff?"

"That pretty young woman," Sheriff Nelson said. "You know, Miss Margrabe?"

"Margrabe? No, I don't think I do know her."

"She's the schoolteacher," Sheriff Nelson said.

"Oh, yes, I have seen her, spoken to her even. I just didn't recall her name."

"I should have said, she *was* the schoolteacher."

"Was?"

"She's dead, Abe. Some inhumane peckerwood murdered her last night. Murdered her in her own bed. Sally White found her body this morning. They were going to do some shopping together, and Miss White went over to her house. When Miss Margrabe didn't answer the door, Miss White let herself in. That's when she found her."

Sheriff Nelson pinched the bridge of his nose, and shook his head slowly. "She was stripped naked, and lying in a pool of her own blood. The son of a bitch cut her throat."

Prichard felt a quiet surge of excitement

264

as he recalled the moment of her death.

"That's a shame," he said.

"Yes, it is. From all I've heard, Miss Margrabe was a sweet young woman. And to think that her friend had to find her like that."

"I don't suppose you have any idea as to who may have done such a thing."

"No," Sheriff Nelson said. "I don't have an idea in hell."

"Well, whoever did it is most likely far from here by now. I can't imagine someone doing something like that, then remaining around town where he could be caught."

"You are probably right. No doubt he is running for his life, as he should be, the inhumane son of a bitch. You know, when it is necessary for the county to hang someone, I am generally the one who has to put the rope around the condemned's neck. Since I've been sheriff I've only had to do it three times, and I don't mind admitting that it has bothered me, every time. It's an awesome thing to take a man's life, even if that man has been condemned by the court. But I tell you true, Abe, if we ever do catch the peckerwood who did this, I will take particular pleasure in hanging him."

"Maybe we'll get lucky and find him," Prichard suggested.

"Yeah. Oh, how about those reward circulars? Anything interesting in the new batch?"

"Not particularly," Prichard said. He pointed to the wall. "As you can see, I posted the new ones, and I destroyed the ones that were no longer valid."

"Good, good," Sheriff Nelson said. "Listen, Abe, if you can watch things here for a while, I think I'm going to go have a drink. After what I saw in that poor young woman's house, I feel the need of one."

"I understand perfectly," Prichard replied. "Go right ahead, I shall stand watch, dutifully."

Sheriff Nelson didn't respond verbally, but he did nod before he left.

Prichard walked back over to the desk and sat down to recall his final moments with Margaret Margrabe last night. It had been good. It had been very good.

CHAPTER TWENTY-TWO

Nearly the entire town of Pecos turned out for Margaret Margrabe's funeral. It was held in the Methodist church, and the pews were filled not only with the parishioners of the church, but with people who hadn't set foot in a church in several years.

When the services in the church were completed, the congregation filed outside. They formed up on either side of the steps as the pallbearers brought Margaret's body through the front door, then placed it in the back of the highly polished, black, glass-sided hearse. The bell of the church began tolling as Gene Ponder, wearing striped pants, a cutaway coat, and a high-topped hat, climbed up on the seat, then started driving the matched team of black horses toward the cemetery. The mourners followed the hearse, not only those who were coming from the church, but the ones who had been waiting outside as well. At the cemetery, her students formed a corridor through which the casket was carried. Even those men who had not attended the funeral were talking about it in the Silver Spur Saloon.

"Charley Keith seen someone goin' into her house," a man who was standing at the bar said. "And if you want to know what I'm thinkin', I'm thinkin' that whoever it was that he seen goin' into the teacher's house, well, more'n likely that's the one what kilt her."

"Who did you say seen 'im? Charley Keith?" one of the other drinkers asked.

"Yes."

"Who the hell is goin' to believe that old drunk?"

"Charley Keith wasn't always a drunk. He was a railroad surveyor once, you know. And they say he was damn good at it too, 'til he started hittin' the bottle."

"Yeah, well, there you go. He started hittin' the bottle, and now you don't never see 'im but what he ain't drunk."

"No, now, that's the thing. You don't ever actual see 'im drunk, 'cause most of the time he can't get enough whiskey to get hisself drunk. And with someone like Charley, who drinks all the time, it takes an awful lot of whiskey to get him drunk."

"Did he say who it was that he seen goin' in there?" one of the others asked.

"No, he didn't say, 'cause he don't know who it was."

"I don't think it matters much anyhow. It's more'n likely that whoever done it is long gone. Hell, I wouldn't doubt but that he's in California now, or maybe Oregon, or Indiana."

"California, Oregon, or Indiana?" one of patrons repeated. He laughed. "That doesn't make sense. Oregon and Indiana are a long way from each other."

"Well, yeah, wouldn't you want to get a long way away?"

Prichard had been standing down at the other end of the bar nursing a beer and listening to the conversation, but not participating in it. Then one of the men spoke to him.

"Deputy Conner, we heard about you catchin' that wanted murderer. Congratulations on that. You'll be gettin' a big reward too, won't you? How you plannin' on spending the money?"

Prichard turned toward them and, with a smile, lifted his beer as if in salute.

"Gentlemen, I don't plan to waste any of it," he said. "I plan to spend every cent on wine, women, and song."

The others laughed.

"No," Prichard said, amending his comment. "I can do without the song. I shall spend every cent on wine and women."

This time the laughter was even more general.

With a good-bye wave to the others in saloon, Prichard left and started walking back toward the sheriff's office, acknowledging the greetings of the others in town. He had gotten away with it. But then, why wouldn't he get away with it? Clearly, there was no one in this town who could match him in intellect. He was absolutely certain that nobody had even the slightest suspicion that he was the one who had killed Margaret Margrabe.

Shady Rest

That afternoon there was a shooting in the Ace High Saloon, and later on that night, when two cowboys got into a fight over a whore at Abby's Place, one of them killed the other.

"Something has to be done," Annabelle told Mayor Trout the next morning. "It has reached the point where decent people are afraid to be out on the street at any time now, not just after dark."

"I agree, something has to be done," Trout

said. "But what?"

"You might ask Matt Jensen if he would accept the position," Annabelle suggested.

"You know him, Miss O'Callahan," Mayor Trout said. "I'm told that you and he had dinner together at the Merchants Club."

"We did. That is true."

"Why don't you ask him?"

Annabelle shook her head. "I have no authority to ask him that, Mayor, and you know it. No, sir, if Matt Jensen is asked to serve as our city marshal, the request is going to have to come from someone other than me."

Trout nodded. "You are probably correct," he said. "Very well, I'll call a special meeting of the city council tonight to discuss it. I'd like you to attend as well. We'll hold tonight's meeting at the Merchants Association Club."

"All right, I'll be there," Annabelle promised.

When Matt played poker with Culpepper, he had a pattern of winning a few and losing a few, and he had lost more than he had won so that, at the moment, he was twenty dollars poorer overall. But the poker had been relaxing and enjoyable and Culpepper did manage to point out some helpful hints that Matt was sure he would be able to employ in some future games. This afternoon, however, Culpepper's table was full, so Matt managed to find another card game, and in this game he won more than he lost. As a result he recovered his twenty dollars, plus an additional ten.

Several times during the afternoon Matt could hear gunshots coming from Plantation Row, though as the other players in the game pointed out, the habitués of that part of town often discharged their pistols for no reason other than entertainment.

"Matt," Hawkins said to him as Matt stepped up to the bar to cash in his winnings, less the 10 percent house cut. "I wonder if you would let me buy you dinner this evening at the Merchants Association Club."

Matt chuckled. "I don't see why not. The ten percent I've given up today would probably pay for the meal, so I'll just feel as if I'm getting my money back. Besides, I ate there the other night with Miss O'Callahan, and I learned that the chef there is an artist with food."

Hawkins chuckled. "What you're sayin' is, he puts out good grub. Well, I'm glad you enjoyed it. Say, seven o'clock?"

"Seven o'clock is fine," Matt said.

■ ■ ■ ■

A little later that afternoon, Matt decided, as a matter of curiosity, to check out Plantation Row, since he had not been there since arriving in Shady Rest. The first establishment he visited was the Pig Palace. After he made his usual cautious entry, he saw, sitting in a high chair at the back of the room, a man holding a double-barreled shotgun across his lap. With a leery eye toward the man holding the shotgun, Matt moved up to the bar and ordered a beer.

"Haven't seen you before," the bartender said. "Just arrive in town?"

"I've been here a few days," Matt replied.

"Poke, don't you know who this feller is?" one of the drinkers at the bar said.

"Should I know?" the bartender replied.

"Why, I reckon you should. He's the town hero right now. He's the one that kilt Morgan, only it turns out Morgan wasn't Morgan. This is Matt Jensen."

The bartender put a beer in front of Matt, and Matt put a nickel on the bar.

"Don't take the man's money, Poke." The person who spoke was a thin man, dressed in black, with a hawk face and a dark van dyke beard. He approached the bar and extended his hand. "Mr. Jensen, I'm Jacob Bramley. I own the Pig Palace."

"Thank you for the beer," Matt said as he picked up the mug.

"Well, it's the least I can do for a genuine hero. The entire town is thankful to you for killing the man who killed our marshal. But of course, Mr. Durbin here" — Bramley pointed to the man with the shotgun, who was sitting on the high chair — "is a little jealous. You see, it was only last month that he killed Quince Calhoun, right after Calhoun had killed Marshal Jarvis. There was no such celebration for Mr. Durbin."

"Believe me, Mr. Durbin could have had my celebration," Matt said. "It wasn't something I asked for, or wanted."

Bramley chuckled. "I can understand that, Mr. Jensen. You are a modest man, and modest men don't have any need for all that folderol. Mr. Durbin, come down here and meet a modest man," Bramley called.

Durbin climbed down from the chair and walked over to the bar. He didn't come up to shake Matt's hand, but just stood at the end of the bar with his right hand near his pistol in a way that, to Matt, appeared to be a little threatening.

"I'm told you've kilt three men since you come to town," Durbin said.

"You were told wrong," Matt said.

"Wait a minute. Didn't you kill two of the men that was goin' to rob the stagecoach? And didn't you kill that terrible murderer, Mutt Crowley?"

"I did."

"Well, in my mind, Jensen, that makes three men."

"Your statement was that I had killed three men since I came to town. The two stagecoach robbers were killed before I came to town."

"Yeah," Durbin said. "Tell me, Jensen, just how many men have you kilt?"

Matt lifted the beer mug to his lips, pointedly doing so with his left hand. He took a sip while keeping a wary eye on Durbin. Finally after taking a drink of the beer, he put the mug down and ran the back of his hand across his mouth to wipe away any of the foam. Again, pointedly, it was his left hand.

"Well, how many, Jensen? Or have you kilt so many that you can't remember?"

"I have never killed a man who wasn't trying to kill me," Matt said. "Nor have I ever killed a man who wasn't facing me."

The last comment was an intentional dig at Durbin, because he knew that Durbin had shot Calhoun in the back. Though Matt was not prepared to argue that Calhoun didn't deserve to be killed.

"Mr. Durbin, why don't you return to the job I'm paying you for," Bramley said.

Durbin fixed one more angry glare toward Matt; then he walked back across the saloon to climb up onto his chair.

"Piano player, I'm paying you to make music, not gawk," Bramley said. "Girls, walk around. I see a lot of lonely men here."

"I'm terrible lonely," one man said, and the others laughed as one of the bar girls hurried over to him.

Music began to spill from the piano, and conversations and laughter resumed.

"Mr. Jensen, I wonder if you would join me at my table for a friendly conversation," Bramley invited.

Matt nodded, then, carrying his beer with him, accompanied Bramley back to his table. He was careful to find a chair that not only placed his back toward the wall, but also enabled him to keep Durbin in sight.

"Mr. Jensen, I'm told that you are a man who moves around quite a bit," Bramley said.

"I can't deny that," Matt replied.

"Have you ever thought of settling down in one place?"

"I've given it some thought from time to time."

"What I'm getting at is this," Bramley said. "Look all up and down First Street. More money is made here on this street than is made in the rest of the town — hell, the rest of the county — combined, and that includes the money the ranchers are making.

"And most of the money made on First Street, is mine." Bramley smiled. "I know what you are thinking. You are wondering how I can say this, when the Pig Palace is just one of the businesses on the street." Bramley held up his finger to make a point. "But, I own a hundred percent of the Pig Palace, fifty-one percent of the Crooked Branch, fifty-one percent of Ace High, and a hundred percent of Abby's whorehouse. Yes, she is just the front."

"It looks like you are doing well," Matt said.

"Oh, I'm doing better than well. I'm doing very well. And here's the thing, Jensen. You could do well too if you would like to throw in with me."

"Throw in with you in what way?"

"I know that you have five thousand dollars coming to you as a reward for killing Crowley. I will sell you forty-five percent of all my holdings for five thousand dollars. The truth is, forty-five percent of my holdings are worth ten times that much, but I'm willing to do that, because with you as a partner, we would soon control the whole town, then the whole county. What do you say?"

Matt finished the beer, then put the empty mug on the table that separated the distance between them. Standing, he looked back down at Bramley.

"I say Hawkins is wrong."

"I beg your pardon?"

"I don't believe you water your drinks," Matt said. He nodded. "Thanks for the beer."

He left the saloon without any further response to Crowley's offer.

CHAPTER TWENTY-THREE

When Matt and Hawkins stepped into the dining room of the Merchants Association Club at seven that evening, they were met by the maitre d'.

"Your table is ready, gentlemen," the maitre d' said, leading them across the otherwise deserted dining room to a long table, around which sat seven men and one woman. The lone woman was Annabelle.

"What is this?" Matt asked.

"I hope you don't mind," Hawkins said. "The truth is, I was less than honest with you when I invited you to dinner tonight. I did so specifically so the city council could meet with you."

There were two empty chairs around the long table, and they were right next to Annabelle O'Callahan. Hawkins maneuvered the seating so that Matt sat next to her.

"So, Matt, we dine here again," Annabelle said.

"So it would seem, Miss O'Callahan," Matt replied a bit cautiously. He had no idea what this was leading to.

"Please, Matt, haven't we reached the point to where you can call me Annabelle?"

"Annabelle," Matt corrected.

"Mr. Jensen, I'm Mayor Trout." The mayor was a dark-haired, dark-eyed man with a full mustache that curved around his mouth like the horns on a Texas steer.

"The gentlemen you see around the table here — Gary Dupree, Melton Milner, Bob Dempster, Earl Cook, Martin Peabody, and George Tobin — are members of the city council. So is Gerald Hawkins, who you know. And of course, Miss O'Callahan, who you also know, is here. Miss O'Callahan is not a member of the city council, but she often sits in on our meetings as a liaison between the council and the Shady Rest Merchants Association."

Each of the men made some sort of acknowledgment as their names were spoken, and Matt nodded back to them.

"I'm sure you are wondering why you are here," Trout continued.

"I thought I was here to have dinner," Matt replied with a smile.

"You are, you are indeed," Mayor Trout said.

"I apologize, Matt, for not being entirely up-front with you," Hawkins said.

"Before we go further with the meeting, I would like to read this proclamation," Mayor Trout said.

Clearing his throat, Trout picked up a sheet of paper upon which a calligrapher had carefully penned the words.

A PROCLAMATION
by the Mayor of the City of
Shady Rest, Texas,
declaring appreciation for
community service.

WHEREAS, it is important that all citizens know and understand the service, courage, and assistance provided by Matt Jensen in preventing a stagecoach robbery, and thereby protecting the passengers, driver and shotgun guard from any further violence; and,
WHEREAS, Matt Jensen did encounter the armed and dangerous murderer of Marshal Devry Pruitt, thereby preventing further harm to any other citizen of Shady Rest; and,
WHEREAS, Matt Jensen provided these vital public services without promise or thought of personal recompense; now,

THEREFORE, I, *OLLIE TROUT,*
Mayor of the City of Shady Rest, Texas,
with the authorization and support of the
City Council of the above-named
community, do award the Certificate of
Appreciation, and call upon all citizens of
the City of Shady Rest, and upon all
patriotic, civic and educational
organizations to observe AUGUST 10,
in honor of *MATT JENSEN,*
who, through his Courageous Deed,
rendered a great service to this
community.

Given this day, by the hand and seal of
Ollie Trout,
and with the authorization
of the City Council of Shady Rest, Texas.

To the applause of everyone around the
table, Trout gave the certificate to Matt.

"Thank you," Matt said. He was as uncomfortable with all this attention, as he
had been with the fireworks celebration on
the day after he had killed Mutt Crowley.
And all things being equal, he would have
preferred being over at Moe's Café now,
having a supper of fried ham and potatoes.

During the dinner, the conversation was
kept casual until the meal was over; then

282

Mayor Trout, who was sitting directly across the table from Matt, posed the question that was the real purpose of the meeting.

"Matt, we — that is, the members of the city council — and, as has also been expressed to me by several of our town's citizens, would like to offer you the position of marshal of Shady Rest. And we are prepared to offer you a salary that is three times higher than anything we've ever paid before."

"Mayor, members of the city council, I appreciate this award" — Matt held up the paper — "and I am honored by your confidence in me, but I know myself pretty well, and I know that I'm not cut out to be a city marshal."

"Why not?" Annabelle asked. "I think you would make an excellent marshal."

"There are ordinances, state and federal laws, to being a city marshal, and those ordinances and laws impose operational restrictions. To be honest with you, there is no way I could operate within those regulations, I am just not the type of person who would make a good marshal."

"I wish you would reconsider the offer," Mayor Trout said.

"It's like I said, Mayor, I'm not really the kind of person who would make a good marshal, though, as long as I am here, I will take a direct interest in the well-being of your community. By the way, you might be interested in knowing that this is the second offer I've received today."

"The second offer?" Hawkins asked.

"Yes. Jacob Bramley offered to make me practically a full partner with him, if I would join him."

"Matt!" Annabelle said with a gasp. "You did turn him down, I hope?"

"I gave it some thought," Matt said. Then, when he saw the expressions on the other faces, he laughed. "But the only answer I could come up with was no."

The others, realizing then that Matt was teasing, laughed in relief.

"Tell me, Mr. Jensen, perhaps you could suggest what type of person would be a good marshal," Mayor Trout asked.

"Sure," Matt replied. "Get someone who can't be killed."

CHAPTER TWENTY-FOUR

The next morning when Bramley came down from his own suite of rooms, which was upstairs and in the back, he stood there drinking a cup of coffee, looking around at the nearly empty saloon. The only customers in the place were the few who had spent the night with one of the whores, or the few who couldn't start their day without a drink.

Durbin came in then, and he walked around behind the bar and poured himself a cup of coffee. He came over to stand by Bramley.

"You ain't the only one Jensen said no to yesterday," Durbin said with a little chuckle.

"What are you talking about?"

"I'm talking about the city asking him to be the new marshal. He turned 'em down."

"Really?"

"That's what I heard this morning."

"You know, Harry, that gives me an idea," Bramley said as he stroked his van dyke. "I think maybe . . . yes, I know it would be. . . . You would be perfect," he said with a broad smile.

"I would be perfect for what?" Durbin asked.

"You would be perfect for the new marshal."

"Wait a minute, what makes you think I would want that job? In case you ain't noticed it, boss, all the marshals we've had so far have been gettin' themselves kilt. Why the hell would I want that?"

Bramley shook his head. "No, no, you don't understand," he said. "If you become the city marshal, we will control the law, and the town. You won't get yourself killed because you won't be enforcing the law — you will be facilitating our breaking of the law."

"I don't understand what any of that means," Durbin said. "Besides, I like the job I'm doin' for you now. And I know for a fact that you are payin' more than I would make as a city marshal."

"Oh, don't get me wrong, Harry. You would still work for me. You would still draw your pay from me, plus what the city would pay you. The only thing is, you would be wearing a badge, and that means that anything you would do, say on your job here

286

would be legal, because you are the law."

It dawned then on Durbin what Bramley was suggesting, and a big smile spread across Durbin's face.

"Yeah!" he said, hitting his fist into his open hand. "Yeah! You're right! That would be a great idea!"

Half an hour later, down at the city hall, the city clerk stepped into the mayor's office. "Mayor Trout, there is a Harry Durbin to see you."

"Harry Durbin? Wait a minute, isn't he the one who works for Bramley? Yes, he killed the man who killed Marshal Jarvis, didn't he?"

"Yes, sir, that's the same man."

"And he wants to see me? What does he want?"

"I'm afraid I don't know what he wants, Mayor. He didn't tell me."

"All right, send him in."

The clerk stepped out of the mayor's office, and a moment later, Durbin came in. For the occasion, Durbin was wearing a clean shirt.

"Yes, Mr. Durbin, what can I do for you?"

"I'm told you are looking for a new city marshal."

"Yes, that's right. We are looking for a city

marshal."

Durbin smiled, and hooked his thumbs under his arms. "Well, sir, you can quit lookin'. I'm volunteerin' for the job."

"Really? Do you have any experience as a law enforcement officer?"

"I ain't got no experience wearin' a badge, but you might remember I'm the one that kilt the son of a bitch that kilt Marshal Jarvis. Besides which, how much experience did Pruitt have?"

Trout nodded. "That's a good question, and the answer is, he had no experience whatever. And, I fear, it was that lack of experience that cost him his life."

"Yeah, well, the difference between me and Pruitt is I'm good with a gun. He wasn't."

"How good? What I mean is, how does one determine how good one might be?"

"I have kilt seven men," Durbin said.

Mayor Trout was startled by the casual way in which Durbin made the announcement.

"I . . . I'm not sure what you are saying to me," Trout said. "Am I to understand that you are validating your application to be our marshal by telling me you have killed seven men?"

"Yeah," Durbin said. "But they was all

288

men like Quince Calhoun. All seven of 'em needed killin'."

"Perhaps so, but I don't know that the mere fact you have killed seven men would qualify you to be marshal."

"Wait a minute, Mayor. You asked Matt Jensen to be the marshal, didn't you? You asked him, but he turned you down."

"That is true," Trout said. "The offer was made, and he did turn us down."

"Well, tell me, Mayor, why did you make the offer to Jensen in the first place? I'll tell you why. You offered him the job 'cause he's kilt lots of men. Fact is, he's kilt more men than I have."

"I . . . that is, that isn't exactly the reason the offer was made."

"But it was part of the reason, if you are honest enough to admit it," Durbin said. "You do need a marshal, and you're havin' a hard time gettin' one, 'cause all the marshals we get here don't live very long. I'm willin' to take that chance."

"That is noble of you, Mr. Durbin," Trout said. "I don't have the authority to hire you out of hand. I'll have to take it up with the city council," Trout said. "But, I can tell you that I will do that. And, I'll let you know what the decision is, as quickly as I can."

"Yeah, you do that," Durbin said as he

turned to leave the mayor's office.

"No, definitely not!" Hawkins said after Mayor Trout presented the idea to the city council. "Don't you know who Durbin is?"

"I know that he works for Jacob Bramley," Mayor Trout said.

"Yeah, he works for Bramley. He's Bramley's gun for hire."

"Gerald is right," Ponder said. "I've already buried two of the men he killed, including one that he shot in the back with a twelve-gauge."

"Well, to be fair to Durbin, you are talking about Quince Calhoun," Dempster said. "And Calhoun was not only a wanted man for murder and robbery, he was the one who, but a moment earlier, had killed Marshal Jarvis."

"Yes, exactly," Mayor Trout said. "Mr. Durbin pointed out to me that the man he killed was the one who killed Marshal Jarvis. Now, this town has heaped honor upon Matt Jensen for doing the same thing, haven't we? There was an impromptu celebration, and we issued a proclamation. How is what Matt Jensen did any different from what Harry Durbin did?"

"Well, for one thing," Hawkins said, "Jensen faced Crowley face to face. Durbin shot Calhoun in the back, with a shotgun."

"I don't see that as a consequential difference," Mayor Trout said. "Both men were murderers, and both had just killed one of our marshals."

"You sound like you are actually in favor of appointing Durbin marshal," Moe Woodward said.

"Why not? We need a marshal, and he is willing to serve."

"Why not? Because we are just asking for trouble if we appoint Durbin, or any of Bramley's men, as our new marshal," Hawkins said. "Hell, as all of you know, most of our trouble comes from Plantation Row. And if you think we have trouble now, just think of the trouble we would have if those people had the law on their side."

"I think Gerald is right," Dupree said.

"So do I," Tobin said.

"I have to agree, Mayor," Dempster said. "Despite the fact that the killing of Quince Calhoun could be called justifiable, I think it would be a huge mistake to hire Durbin."

"All right," Trout said. "I will inform Mr. Durbin that the city council has turned down his request."

Shortly after Durbin was told that his application to be the new marshal was rejected, Bramley held another meeting of the Plantation Row Citizens' Betterment Council.

"Gentlemen, and lady," Bramley said, acknowledging Abby's presence. Abby hooted at the acknowledgment.

"Bless your heart, darlin', for callin' me a lady, which I ain't," Abby said. "But I am a woman, as I'll be glad to show you anytime you're of a mind."

Foster and Gimlin laughed.

"Abby, I may just surprise you someday, and take you up on that offer," Bramley said. "But right now, I've got other things on my mind." He turned back to the others who were present at the meeting.

"It has come to my attention that what we need is to have a lawman on our side. And to that end I sent Harry Durbin to see Mayor Trout to volunteer to be the new town marshal. Trout, in turn, took it to the city council."

"So," Gimlin said with a big smile. "Do we have a new city marshal?"

"No, they turned him down," Bramley said.

"Well, hell, why did you call this meeting then?" Foster asked.

"We don't have a new marshal," Bramley said. "But we have something even better.

Harry, come on in here!" Bramley called.

Durbin stepped into the back room then, prominently displaying a star on his shirt.

"What is it with the star?" Foster asked. "I thought you said the city council turned him down."

"Yes, he has been turned down as the city marshal. But, you are now looking at the newest deputy sheriff in the country. And as such, he will have authority over whoever is eventually appointed as the city marshal." Bramley gave the others a broad smile.

"Folks, we are the law. And the first thing I propose is that we refuse to pay these new taxes the city has placed on us."

The first thing the new deputy did was visit the mayor's office.

"Tell the mayor I want to see him," Durbin said.

"Oh, I'm not sure the mayor has time to see anyone this morning," the clerk said.

Durbin pointed to the star on his shirt. "You tell him that the deputy sheriff of Pecos County demands to be seen."

"Yes, sir," the clerk replied meekly.

"You're the deputy sheriff?" Mayor Trout asked, when Durbin stepped into his office.

"Yeah," Durbin said. "If you had appointed me city marshal like I asked, I would be working for you. But I don't work for you now, and I'm here to tell you that nobody on First Street will be paying this new tax."

"They have to pay it," Mayor Trout said. "It's the city law."

"I don't enforce the city law," Durbin said.

The news of Harry Durbin's appointment as a deputy sheriff spread quickly through the town as Durbin began making the rounds, "enforcing" the law. He arrested a couple of cowboys who were coming out of the Texas Star for "public drunkenness" though neither of the young men were noticeably drunk. On the other hand, within an hour after the two young cowboys were arrested, some men who actually were drunk started having target practice in the middle of Plantation Row, and the new deputy did nothing to stop them.

Then, on the same day Durbin was appointed as deputy sheriff, he stopped a freight wagon on the road leading into town.

"What is it, Deputy?" the driver asked.

"I need to inspect your load," Durbin said.

"Inspect it? Inspect it for what? It ain't nothin' but whiskey and beer for Mr. Hawkins."

"Do you have your beer and whiskey permit?"

"Beer and whiskey permit?" the driver asked in confusion. "What beer and whiskey permit? I don't know what you are talkin' about."

"It's a new law. You can't bring beer and whiskey into Shady Rest without having a permit, signed by the liquor commissioner."

"Well, who is the liquor commissioner?"

"I am," Durbin said. "That's one of my jobs."

"Oh, well, then why don't you sign them for me, so I can get on about my business?"

"The permit will cost you one hundred dollars," Durbin said.

"One hundred dollars? I ain't got that kind of money on me!"

"Then you are goin' to have to unload your wagon, right here."

"I can't do that!" the wagon driver complained. "This here load belongs to Mr. Hawkins. He's done paid for it."

Durbin pulled his pistol and pointed it at the driver. "I'm the law," he said. "And I'm tellin' you to unload your wagon, right here, and right now."

With the gun pointed at him, the driver had no choice but to unload the wagon, meaning that he had to roll the beer barrels down the incline by himself. It took him the better part of an hour, but he was able to do it without losing one barrel.

"What do I do now?" the driver asked.

"You turn your wagon around and go on back to where you come from," Durbin said.

Again, it was the threat of the gun that convinced the driver to acquiesce to Durbin's demand.

Durbin watched until the driver was out of sight; then he gave the signal, and another wagon, belonging to Jacob Bramley, pulled up to take on the beer that had been "confiscated" for lack of a whiskey and beer permit.

CHAPTER TWENTY-FIVE

Pecos

"What has it been, Sheriff, a week since the senseless and brutal murder of that young schoolteacher?" Prichard asked. "Are there any leads?"

"One lead, though I don't know how productive it will be. And, I don't know how credible the witness is."

Prichard felt a quick bolt of fear.

"Witness? Do you mean to tell me that there was someone who witnessed the killing?"

"No, nobody saw the actual killing, but Charley Keith did see a man go in through her back door."

"Charley Keith. Wait a minute, I haven't been here all that long, but I have heard of him. Isn't he the town drunk?"

"Yes, and that's the problem. I don't know how credible Charley Keith would be as a witness. I mean, even if he is telling the truth, and I have no reason to doubt him, but if we had a suspect, and brought him to trial on Charley's word, I'm pretty sure a good lawyer would be able to challenge his . . . what's the word I'm looking for?"

"The word you are looking for, Sheriff, is credibility," Prichard said.

"Yes, credibility. And that's too bad too, because Charley told me he was in the back alley when he saw someone knock on her door. Then he saw the door open, and he saw the man go inside."

"What is your level of confidence in that report?"

"I believe him. I've known Charley Keith for a long time, even before he became a drunk. He has his faults, but he's never been a blowhard, he's never been a man to spread tall tales. If he said he saw the man, then I believe he saw him."

"Did he get a good look at the man? I mean, if he saw him again, do you think he could recognize him?"

"No, and that's the next problem. I asked Charley if he could identify the man again if he saw him, and he said that he didn't think he could. It was too dark. You know what I'm thinking?" Sheriff Nelson asked.

"What?"

"I'm thinking that Miss Margrabe may

have had a man friend, and she didn't want anyone to know anything about it. You know there was a clause in her teaching contract that said she couldn't be married. There was also a morals clause, meaning she couldn't be seen with any men. I think all we have to do is find out who she was seeing, and we'll have our man."

"You are probably right," Prichard said. "But you say that Keith can't give you a description?"

"No. Like he said, he was back in the alley, and you know there are no lamps back there. Well, as a matter of fact, there aren't any streetlamps at all where Miss Margrabe's house was, so it was too dark for him to actually see anything."

"I have an idea," Prichard said.

"What's that?"

"The killer doesn't know that he was seen. And the killer doesn't know that he can't be identified. Suppose we put the word out that we have a witness, someone who saw, and can identify, the killer?"

"What good would that do?"

"If nothing else, it would get the killer nervous, maybe so nervous that he might try something that would inadvertently cause him to fall right into our laps?"

"Yeah!" Sheriff Nelson said. "Yeah, that's

a great idea. We could . . . no, no wait," he said. "If we did that, it could make Charley Keith a target. I wouldn't want to do that."

"We don't have to say who the witness is," Prichard said. "All we have to do is say that we have a witness."

Sheriff Nelson smiled, and nodded. "All right, we'll do that. I'll start spreading the word around that we have a witness."

Prichard watched Sheriff Nelson leave; then he went over and poured himself a cup of coffee. He laughed as he took a swallow and, because of the laughter, had to spit some of the coffee out. It was fun, playing the sheriff for a fool.

Shady Rest

When Matt came down from his hotel room the next morning he was surprised to see Annabelle waiting for him in the lobby.

"Miss O'Callahan," he said, walking toward her as she stood up from the sofa.

Annabelle raised her finger and wagged it back and forth. "No, no, it's Annabelle, remember?"

"Annabelle," Matt said with a smile. "What are you doing here?"

"I came to ask a favor of you."

"Sure, anything," Matt answered. "Except I hope you aren't going to ask me to serve

300

as city marshal."

"No, it isn't that. Besides, we have a deputy sheriff now."

"So I've heard. What is the favor?"

"I want you to teach me to shoot a gun. I think that in a town like Shady Rest it is almost imperative that someone be able to shoot well enough to defend themselves. And I believe that would go for a woman, as well as for a man."

Matt smiled, and nodded. "I can't argue with that," he said. "I think you're right. When do you want your first lesson?"

"This afternoon, right after you buy my lunch," Annabelle said. "As I recall, you did offer to buy lunch for me, didn't you? That was several days ago, but I assume the offer is still valid."

"It is absolutely valid. That is, if Moe's is all right."

"Moe's would be fine," Annabelle agreed. "I'll meet you there at noon."

Pecos

At the opposite end of the town from the sheriff's office, in one of the stalls of the livery, Sheriff Nelson and Charley Keith were engaged in conversation. Nelson had not come to the conversation empty-handed, having brought a pint of whiskey as

301

a bribe to get Keith to talk to him.

"Damn," Keith said as he examined the bottle. "This really is a blended whiskey, and not the kind of blending I have to do." He pulled the cork and held the bottle opening under his nose as he inhaled. "It smells like a little bit of heaven," he said. He turned the bottle up and took a long, Adam's-apple-bobbing swallow.

"Ah, yes. I thank you, Sheriff. With all my heart, I thank you."

"I thought you might appreciate that, Charley."

Keith took another swallow; then he wiped his lips with the back of his hand and looked directly at the sheriff.

"Now, what is it that you want?"

"I want to talk about the man you saw going into Margaret Margrabe's house on the night she was killed."

'The poet, you mean?"

"The poet? What do you mean, the poet?"

"The fella that went into the teacher's house," Keith said. "He stood there on the back porch and spoke a poem to her."

"Do you remember the poem?"

"Sort of," Keith said. "It was somethin' like 'love me with everything you are.' Them might not be the exact words, but they was somethin' like that."

"How do you know it was a poem?"

"I know 'cause of the way he was sayin' it. I mean it wasn't like it is when someone is just talkin' to another person. He sort of said the words like he was on stage or somethin'. Also, a couple of the words rhymed, but right now I can't rightly tell you which words it was that was rhymin'."

"Charley, do you think you would recognize this person if you saw him?"

"No, it was too dark," Keith said. "I wouldn't be able to recognize him by seein' him."

Sheriff Nelson sighed. "Damn, I was hoping you might recognize him."

"I would recognize him."

"You just said you wouldn't."

"I said I wouldn't be able to recognize him by seein' him." Keith smiled. "But you didn't ask if I would recognize him if I heard him talk. Because I would. Especially he was to talk like as if he was recitin' a poem, or somethin'."

"Charley, I thank you for this information," Sheriff Nelson said. "But for now, let's just keep this between you and me, all right?"

"All right, Sheriff, if you say so," Keith agreed.

"Hello, Matt. Hello, Miss O'Callahan," Moe said as the two went into the café. Matt had eaten several meals here now, and had befriended Moe.

"What's for lunch today, Moe?"

"Pork chops, potatoes, turnip greens, and cornbread."

Matt smiled at Annabelle. "Not as fancy as the dinner we had the other night, but it sounds good to me."

"It sounds good to me as well," Annabelle said.

After lunch, Matt rented a buckboard and team, and he and Annabelle drove about two miles out of town, where he started his instruction. She had her own pistol, a thirty-two caliber, and she took it out to show Matt.

"I bought this a few months ago. I hope it's all right."

"If you shoot it accurately, trust me, it's all right," Matt said. "Let me see how you hold it."

Annabelle held the pistol, balanced it in her hand.

"Looks like you're holding it all right. Let me see what you can do with that rock there, about twenty feet in front of you. That

304

dark red one. See if you can knock a chip off it."

Annabelle lifted her hand and without pausing to sight along the barrel, she pulled the trigger. A spark flew from the rock, and the strike of the bullet left a white mark.

"That's not bad. But if you hadn't pulled the trigger you would have hit it dead center," Matt said. "Pulling the trigger pulled the gun off target."

Annabelle laughed. "Now you're teasing me," she said. "How do you shoot the gun without pulling the trigger?"

"Like this."

Matt drew, fired, and put the pistol back in his holster in a motion that was so fast that Annabelle couldn't believe her eyes. And on the red rock, there was a white chip in the dead center.

"That's very impressive, Matt, but don't tell me you didn't pull the trigger."

"I didn't. Look, wrap your hand around the butt of your pistol, and put your finger on the trigger, and I'll show you."

Annabelle held the pistol as Matt directed, then raised it in the direction of the rock. Matt wrapped his hand around hers.

"Now, aim the pistol, but don't think of shooting it. We'll shoot it together."

Annabelle pointed the gun toward the

305

rock, and Matt, slowly began to squeeze
down on her hand.

"Do you feel that?" Matt asked.

"Yes, I do," Annabelle answered in a
breathy voice.

Matt either didn't get the inference of her
answer, or paid no attention to it. Instead,
he continued to squeeze her hand until
quite unexpectedly, as far as Annabelle was
concerned, the pistol just seemed to go off
in her hand.

"Oh!" she said, jumping in surprise.

Matt chuckled. "Look where you hit," he
said.

Looking toward the rock, Annabelle saw a
new white chip, right next to the one that
Matt had put there.

"Oh, did I do that?" she asked. Then she
answered herself. "No, you did it."

"Huh-uh, you are the one who aimed the
pistol. All I did was help you squeeze off a
shot. Now, try it again, without my help.
Remember, just squeeze. That rock's getting a little used up, try that one." He
pointed to another one; this one was sort of
a blue green.

"That one is too far away."

"Try it."

Annabelle aimed and squeezed. The gun
went off in her hand, bucked up slightly,

and, as before the strike of the bullet brought a spark and left a scar, right in the middle of the rock.

"Oh, that's wonderful!" Annabelle said.

"Keep this up, and you'll give Annie Oakley a run for her money," Matt quipped.

In town at the Pig Palace, Lila walked over to the table where Carter and Fletcher were drinking whiskey.

"What about it, boys?" she asked, smiling as seductively as she could. "Would you like another visit like the one we had last week?"

"What do you mean?" Fletcher asked.

Lila leaned over, put her hand down, and let it rest on Fletcher's crotch. "I mean when I had the two of you at the same time. I've never had such a good time since I've been on the line. I think I proved I was woman enough for you two boys. Now, are you two men enough to do it again?"

"What are you going to charge us?" Carter asked.

"Same thing I charged you last time. Five dollars."

"Wait a minute, you're the one that asked us. I think we ought to get more of a bargain this time," Carter said.

"What about four dollars?" Lila suggested.

"Four dollars? Yeah, let's go," Carter said,

and he and Fletcher followed Lila up to her room.

"Here's your four dollars," Carter said as soon as they got upstairs to Lila's room. Carter was holding out two one-dollar bills, and Fletcher was also holding two one-dollar bills.

"Huh-uh," Lila said. "Four dollars ain't goin' to do it, honey. It's goin' to cost you one hundred dollars."

"One hundred dollars? Are you crazy? Hell, the most expensive whore I ever had only cost me ten dollars! You think we are goin' to pay you a hundred dollars just to go to bed with you?"

"That's not what you're payin' for," Lila said. She walked over to a chest of drawers and opened the top drawer, then pulled out two sheets of paper. She showed the papers to the two men.

"What's this?" Fletcher asked.

"For me, it's fifty dollars apiece from each of you," Lila said. "For you, it's your chance to stay out of jail."

```
┌─────────────────────────────────────┐
│              WANTED                  │
│         for Bank Robbery             │
│           and MURDER                 │
│         WILLIAM CARTER               │
│            $1,500                    │
│          to be paid by               │
│          WELLS FARGO                 │
└─────────────────────────────────────┘

┌─────────────────────────────────────┐
│              WANTED                  │
│         for Bank Robbery             │
│           and MURDER                 │
│         LENNY FLETCHER               │
│            $1,500                    │
│          to be paid by               │
│          WELLS FARGO                 │
└─────────────────────────────────────┘
```

"What the hell! Where'd you get these?"
Carter asked.

"It don't matter where I got 'em, honey,
the point is I got 'em," Lila said. "And if
you don't give me one hundred dollars, I'll
give these to Mr. Durbin. I'm sure he would
be willing to pay me somethin' for 'em.
After all, he stands to make three thousand
dollars out of it."

CHAPTER TWENTY-SIX

"Shady Rest wasn't always like this, you know," Annabelle told Matt as, after the shooting lesson, they sat for a while on the bank of Painted Rock Creek. The water was so clear in some places, that it was easy to see the pebbles that lay on the bottom some four feet deep, while in other places the stream broke into white froth where it tumbled over the large rocks.

"When I first came here, it was a nice community, with good people. That's why I invested everything I had in building my dress shop."

"What happened to the town?" Matt asked.

"Jacob Bramley is what happened to it," Annabelle said. "The trouble started when he arrived. He bought the Pig Palace and turned it into a gathering place for the absolute scum of the earth. Then, gradually, all of First Street became a den of inequity.

"For a while it was tolerable, because the troubles stayed on First Street, and it was almost as if we were two separate towns, Plantation Row, and the rest of Shady Rest. But, as you have seen, the evil is beginning to spill off Plantation Row, and contaminate the rest of the town.

"Well, I have too much invested here, in money, labor, and personal commitment, to let Bramley and the others take it away from me. I don't intend to stand by and let that happen. I will fight them."

Matt was a good judge of character and had already decided that Annabelle was a woman with metal under the surface. He was seeing in her eyes now both fire and ice.

"Annabelle, I know that you are disappointed that I refused to accept the position of city marshal," Matt said. "But just because I didn't accept the position doesn't mean that I have no interest in the conditions here. It's just as I said. As city marshal I would have my hands tied by rules, and regulations. I promise you that whoever the town selects as marshal will have my support."

"Whoever the marshal is will need your support," Annabelle said. "Especially since Bramley now has his own law with *Deputy*

Sheriff Durbin." She set the words "deputy sheriff" apart, to show her disdain for the idea.

"An outlaw with a badge is still an outlaw," Matt said.

"Yes," Annabelle said. "That's my thought exactly."

Annabelle reached up to put her hand on Matt's cheek; then she kissed him. When she pulled away from him, her face held an expression that was halfway between laughter and embarrassment.

"I think we should get back to town now," she said. "It isn't good for business for me to keep my shop so long closed."

"All right," Matt said. Standing first, he reached down to help Annabelle up.

Annabelle held her pistol out to look at it. "Now that I know how to shoot this, I'm going to have to get a holster," she said.

Back in the Pig Palace, Carter and Fletcher were standing at the foot of the bed in Lila's room, looking down at the naked woman. Her head was turned to one side, and there were bruises on her neck.

"I don't know, maybe we shouldn't of done that," Fletcher said.

"What do you mean, maybe we shouldn't have done it? We didn't have no choice. She

312

found out who we was. You seen them posters same as I did. She was goin' to show 'em to Durbin if we didn't come up with a hunnert dollars. You got fifty dollars left?"

"No, not since we give that money to Mutt. Which we never did get back," Fletcher said.

"Yeah, well, I don't have fifty dollars left either," Carter said. "So, it's like I said, we didn't have no choice."

Carter picked up the wanted flyers Lila had shown them.

"I wonder where the hell she got these. I didn't even know there was any wanted flyers out on us. Hell, if we had known that, we could a' changed our names just the way Mutt did. If we had changed our names, she wouldn't a' known who we was. I mean, there ain't no description or nothin' like that on 'em, there's just our names."

"What are we goin' to do with her now?" Fletcher asked.

"We're goin' to hide the body."

"How? We can't just take her downstairs. Maybe you ain't never took no notice, but there ain't no back way out of here. The only way out is through the bar."

"We aren't goin' to take her out," Carter said. "We're goin' to leave her here."

"And do what? Hide her under the bed?

313

She'll be discovered, and once they find her, they'll know we done it. I mean, there ain't no one in the bar that don't know we both come up her with her. Half the people in the bar seen us leave."

"We'll put her there," Carter said, pointing to big trunk.

"Hell, she can't fit in that trunk."

"We'll make her fit."

"Yeah!" Fletcher said with a demonic chuckle. "Yeah, we'll make her fit. That'll be a good place to hide her."

"Come on, you're goin' to have to help."

"I tell you what, Bill, I don't like the way she's lookin' at us," Fletcher said. "I mean, look at 'er. It's givin' me the willies, I tell you."

"She ain't lookin' at us. She ain't lookin' at nothin'. She's dead."

"Her eyes is open."

As Fletcher said, Lila's eyes were open, bulging, and still reflecting the terror of her last few seconds of life.

Carter opened the trunk, then lifted out several dresses, scarves, and shawls until the trunk was empty.

"All right, let's get her in there."

The two men lifted her from the bed.

"Damn!" Fletcher said. "I didn't have no idea she was this heavy."

It took some bending and twisting of legs and arms, but after a couple of tries, Carter and Fletcher managed to get her body stuffed down into the trunk. Once they had her in the trunk, they covered her up by putting the clothes and other articles back over her.

"There," Carter said as they closed the trunk. "Now, even if someone happened to open the trunk, they won't see her unless they start emptying it."

"And more'n likely they ain't nobody goin' to do that until she starts in to stinkin'," Fletcher added with a chuckle.

"Let's go have a drink."

"What? Are you serious? Don't you think maybe we ought to get out of here?"

"Not yet. Now we are going to go downstairs and ask the bartender where Lila is. After all, we gave her good money to go with us, but she never showed up."

"What do you mean she never . . ." Fletcher started; then he laughed. "Yeah," he said. "She never showed up. That's good. That's real good."

"What do you mean, where is she?" Poke asked. "I thought I seen the three of you go up together."

"Yeah, you did see us go up together,"

Carter said. "But when we got to the top of the stairs she told us to go on into her room and wait for a couple of minutes while she went out to the privy. And that's what we done, only she didn't come back."

"Maybe she come back when you two come back down here," Poke suggested.

"No, I don't think so. You can go up and look for yourself, if you want to," Carter said. "She ain't there."

"I can't leave the bar," Poke said. "But Mr. Bramley is right over there, you can go talk to him."

Fletcher and Carter went over to a table where Bramley was playing a game of solitaire.

"We got a bone to pick with you," Carter said.

Bramley played a red nine on a black ten before he looked up at the two men.

"And what would that be?" he asked.

"Me 'n Fletcher here paid one of your whores to go to bed with us, but she took the money 'n never showed up."

"Which means you owe us five dollars," Fletcher said, adding a dollar to the price Lila had actually quoted to them.

"Why would I owe you anything? Did you give the money to the whore?"

"Yeah, we told you we did."

"Then she's the one that owes you the five dollars."

"All the whores here work for you, don't they?" Fletcher asked.

Bramley sighed. "Which whore are you talking about?"

"Lila. I don't know her last name."

Bramley chuckled. "You don't know her first name, either. Whores never use their real names. Why don't you go on up to her room? More 'n likely she's up there, now, waitin' on you."

"No, she ain't up there. She told us to wait in her room for her, which is what we done, but she never come."

"We? What do you mean? Both of you were waitin' on her?"

"Yeah."

"At the same time?"

"Yeah, that's what we done once before, and she said she'd do it again."

"Well, if anyone would do something like that, it would be Lila, I reckon. Are you sure you were in the right room?"

"Like I told you, we been with her before, so we know which room was hers. Besides which, you can ask Poke if you want to, he seen the three of us go up together, so he can prove we was with her. She said she was goin' to use the privy and would be right

317

back, only she didn't never come back. We was in her room for sure. It's the second room on the right at the top of the stairs. That's her room, ain't it?"

"Yes, that's her room. All right, come on, we'll go up and look together," Bramley offered.

"It won't do no good. She ain't there."

"Let's look anyway."

Fletcher and Carter followed Bramley up the stairs. When they got to the door to Lila's room, Bramley knocked.

"Lila? Lila, are you in there? I got a couple of men here complaining that you took their money, but didn't do anything for 'em." Bramley knocked again. "Lila? Open the damn door!"

"The door ain't locked," Fletcher said. "I know 'cause me 'n Carter was both was just in here."

Bramley opened the door and the three men stepped inside. The room was empty, and the bed made.

"Damn," Bramley said. "I wonder where she went."

"Is that all you're goin' to say?" Carter asked.

"What do you mean?"

"Like we told you, we give her five dollars and we didn't get nothin' for it. I mean,

318

that don't look very good for your business, does it?"

"All right. Come downstairs, I'll give you your money back," Bramley said. "I can always get the money from Lila when she finally does show."

"Yeah, that's pretty much what we was thinkin' too," Carter said.

Two days later Jake Bramley was playing solitaire at "his" table in the back of the saloon when Barb and Monica came over to speak to him. Barb was the younger of the two girls, but only marginally better looking. Both of them, though, realized that they were near the end of their effective lives as prostitutes, the Pig Palace being practically the last stop for them.

The two women stood by the table for a long moment without speaking, until finally Bramley broke the silence.

"Have you just come to watch me play Ole Sol? Or is there a purpose to the two of you standin' there like a couple of moon-faced heifers?"

"Mr. Bramley, me 'n Barb are worried about Lila," Monica said.

"What about her?"

"Well, maybe you ain't noticed, but there ain't nobody seen her for two or three days.

It ain't like her to just run off like that."

"Have you checked down at Abby's?" Bramley asked. "Maybe she's gone back to workin' there."

Barb shook her head. "No, she ain't gone back there, I checked with some of the girls that work there. Besides which, you might remember, she and Abby had a big fallin' out, which is why she come here to work in the first place."

Bramley was holding a card in his hand, looking at all the possible matches. "Shit!" he said in frustration, when he saw that he had no further plays in the game. He gathered up the cards, then looked up again at the two worried women.

"What about the Crooked Branch, or Ace High? Have you checked with Foster, or Gimlin?"

He laid the cards out for a new game.

"No, sir, we ain't checked with them, but we've asked some of the other girls," Monica said. "I'm tellin' you, Mr. Bramley, there ain't nobody seen her in two or three days."

"If that bitch ran off and took my clothes with her I'm goin' to have her ass," Bramley said.

Because he wanted the women who worked for him to dress a certain way, he bought all their clothes, though he was very specific in the arrangement he had with them. The women could wear the clothes as long as they worked for him. But if they left the Pig Palace for any reason, the clothes had to stay.

"Mr. Bramley, I don't think Lila would do that," Barb said.

"You don't, huh? All right, go up to her room," Bramley ordered. "Go through her trunk and take out all her clothes. Even if the bitch does come back now, she doesn't work here, anymore. You two can divide her clothes between you."

"Oh, I want the red one," Barb said excitedly as they started back toward the stairs.

Bramley was several cards into his new game when he heard the screams from upstairs.

"What in the hell has gotten into them? What are they screaming about?" Bramley asked, irritably.

"You want me to go find out?" Durbin asked. Even though Durbin now wore the badge of a deputy sheriff, he still spent most of his time in the Pig Palace Saloon, declaring it to be the "office of the deputy sheriff." He also continued to draw, in addition to the salary of a deputy sheriff, the much more generous salary Bramley was paying him to provide security for the saloon.

"Yes, go find out," Bramley ordered.

When Durbin reached the second floor he saw Barb and Monica standing in the hall, clinging to each other, their faces reflecting terror.

"Mr. Bramley wants to know what the hell is wrong with you two," Durbin said.

Monica pointed toward the open door. "She's in there," she replied in a weak voice.

"Who is in there?"

"She is."

Realizing that, for some reason, the two women were too frightened to give him much information, Durbin went into the room. He saw dresses, scarves, and other items scattered around, but nothing else. The lid of the trunk was up, but because the lid had been opened from the other side of the trunk, it blocked his view down inside. He walked around to the other side to look into the trunk, and that was when he saw Lila's nude body, her arms and legs twisted into a position that would allow her to fit into the confined space.

Lila's skin was a clammy bluish white, and her eyes were open and bulging almost out of their sockets. Durbin reached down into the trunk, lifted her body out, then lay it down on the bed. It was hard to pick her up and maneuver her because rigor mortis had set in, causing her arms and legs to remain in the contorted position in which Durbin found them.

Leaving her twisted body on the bed, he went downstairs to inform Bramley.

"That whore that's been missin'? Well, she ain't missin' no more. She's layin' up there on her bed now, deader 'n hell."

"Damn," Bramley said. "I sort of figured somethin' like that might have happened. Sumbitch! Here's the card I was lookin' for! Ha! I got this game won!"

CHAPTER TWENTY-SEVEN

At that very moment, Carter and Fletcher, unaware that Lila's body had been discovered, were down at the Texas Star, the saloon that was most distant from the Pig Palace. They were sitting at a table separated from the others in the saloon by mutual choice. They didn't want to be with any of the other customers, and none of the other customers wanted to be with them. The women who worked at the Texas Star had learned the first time Carter and Fletcher ever came to the saloon that they were not good company. As result, not one bar girl had come anywhere close to them for the whole time they'd been there.

"You know what I'm thinkin'?" Carter asked, speaking quietly.

"What?"

"I'm thinkin' maybe it's time we was gettin' on. If Jensen ever puts it together that we was with Mutt, he's likely to come after us. And even if he don't, if that whore come by some wanted posters on us, like as not Durbin will too. And I know that son of a bitch, he'd just as soon kill us as look at us, especially if he thinks there's some reward money in it for him."

"Yeah, and I'd just as soon not be here when they find the whore's body, either," Fletcher said.

"I ain't worried about that. First of all, by now, I mean what with us not runnin' 'n all, I don't think it's likely they'll think we done it. Hell, whores is always gettin' kilt. Besides which, I doubt Bramley, or anyone else down there, cares one way another. It's them reward posters I'm worried about.

"Problem is, we ain't got practically no money left at all."

"That's all right. I plan to do somethin' about that before we leave."

"You mean, hold up the bank?"

"No, there's only two of us, and I don't know that just the two of us could hold up a bank. But if we was to rob some small business, say one that was out on the edge of town so that we could just ride off, it would be an easy way get some money. Not much, but enough to get us out of here."

"What business you got in mind?" Fletcher asked.

"What about the grocery store? It's the last store in town and there ain't likely to be anyone there that's wearin' a gun, especially if we go when there's no customers. And because it's right on the edge of town, we can just grab whatever money there is in the store, then hightail it on out of here."

"Yeah, that's a good idea," Fletcher said.

Fifteen minutes later, after the two men tied their horses up at the hitching rail in front of Rafferty's Grocery Store, they took a quick look around to see if anyone was watching them, then went inside. The store was redolent with the familiar smells of flour, smoked meat, ground coffee, cinnamon, and other spices. Sixteen-year-old Michael Rafferty, who was the son of the store owner, was sweeping the floor when Carter and Fletcher came in. Michael looked up and smiled.

"Yes, sir, somethin' I can do for you?"

"You runnin' this store by yourself, are you, boy?" Carter asked.

"I am right now. Pa's takin' care of business downtown. But if you need to buy somethin', I can help you."

"What if I give you a bill that's bigger'n what the thing costs?" Carter asked. "Would you be able to give me change? I ain't goin' to do business with you if you can't give me change."

"Yes, sir, I can give you change. Pa give me the key to the cashbox," Michael said.

"Well, that's good. We'll just do a little shoppin' then."

Michael walked around behind the counter. "What can I get for you?" he asked.

"A pound of flour, two pounds of bacon, a pound of coffee, and a couple pounds of beans ought to do it," Carter said.

Efficiently, Michael moved back and forth along the shelves behind the counter, making the selections, then bringing them back to the counter. There he wrapped everything in wrapping paper, and tied it off into a couple of neat packages. Then he put the packages into a paper sack.

"That will be a dollar seventy-five, please," Michael said with professional courtesy.

Carter put a dollar on the counter. "I'll be wantin' change for this," he said.

Michael looked at the dollar, then back at Carter, and laughed. "You're foolin' me," he said.

"No, I'm not."

"Mister, you've only put one dollar here. I'll be needin' seventy-five more cents, or, another dollar, then I can give you some change," he said.

Carter drew his pistol and aimed it at Michael, pulling the hammer back. "I tell you what," he said. "I'll just be keeping this dollar, and I'll take everything else you have in the cashbox."

"What? Mister, are you robbin' me?" Michael asked, incredulously.

"What do you think, Lenny? This boy ain't as dumb as he looks," Carter said. "Open the cashbox, boy, and give us all your money," Carter said.

With shaking hands, Michael emptied the cashbox of thirty-six dollars and fifty-five cents, then handed the money over to Carter.

"This is it? This is all the money you have?"

"Yes, sir," Michael said in a shaky voice. "Pa took the rest of the money to the bank. This here money is only just what he left me for makin' change."

"Come on, Bill, it'll have to do," Fletcher said. "Let's get out of here."

Carter dropped the money down in the bag with the groceries just as the front door to the store opened and someone came in.

"Hello, Michael! Can we go fishin'? Or has your pa got you workin'?" the young men who stepped in through the front door called.

"Kelly! Go get the marshal! I'm bein'

robbed!" Michael shouted.

Carter and Fletcher both turned toward the man who had just come in, a cowboy who worked at one of the neighboring ranches. Both Carter and Fletcher fired at him, and the cowboy went down. Michael took that opportunity to dash out the back door so that, by the time the two robbers turned back, he was gone.

"Where the hell did he go?" Fletcher asked.

"It don't matter," Carter said. "Let's go! We need to get out of here!"

Clutching the paper sack, the two men dashed out the front door, mounted their horses, and galloped away.

Michael, who was hiding behind the privy that was between the store and the house, watched the two men ride off to the north. He stayed hidden, not going back into the store until he was certain they were well away.

Once he was back inside, Michael ran to the downed cowboy, kneeling on the floor beside him to see if he could do anything to help, but the man on the floor was dead. The young cowboy, Kelly Tucker, was a friend of Michael's, and often came to the store as much to visit with Michael as to buy anything.

With tears in his eyes, Michael shut and locked the door, hung out the CLOSED sign, then walked down to the marshal's office to report what had happened.

Matt dropped Annabelle off at her shop, then took the buckboard and team back to the livery to turn it in. That done, he walked across the street to the Texas Star. Hawkins met him as soon as he stepped inside.

"We had a robbery while you were gone," Hawkins said to Matt.

"What, here? You mean you were robbed?"

"No, it was Rafferty's Grocery. All they got was thirty-six dollars, but they killed young Kelly Tucker. Kelly was a cowboy who worked out at the Crooms Ranch. He and young Michael Rafferty were good friends, and Kelly had come to invite Michael to go fishing. Michael said the robbers opened up on him as soon as he stepped in through the front door."

"Do they know who did it?"

"From the description the Rafferty boy gave, it sounds like it might have been Bill Carter and Lenny Fletcher. Do those names mean anything to you?"

Matt shook his head. "I'm afraid not," he said.

"Well, they came into town about the same time that Mutt Crowley did. You most always saw the three of them together. Carter and Fletcher were in here this morning, but, generally, they hung out down on Plantation Row."

"I'm sure our new deputy sheriff is hot on their trail," Matt said, sarcastically.

"I believe Durbin's words were that they were 'most likely out of the county, by now.' How the sheriff was ever convinced to give the buffoon a star, I'll never know. If he's a lawman, I'm a ballet dancer."

Matt laughed at the outlandish comparison.

Pecos

Prichard was standing at the bar in the saloon, and had just lifted the beer mug to his mouth when, in the mirror, he saw two familiar faces come into the saloon. What were Carter and Fletcher doing here? And where was Mutt?

He watched them in the mirror until they found a table; then, carrying his beer with him, he walked over to them.

"Hello, Prichard," Fletcher said.

Prichard's eyes flashed in anger, and he glanced around quickly to see if anyone had heard Fletcher's greeting.

"The name is Conner," he said. "Deputy Sheriff Abe Conner."

"I meant Conner," Fletcher said, contritely.

"What are you two boys doin' here? Where's Mutt?"

"He's dead," Carter said without prelude.

Prichard blinked his eyes in shocked surprise. "Dead?"

"Yeah."

Prichard sat down at the table with the two men; then he ran his hand through his hair. "What happened? How did he die? Or was he killed?"

"He was kilt all right," Carter said. "He was shot by a man named Matt Jensen. Do you know him?"

"Indeed I do," Prichard said. "I have never met him, but I certainly know who he is. He was the reason my brother was facing the hangman's noose up in Trinidad. Do you know any of the particulars?"

"Neither one of us seen it," Fletcher said. "But what we heard was that whenever Jensen seen Mutt, he recognized him, and told the marshal about it. Then Mutt, he kilt the marshal, and Jensen kilt Mutt."

"And where is Jensen now?"

"He's back in Shady Rest," Carter said.

"We tried to kill 'im, we took a shot at

'im, but we missed," Fletcher said.

"And you didn't make another try?"

"We couldn't stay around long enough," Carter said. "We, uh . . ." Carter looked around to see who was close enough to overhear him Then he leaned across the table to speak very quietly. "We kilt us a whore, then we kilt some cowboy while we was robbin' a grocery store. More'n likely nobody cares about the dead whore, but they're likely to get upset over the cowboy we kilt."

"So we thought we'd better come over here and find you," Fletcher said. "Bein' as you're deputy sheriff, why we figured we'd be safe over here."

"Did you know there are reward posters out on the two of you?" Prichard asked.

"Yeah, we seen 'em. The whore had 'em, but I don't know where she got 'em."

"So that's why we kilt her," Fletcher said.

"And that's also why we robbed a store 'cause we was near 'bout out of money, and we figured we needed to come over here," Fletcher said.

"All we need is a place to hide out for a while," Carter said

"All right," Prichard said. "I tell you what, there's an old abandoned cabin about a mile north of here. You two go hide out there

333

until I come for you."

"When will that be?"

"I've got some money coming. Soon as I collect that, I'll come get you."

"Where will we be a' goin', do you think?" Fletcher asked.

"I don't think, I know where we are going," Prichard said. "We're going to Shady Rest."

"Shady Rest? Why the hell would we want to go there? We just left there," Carter said.

"Because we're going to kill Matt Jensen."

"Look, I don't know how much you know about Matt Jensen, but I'm not even sure that the three of us could face him," Carter said.

"Tell me about Shady Rest. What kind of law do they have there?"

"Ha! They don't have no law at all," Fletcher said.

"No law?"

"No, not since Mutt kilt the marshal. All they got is a deputy marshal, and from what I hear, he don't want to be the marshal," Carter said.

"Don't forget Durbin," Fletcher said.

"Who is Durbin?"

"Durbin is a deputy sheriff, but he works for Jacob Bramley," Carter said. "Which means the town don't have any law, 'cause the law belongs to Bramley."

"And who is Jacob Bramley?"

"Bramley sort of runs things on his side of town — you know, the saloons, whores, that sort of thing," Carter said. "And the other saloon owners and the woman that runs the whorehouse, they all sort of listen to him."

Fletcher laughed. "They call that side of town Plantation Row."

"Am I to understand that the town of Shady Rest is a town divided?"

"Yeah," Carter said. "You could say that. There's all the people over on Plantation Row, then there are the 'good' people."

"How do the people on Plantation Row feel about Matt Jensen?" Prichard asked.

"I don't know. I don't think they think about him one way or the other."

"Then we shall have to change that," Prichard said.

CHAPTER TWENTY-EIGHT

"When can I expect the reward money?" Prichard asked Sheriff Nelson, when he returned to the sheriff's office.

"I've notified the state," Nelson replied. "We'll have to wait until they transfer the funds. Twenty-five hundred dollars is a lot of money. I don't have that much in sheriff's funds."

"Yes, but how long? The reason I ask, is I think I may be moving on."

"So soon?"

"It may seem soon, but I've already stayed here longer than I normally stay anywhere. And as they say, *volvens lapidem non congregabo musco.*"

"You want to tell me what the hell you just said?" Sheriff Nelson asked.

"A rolling stone gathers no moss."

"Why didn't you say so? Hell, I've heard that expression before."

Prichard laughed. "Because that's not the

way Erasmus said it. He said it in Latin."

"You are an educated man, aren't you, Conner?"

"University of Colorado."

"What are you doing, wandering around like you do? With your education, you could be a doctor or a lawyer, or someone important."

"Ah, but therein is the rub," Prichard said. "I have a Bachelor of Arts degree, and for a while, I was an assistant professor of English in a small college. If you want to discuss the great masters of painting, or literature, or poetry — and, as I have just so superciliously demonstrated, if you would like to do so in Latin — then I am your man."

"Poetry? Do you know poetry? I mean, do you ever recite it?"

"Oh yes, I often recite poetry. And there is one by Robert Browning that perfectly fits my wanderlust. Would you like to hear it?"

"Yes, yes, I would."

Striking a pose as if on stage, Prichard began to recite in rolling sonorous tones.

"Boot, saddle, to horse, and away!
Rescue my Castle, before the hot day
Brightens the blue from its silvery grey."

"Yes," Sheriff Nelson said. "Yes, I like that. Listen, how about watching the place for me for a while. I'll go down to the telegraph office and send another wire to Austin to see what the holdup is on your money."

"Thanks, Sheriff, I am most appreciative."

"I'm glad to do it," Nelson said with a nod as he put his hat on, then left.

As Nelson walked away from the sheriff's office, he wondered if he was crazy for being suspicious of Conner. Conner had been a good deputy — he had been an exceptional deputy as far as that goes. As a case in point, he had recognized the outlaw Holder, chased him down, and brought him to justice. Of course, he had brought him in dead, rather than alive, but at least the bullet hole was in front.

Conner had also shown his prowess with a pistol when he had a run-in with Teddy Rogers. He'd killed Rogers, but everyone who'd witnessed the fight, and many had, had testified that Conner had been pushed into the fight by Rogers, so that he'd had no choice but to kill him. And truth to tell, Sheriff Nelson had always known that Rogers was a hothead who was going to get himself into deep trouble someday.

That's why, when it happened, Nelson had not been shocked, nor had it been hard for him to believe the witnesses who'd testified on Conner's behalf. Afterward, Conner had even apologized to the Rogers family, and they had accepted the apology.

So why, now, was there something about Conner that was bothering him? Was it because of his arrogance about his education? All right, Conner was a bit of a puffed-up peckerwood, speaking Latin and such, and Nelson had to admit that he was finding that a little irritating. But there was something else that bothered him. He knew that the young schoolteacher had been an educated woman, and he knew that she had been a little pompous herself, that she wouldn't have had anything to do with a man whom she'd felt wasn't her equal in education and intelligence. In Pecos, there were damn few such men who would meet that standard. But Conner, with his education, and the way he talked, would certainly have to be classified as one who would meet her standards.

And then there was the poetry. Charley Keith had said that the man he saw going in through the back door of Margaret Margrabe's little house on the night she was killed had recited poetry. Had that man been Conner? Sheriff Nelson knew — or if he didn't know, he at least had a passing acquaintance with — most of the men who lived in and around Pecos, and Conner was the only one he knew who had even a passing interest in poetry.

Keith had said that he thought he would be able to recognize the voice if he heard it again, and Sheriff Nelson was about to put that to the test.

Sheriff Nelson found Charley Keith sitting on the front porch of the hardware store and, again, he bought the man's time with a pint bottle of whiskey. He told Keith that he wanted him to go down to the sheriff's office, and stand just under the open window.

"What do you want me to do while I'm standin' there?" Keith asked.

"All I want you to do is listen," Sheriff Nelson said.

"Listen to what?"

"Just listen. It may be nothing. But if it is what I think it is, you will know without being told."

"All right," Keith said. He started to pull the cork on the bottle.

"No, not yet," Sheriff Nelson said. "Wait until after."

"After what?"

"After you listen."

"Sheriff, I'm the drunk here, but I swear, you aren't making any sense at all."

"If I'm making sense, it will all make sense," Nelson said. "If I'm not, well, you can keep the whiskey anyway, so what do you have to lose?"

When they reached the sheriff's office, Nelson held his finger across his lips, cautioning Keith to be quiet; then he placed him just under the window that was open on the side of the building. With Keith in position, Nelson went back inside. He saw the deputy sitting at the desk, reading a newspaper.

"Any problems while I was gone? Any wives coming to complain about their husbands or anything like that?" Nelson asked.

Prichard chuckled. "No, nothing like that."

"Say, Abe, that poem you said a while ago, I been thinkin' about it. Do you know any more of it?"

"Sure I do," Prichard replied. "I know the entire poem."

"Say it for me. I sure do like the way you do poetry. It's like an actor on stage, or something."

"Why, Sheriff," Prichard said. "Can it possibly be that I am to have a fellow lover of poetry in this cultural desert?"

"Well, I do like poetry," Sheriff Nelson said. "And I'm told that Miss Margrabe liked poetry as well."

Nelson studied Prichard's face as he made the comment, but saw no reaction.

"Did she? Well, it's too bad she's gone, perhaps we could have found common interests. But, you wanted to hear the poem."

"Yes."

Again, Prichard assumed a studied pose, then began reciting.

"Boot, saddle, to horse, and away!
Rescue my Castle, before the hot day
Brightens the blue from its silvery grey.

"Ride past the suburbs, asleep as you'd
    say;
Many's the friend there, will listen and
    pray
God's luck to gallants that strike up the
    lay,
Boot, saddle, to horse, and away!

"Forty miles off, like a roebuck at bay,
Flouts Castle Brancepeth the
    Roundheads array:

342

Who laughs, Good fellows ere this, by my
    fay,
Boot, saddle, to horse, and away!"

Finishing his recitation, Prichard looked toward Sheriff Nelson for his review, but before either man could say a word, Charley Keith burst into the room.

"That's him, Sheriff!" Keith shouted. "Now I know why you wanted me to stand out there under the window. That's the same voice I heard sayin' poetry that night. That's the man that I saw going into the schoolteacher's house!"

Sheriff Nelson turned toward Prichard to question him, but it was too late. Prichard already had his gun in his hand. He fired twice, and both men went down.

Less than thirty seconds later, Prichard was on his horse, galloping away.

Abandoned cabin

The small, one-room cabin was empty of all furniture except for one broken chair. There was a built-in shelf to one side, and a water pump stuck up through the shelf.

Carter tried the pump, moving the handle up and down quickly. Except for some squeaks, clanks, and dust billowing from the mouth of the pump, his effort to get

343

water produced no results.

"I sure as hell hope Prichard ain't plannin' on us stayin' here for long," Fletcher said he picked up an empty, rusty can. "There ain't a damn thing here."

"That's why they call it abandoned," Carter said.

"Hey, Carter, now that Prichard is the sheriff an' all, you don't think he'd turn us in for the reward, do you?"

"No."

"Why not? I mean, he's wearin' a badge now. And I don't trust nobody that's wearin' a badge, whether I know them or not."

"Trust don't have anything to do with it," Carter said. "You seen him when we told him that Mutt got kilt. He wants to go back there and get revenge."

"Yeah, well, here's the thing. I ain't all that ready to go back to Shady Rest, what with we kilt a whore and that fella at the grocery store," Fletcher said.

"I've told you before, I don't think anyone is goin' to get all that upset about Lila gettin' kilt. I mean she warn't nothin' but a whore, and there don't nobody care nothin' about whether or not a whore gets kilt, least of all Bramley. It happens all the time," Carter said.

"What about the man we kilt at the store?"

Fletcher asked.

"Yeah, well, Durbin is the law there now, remember? And I don't see him gettin' all upset about some cowboy gettin' hisself kilt either. Prichard is a pretty smart man. If he says he can fix it so we can go back, I believe him."

"I wonder how long we're goin' to have to stay here in this place."

"No long," Carter said, as he looked out the window. "Not long at all."

"How do you know?"

"I know, 'cause Prichard is comin' up the road now, ridin' like a bat outta hell."

Deputy Curly Lathom, who had picked up the sobriquet because he had been bald since his early twenties, spent most of his time around Fort Stockton. Today, he rode into Pecos to visit with Sheriff Nelson, but when he went into the sheriff's office, he discovered both Nelson and another man lying on the floor. At first he thought they were dead, but he bent down to examine them, he discovered that they were both alive.

"Sheriff! Who did this?" Deputy Lathom asked.

"Conner did it," Nelson said. "It was Deputy Abe Conner."

345

"Wait here," Lathom said. "I'll get the doctor."

Despite his wound, Sheriff Nelson chuckled. "Now, Curly, you tell me just where the hell you think I might go."

"I'll be right back," Lathom said.

CHAPTER TWENTY-NINE

As had become his custom in the time since arriving in Shady Rest, Matt had taken another long ride out into the countryside. He had two reasons for doing this. One was just to get out of town for a while, since there was nothing to do in town except spend his time in the saloon, and the other reason was to give Spirit a little exercise.

Spirit (this was his third horse so named) did not enjoy being cooped up for too long, and Matt knew that he enjoyed, and needed, these long rides as much as Matt did. Today, Matt had explored the Guadalupe Range for most of the day, having a lunch of jerky and water at noon. But now, looking to the west, he saw that the clouds were building up into towering mountains of cream, growing higher and higher and turning darker and darker, until the sky in the west was nearly black as night.

"I tell you what, Spirit. We need to start

back to town. I think we're about get us a regular gully washer."

Matt remounted, and turned Spirit back toward Shady Rest. Soon thereafter, the air stopped stirring, and it became very hushed, with only the sound of Spirit's hoofbeats interrupting the quiet. Matt thought about putting him into a gallop, but decided not to risk it, for fear of injuring him.

"We're goin' to get wet, boy. There's just no way around it." He reached down to pat Spirit on the neck. "But we aren't made of sugar, so we'll be all right."

There was a strange, heavy feeling in the air, and Matt kept an eye on the sky. He could tell that Spirit also sensed that something was about to happen.

He remembered an incident once when he was still quite young and riding on his very first horse, also named Spirit, and given to him by Smoke Jensen. The horses, then, had seemed to be reacting to a change in the weather, and Matt had commented on it to Smoke.

"They can smell the sulfur, boy," Smoke said.

"Smell the sulfur? What does that mean?"

"That means that the very gates of hell are about to open."

This was a day like that one had been, and Matt could see the lightning, now but flashes buried deep in the clouds, each flash coming several seconds before the thunder, low and rumbling. Then the lightning broke out of the clouds. It streaked down the distant horizon, stretching from the clouds to the ground, and after each strike the following thunder came more closely on the heels of the flash.

Then the winds came. At first it was no more than a gentle freshening, still hot and dry with the dust of the prairie. But the wind increased and Matt could feel a dampness on its breath.

The intensity of the lightning increased. Instead of one or two flashes, there were ten or fifteen huge, jagged streaks, each streak giving birth to at least half-a-dozen more splitting off from it. Now the thunder, which was hard and sharp, followed so closely that it was almost concurrent with the lightning. After each flash, the thunder rolled with a long, deep-throated roar.

"Get ready, Spirit, here it comes," Matt said as he put on his poncho.

The rain came then, sweeping down from the west, and he was able to watch it approach, a giant, gray wall. The lightning streaked and the thunder crashed, and then the rain was upon him, the water cascading down on him with as much ferocity as if he had been standing under a waterfall. Matt was drenched, and he felt wet clear through to the bone.

The skies had opened over Shady Rest, and because of the deluge, no one was out and about. That meant that none of the stores in Shady Rest were doing any business. Annabelle was standing at the front window of her shop, watching the rain. It dripped from the eves, and the water stood in pools. There were no horses tied to any of the hitching posts, and the street was empty. Across the way, she saw Roy Clinton standing in the doorway of his apothecary, looking out at the rain. Near the apothecary, a cat was crouched under the slight overhang of the boardwalk, trying to pull itself back far enough to keep from being drenched, though Annabelle could see that the effort wasn't successful.

At the far end of the street she saw a horse and rider approaching and felt sorry for anyone who happened to be out in weather like this. Then she recognized him. It was Matt Jensen! Before she realized what she was doing, she stepped out into the rain and waved at him, bidding him to come over.

Seeing Annabelle standing in front of her

shop, waving at him, Matt turned Spirit toward her.

"Come in out of the rain," Annabelle invited, her voice thin in the downpour.

"I need to get my horse out of the rain as well," Matt called back.

"I have a lean-to out back."

Matt nodded, rode Spirit around to the back of the shop, dismounted, then led his horse into the shelter.

"You'll be all right here, for a while," Matt said as he wrapped the reins around a stanchion.

When Matt went inside the shop, Annabelle met him with a towel. Matt dried himself off as best he could; then he handed the towel back. "You look like you could use it as well," he said.

Annabelle smiled. "Yes, I did get a little wet, didn't I? We both need some dry clothes."

"I guess we do. The problem is, I don't seem to have any handy at the moment."

Annabelle smiled. "Yes, you do," she said.

"What do you mean?"

"I not only sell dresses to women, I also have some nice robes for men. Suppose I pick one out for you, then we can go up my apartment and both of us get into some dry clothes?"

"Let me get this straight," Matt said. "You are inviting me up to your apartment, where we are both going to take off our clothes?"

Her smile was bold and self-confident.

"Yes," she said, as she turned the sign around in her door from OPEN to CLOSED.

Annabelle's apartment upstairs was diffused by gray rain-light, so Annabelle struck a match and lit a lantern, which pushed out a little golden bubble of light. She raised the match to her lips and blew it out. "You can change out here," she said. "I'll go into the bedroom."

Matt nodded, and as soon as she went into her bedroom and closed the door, he began stripping out of his wet clothes. A moment later he had them draped over the cold radiator, and he put on the red flannel robe she had given him.

He waited for a long moment for her, and when she didn't reappear he decided that she must be waiting to hear from him that it was all right for her to come back out. He knocked lightly on the bedroom door.

"Annabelle?" he called. "You can come out, now."

"Or, you can come in," Annabelle replied.

Matt found the answer curious, but he opened the door to step inside. There, he saw her, wearing nothing but a thin, cotton sleeping gown. The nipples of her breasts were prominent against the cloth.

"Annabelle?" Matt asked.

"You don't really want to go back out into the rain, do you, Matt?" Annabelle asked. She put every ounce of seduction she could muster in her voice, and she thrust her hip out to one side, accenting her curves. She'd planned for it to be a provocative pose, and it was.

"Perhaps I should blow out the lantern," Matt suggested.

Smiling, Annabelle pulled her sleeping gown over her head, then stood naked before him.

"I was hoping you would say that," she said

The next morning Annabelle went to see Mayor Trout, carrying with her a carefully wrapped package.

"Miss O'Callahan," Mayor Trout said. "What a delight to have you call on me. What is in the package?"

"I have finished the dress I was making for Mrs. Trout," Annabelle said. "I thought perhaps, since you have already paid for it, that you might like to deliver it to her personally."

"Yes, what a wonderful idea!" Mayor Trout said. "And aren't you nice to think of it."

"Now, Mayor, I have a request to make."

"Of course, Miss O'Callahan. Anything, just ask."

"Good, I'm glad you feel that way. Mayor Trout, I want you to appoint me to the position of city marshal."

"What?" Trout said, his voice a gasp at the request.

"I want to be appointed as the next city marshal."

"Why in heaven's name would you ask something like that? That is absurd. And were I to grant that request, I would be insane."

"Do we or do we not need a city marshal? Or, are you ready to turn all the law enforcement over to Deputy Durbin?"

"No, I — that is, yes, we do need a city marshal."

"And have you been able to find someone to take the job?"

"No," Mayor Trout admitted.

"Then, I ask you, why do you turn me down? You need a city marshal, and I want the job."

"I . . . I'll have to take this up with the city council."

"When?"

"I'll call a special meeting this afternoon."

"Good. Now, I have one more request."

"What might that be?" Mayor Trout asked in a resigned voice.

"I want to be present at the meeting of the city council. I want to plead my own case."

Mayor Trout sighed, and ran his hand through his hair. "All right, we'll meet at three o'clock, here, in the city hall."

Matt was having his lunch at Moe's when he saw Hawkins coming toward his table.

"You're going to join me for lunch? Good," Matt said.

Hawkins ordered his meal, and Matt told the waiter to hold his own lunch back until Hawkins was served.

"There's going to be a meeting of the city council at three this afternoon," Hawkins said. "You might be interested in the subject."

Matt took a swallow of his coffee before he answered. "I hope it isn't another attempt to get me to accept the job of city marshal."

"It isn't," Hawkins said. "Oh, it is about the city marshal, but you aren't the one they'll be considering."

"You mean they have a volunteer for the job?"

"Yes."

"Good. Once you have a new city marshal, tell him he can count on my support."

Hawkins smiled. "I'll tell her," he said.

Hawkins's reply came just as their meals were being delivered, and Matt was paying attention to the placement of his plate. But he looked up quickly.

"What did you say? You will tell *her*?"

Hawkins chuckled. "I thought that would get your attention."

Matt recalled something Annabelle had said on the day he had given her a shooting lesson.

"Well, I have too much invested here, in money, labor, and personal commitment, to let Bramley and the others take it away from me. I don't intend to stand by and let that happen. I will fight them."

"I'll be damned," Matt said. "You're talking about Annabelle O'Callahan, aren't you?"

"Yes," Hawkins said. "Wait a minute. How do you know that? Did you know that Miss O'Callahan was going to do this?"

"No, I can't say that I knew she was going to do this," Matt said. "But neither can I say that I'm surprised."

"Well, I'm surprised," Hawkins said. "I'm damn surprised."

"What time did you say the city council was going to meet?"

"At three o'clock this afternoon."

"Do you suppose they would let me attend the meeting?"

"You can come as my personal guest," Hawkins said. "That way there will be no question."

There was a room in the back of the city hall that was set aside just for the city council meetings. It had a long conference table in the middle, with enough chairs around it not only to accommodate the council members, but any visitors who might be required to appear before the council. Matt accompanied Hawkins to the meeting and, as of three minutes until three, he looked around the table to see, in addition to the mayor and Hawkins, the other council members: Dupree, Milner, Dempster, Cook, Peabody, and Tobin

Matt was the only non-council member present, and he sat in one of the chairs that was separated from those occupied by the council members.

"Mayor, is it true what I heard?" Dupree asked. "Are we here to decide whether or not to appoint a woman as our marshal?"

"Yes," Mayor Trout answered.

"Well, that is the dumbest thing I've ever heard," Dupree said. "Let's just vote on it now. We can all vote no, and get this silly business over with so we can go back to work."

Mayor Trout shook his head. "I promised her that she would be able to address the council."

"Well, where is she?" Dupree asked. "It's three o'clock and . . ."

"I'm here," Annabelle said.

CHAPTER THIRTY

Looking toward the door, the men gasped, not at the sudden appearance of Annabelle, but at the way she looked. Annabelle was not wearing a dress. She was wearing denim trousers, and a white shirt, tucked down into her trousers. Around her waist she was wearing a belt and holster, and in the holster, Matt saw the same pistol she had brought to her shooting lesson. She was also wearing a man's hat, beneath which her red hair tumbled to her shoulders.

For a long moment all the men around the table stared in surprise at Annabelle's unexpected appearance. As the owner and seamstress of the Elite Shoppe, she'd never been seen in anything except a dress, and not just any dress, but very elegant dresses of her own design and make. And yet, she had never looked more like a woman than she did now, in this outfit.

"Uh, Miss O'Callahan, if you would take

a seat, we'll get the meeting started," Mayor Trout said, once he found his voice.

So shocked were the men that none of them thought to stand, except Matt, who not only stood, he also held out a chair for her, a chair that was next to his own. Not until then did the other men stand, rising awkwardly and discordantly until she took her own seat in the chair Matt had proffered.

Once they were seated again, Mayor Trout called the council to order. "Gentlemen," he said. "I think all of you are already aware of the purpose of this meeting. We are here to consider the appointment of Annabelle O'Callahan to the position of city marshal."

"That's not even possible, is it?" Milner asked. "I mean, seeing as women can't vote, how can they hold a political office?"

"Mr. Dempster?" Mayor Trout asked.

"There is no legal reason why she cannot be appointed as city marshal," Dempster said. "And the operative phrase is appointed, for that is what the position is . . . appointed, not elected."

"Well, gentlemen, there it is. According to the city attorney, there is no legal reason why we cannot appoint Miss O'Callahan to the position of city marshal."

"Then let's vote," Milner said.

"Mr. Mayor," Annabelle said. "I believe you said that I would be allowed to address the council?"

"Yes," Mayor Trout said. "Yes, I did, and you may do so."

"Thank you, Mr. Mayor, and thank you, honorable members of this council, for giving me this opportunity to plead my case.

"I know that you may question whether I, or indeed whether any woman, could perform the duties of a city marshal. But before you cast your vote using that as your criteria, I would like to tell you the story of Molly Pitcher. That is how she has come to be known, though her real name was Mary Hays.

"At the Battle of Monmouth in 1778, Mary Hays was bringing water to the parched soldiers, doing so under heavy fire from the British. During that battle, Mary's husband fell, wounded, and as they carried him from the battlefield, Mary took her husband's place, swabbing and loading the cannon so that the battery could continue to keep up the fire. At one point a musket ball passed between her legs, tearing off the bottom of her skirt, but Mary continued loading the cannon.

"After the battle none other than General George Washington recognized her courage, and made her a noncommissioned officer. She has come down through history to us as Molly Pitcher, or the name she used for the rest of her life, Sergeant Molly.

"Now, gentlemen, I am not comparing myself with a genuine heroine of the War of Independence, but I do use that as an example to show you that honor, courage, and duty are not the exclusive domain of men. I ask for the appointment, and I promise you, I will serve the city well."

"I have a question, Miss O'Callahan," Dupree said. "Do you have a personal reason for wanting this position?"

"My reason is both personal and public. Too many of our families are leaving town, and if this trend continues, it may well reach the point to where the outlaws outnumber the decent citizens. And when that happens, we will cease to be a town. I, and nearly every other business in town, would be forced to close, and in doing so, would likely lose so much money that I may not be able to start anew, somewhere else. I like Shady Rest, I don't want to see the town die, and I am willing to fight to save it."

"At the sacrifice of your own life?" Milner asked. "Don't forget, we've had four marshals killed already. What do you have to offer that the other four marshals didn't have?"

"I am a woman," Annabelle said. "Initially, that will give me an element of surprise."

"Initially," Tobin said. "But what happens after that initial surprise wears off?"

"She'll have the support of a deputy," Matt said.

"Ha!" Dupree said. "Are you talking about Prescott? What kind of support do you expect that old coot to provide?"

"I don't share your opinion of Deputy Prescott," Matt said. "But he isn't the deputy I was talking about."

"What do you mean he isn't the deputy you were talking about? He's the only deputy there is," Dupree said.

"If you appoint Miss O'Callahan as marshal of the city of Shady Rest, I will apply to her for the position of deputy marshal," Matt said.

Annabelle smiled at Matt. "And I will accept his application," she said.

"Gentlemen, I don't know about the rest of you, but I am won over," Tobin said. "And I move the question."

"All who favor hiring Miss O'Callahan as city marshal for the city of Shady Rest, say aye," Mayor Trout said.

To the man, including Dupree, the vote was "Aye."

■ ■ ■ ■

That very afternoon, Annabelle made her first foray onto Plantation Row. Her first stop was Abby's whorehouse. Squaring her shoulders she marched up to the house, opened the door, and walked inside. A large woman, smoking a cigar, was standing behind a counter, looking down at something.

"All the girls is busy right now, honey," Abby said around her cigar, without looking up. "You can have a seat and wait, or you can come back in about half an hour."

"This place is closed, as of now," Annabelle said.

"What?" Abby asked, looking up in surprise, not only at what had been said, but at the fact that the words had been spoken by a woman.

"You have been operating this place without a business license, and without having your girls get regular checkups from the doctor. By order of the city council, this place is closed," Annabelle said. "Get all of your women down here, now."

"The hell I will!" Abby said, and she started toward the back wall, where Annabelle saw that there was a shotgun. Annabelle drew her pistol, aimed at the window near the shotgun, and fired. The sound of the shot startled even her, but the window was shattered, and with a little squeal, Abby jumped back.

"Are you crazy?" Abby shouted.

"Get the women down here, now," Annabelle said, holding the smoking pistol.

Within the next ten minutes, all six of Abby's "girls" were gathered in the downstairs parlor. The men, a couple of them carrying their boots, were hopping around on bare feet.

"What is this?" one of the men asked. "What's going on here?"

"All of the men, out now," Annabelle said, waving her pistol toward the door.

"I ain't goin' nowhere 'til I get finished," one of the men said, angrily.

Annabelle pointed her pistol at his crotch. "If you don't go now, you won't have anything to get finished with," she said.

One of the whores giggled.

"I think she means it, Cootie," one of the other men said. "Let's get the hell out of here before that crazy woman shoots us all."

Matt was outside, leaning against an Alamo tree that was growing on the side of the road.

"I tell you what I'm goin' to do," one of the men said. "I'm goin' to go back in there and shoot that crazy woman."

"I don't think so," Matt said.

"What? Who the hell are you? What are you doin' here?"

"The name is Jensen. Deputy Matt Jensen. And I'm here to help the marshal, if she needs any help."

"If she needs any help? Wait a minute, are you tellin' me that crazy woman in there is a marshal?

"That's exactly what I'm telling you."

When the stagecoach left Shady Rest the next morning, Abby Dolan and the six girls who worked for her were on the coach. The house where they had been doing business was empty.

The Crooked Branch was the next business that Annabelle went after. But this time, she didn't go in alone. Both of her deputies, Matt and Wash Prescott, were with her. Prescott was carrying a double-barrel shotgun; Annabelle and Matt both had their pistols holstered.

Foster had been warned that they were coming, and he was standing there, waiting for them. He ran his hand over the top of his bald head, and stared at the three with almost colorless eyes that had neither lash nor brow.

"I heard what you did to Abby's Place," Foster said.

"Did you?" Annabelle asked. "Good, then you know that I am serious. Mr. Foster, you have not paid the excise tax. You are operating a brothel without a license, and your girls are not getting regular medical examinations. Until you bring the Crooked Branch into compliance, I am going to have to shut you down."

Foster stretched his mouth into the misshapen gash of an evil smile. "Wade, Luke," he said quietly. "Take care of this little — problem — would you?"

From the overhanging balcony of the second floor, a man suddenly rose, holding a rifle to his shoulder. At the same time another man stepped out from behind the piano, with a pistol in his hand.

Matt drew and fired before the man on the balcony could shoot, and then, on top of the sound of Matt's pistol shot, came the roar of the shotgun Prescott was holding.

Wade, the man on the balcony, fell across the banister, then flipped over it and came crashing down on his back. Luke, the man Prescott had shot, was driven back onto one of the tables, his stomach opened up by the shotgun blast.

Foster looked first at one and then the other, totally shocked by what he had just seen. When he looked back around, he saw that Annabelle was now holding a pistol.

"As I was saying," Annabelle said. "This place is closed, and it will remain closed until you can bring it into compliance."

Within two weeks, Shady Rest went from being the wildest town in Texas, to being the most peaceful. There was no longer a daily sound of gunfire, no longer did drunken cowboys "huzzah the town" by riding up and down the street shooting their guns, not only into the air but into the buildings. The change in the complexion of the town was almost entirely the result of Plantation Row being pacified.

But while that change was appreciated by the citizens, and good for the legitimate businesses of town, it had just the opposite effect on Plantation Row. There, the business that the saloon owners had once enjoyed was almost brought to a standstill. And a meeting of the Plantation Row Betterment Council was called, not by Bramley, but by Fred Foster and Red Gimlin.

"What are we going to do about this?" Foster asked. "She has already closed down

Abby's Place, and my place. I got it open again by paying the back taxes, and getting a license to run a whorehouse, but she's got the place so orderly now that it's more like a mortuary than a saloon. Hell, the customers are afraid to get drunk, and that means they're only spendin' about half of what they was."

"Yeah," Gimlin said. "The same thing is happenin' in my place. I paid the taxes, and I got a license for the whores, but we ain't doin' near the business we once was. Folks come to my place lookin' to have fun, not go to a Sunday school class."

"I thought you said we had the law on our side," Foster said. "I mean, hell, your man has a badge. What good is it for him to have a badge if he don't use it?"

Bramley nodded, then looked across the room where Durbin was sitting in his high chair, overlooking the saloon floor. The floor was relatively quiet because, even though the new marshal hadn't come into the Pig Palace yet, the effects of her efforts were evident from the low-key behavior of the customers. There were fewer drunks because fewer men were drinking, and those who were drinking weren't drinking as much. Bramley signaled for Durbin to come over.

Leaving the shotgun on his chair, Durbin

369

climbed down, then walked over to the table where Bramley, Foster, and Gimlin had been holding their meeting.

"Yeah, boss?"

"Durbin, you are a deputy sheriff, right?"

"Yes, sir, I am. I ain't never seen the sheriff yet, but you got me this job, so I am a deputy."

"As a deputy sheriff, your authority exceeds that of the marshal, or either of her deputies," Bramley said. "You are aware of that, aren't you?"

"Yes, sir, you done told me that."

"Good, I'm glad you know. Now, here's what I want you to do. I want you to arrest the marshal and both of her deputies, and throw 'em all three in jail."

"What do I say is the reason?"

"Reason? What reason? You don't need a reason, Durbin," Bramley said, his voice showing his exasperation. "Just do it!"

CHAPTER THIRTY-ONE

When Wash Prescott walked down Railroad Avenue, carrying a shotgun, there was a bounce in his step. He had found a degree of self-respect that he hadn't known in many years.

"Mornin', Deputy," Roy Clinton greeted.

"Good mornin' Mr. Clinton."

As he continued his morning walk, he exchanged greetings with pedestrians and riders. Seeing a woman laden with packages about to get into a surrey, he hurried over to help her, putting the packages in the back, then assisting her into the vehicle. A dog ran up to him and, smiling, Prescott reached down to rub the dog behind the ears.

As he resumed his walk, he began singing, softly, "My Darlin' Clementine." As he passed the feed and seed store, Maurice McGill spoke to him.

"You're in good voice this mornin',

Deputy. Think we'll get rain today?"

"Kinda feels like it, don't it?" Prescott replied.

People who had rarely spoken to him before now greeted him with respect, and their respect built up Prescott's self-respect. In the café this morning, Moe had brought him a second cup of coffee and a sweet roll, even though he hadn't asked for it. The meals were furnished free to the marshal and deputies, paid for by the city, so Prescott had been eating at Moe's for some time now, but never before had Moe brought him extra coffee and a sweet roll for no reason at all.

It's funny, if someone had asked him a month ago if he would ever work for a female marshal, he would have told them they were crazy. But Annabelle O'Callahan had more brass than anyone he had ever met before. He was not only willing to work for her, he was proud to work for her. Yes, sir, this town had been cleaned up, and he had been part of it.

Mark Worley was sweeping the front porch of his leather goods store, and he paused for a moment as Prescott passed by.

"Good morning, Mr. Worley," Prescott said.

"Deputy," Worley replied with a nod of

his head.

"Have you heard?" Worley asked. "The Andersons aren't moving away after all. They said that, now that the town has been cleaned up, they're goin' to stay."

"Lou Anderson is a good man," Prescott said. "We need people like him to help us grow."

"Yes, sir, that's exactly what I was thinkin'," Worley said.

Worley went back to his sweeping as Prescott continued his morning walk. As he walked away, Harry Durbin suddenly stepped out of the gap between Worley's Leather Goods Store and Dupree's Emporium. This put him behind Prescott, and he had his pistol in his hand, pointing it at Prescott's back.

"You're under arrest, Prescott! Throw down that scatter gun!" Durbin shouted at the top of his voice.

Startled, Prescott whirled around, and that's when Durbin fired. The bullet hit Prescott in the forehead, and he went down, dead before he hit the boardwalk.

"What? What the hell happened?" Worley shouted, dropping his broom and hurrying toward the fallen deputy.

"Hold it right there!" Durbin shouted, pointing his pistol at Worley. Worley stopped, and backed up with his hands in the air.

Dupree and a few of his customers came out of the store, and they saw Prescott lying dead on the on the weathered boards of the walk. He was on his back with his arms thrown out to either side, as if he were on a cross.

By now several other townspeople were hurrying toward the scene where Durbin stood, still holding his pistol, though by now all the smoke had dissipated.

"You killed him," Worley said. "Why did you kill him?"

"I didn't have no choice," Durbin replied. "You heard me shout at him, I told him he was under arrest. He turned toward me with the shotgun. If I hadn't kilt him, he would have kilt me."

"The truth is, I don't think we have any real basis to issue a warrant," Bob Dempster said, talking to Matt, Annabelle, and the mayor.

"What do you mean, we don't have any authority?" Annabelle said. "Durbin killed Wash. He shot him right between the eyes, and we have half a dozen people who will say that they saw it."

"That's just it," Dempster said. "If he had shot Wash in the back, we might have a case.

But he shot him in the front, and that same half a dozen people will say that Durbin told him he was under arrest, and ordered him to throw down the gun. If Wash had dropped the gun before he turned around, we could issue a warrant. But Wash was still holding the gun when he was shot, and that could be construed as a threat to the arresting officer."

"Arresting him for what?" Annabelle said. "You can't just arrest someone without a reason."

"He had a county arrest warrant for the murder of Luke Warren."

"That wasn't murder, it was self-defense," Matt said. "Hell, they could just as easily put out a warrant on me, for killing Wade Matthews."

"I'm sure that the case would have been dismissed before it ever got to court," Dempster said.

"And I'm just as sure that Durbin never intended it to go to court," Matt said. "I think Durbin intended to kill Wash."

While Matt and Annabelle were meeting with the city attorney, Durbin released Brax Barlow from jail, then took him down to the Pig Palace to meet with Jacob Bramley.

"Would you like a whiskey?" Bramley asked.

"I ain't got no money," Brax said. "I been in jail."

"Harry, get our new friend a whiskey," Bramley said. "Bring the whole bottle."

"All right."

Durbin brought a bottle to the table, and Bramley poured a glass, then slid the glass across the table toward Brax.

"Enjoy," he said.

Brax tossed the drink down quickly, then swiped the back of his hand across his mouth.

"Damn," he said. "You don't know how much I been wantin' that."

"I thought you might be a bit thirsty."

Brax looked at Bramley, then at Durbin. "I don't get it," he said.

"What is it you don't get?"

"How come the law got me out of jail, then brought me here to you?"

"Well, let's just say that he delivered you to my custody."

"What does that mean?"

"That means that you are out of jail, but I am responsible for you."

"Oh. Well, I thank you for that."

"I want more than thanks," Bramley said. "I look at this as sort of a bargain between the two of us. I do something for you, and you do something for me. Or, if you don't agree with that, I can have Deputy Durbin return you to your cell."

"No, no, I agree. I'll do whatever it is you want me to do."

"I'm told you tried to kill Matt Jensen."

"Yeah," Brax said. "The peckerwood kilt my two brothers."

"You also mentioned, a moment ago, that you didn't have any money."

"I ain't got one red cent."

"Suppose I offered you a way to make some money, and to get revenge for your two brothers? Would you be interested in such a deal?"

"Yeah, I would be."

"You'll find Matt Jensen over at the Texas Star. I'll give you twenty-five hundred dollars to kill him."

"What good would the money do if I murdered him? I'd get hung."

"Not if it is a fair fight."

"Mister Bramley, there don't nobody go up ag'in Jensen in a fair fight and win."

"Suppose you had an edge?"

"What kind of edge?"

"For one thing, he won't be expecting to see you. He thinks you're still in jail. And if he's sittin' down, like he most of the time is

377

when he's over at the Texas Star, well, he won't be able to get to his gun."

"Twenty-five hundred dollars?"

"As soon as I get word he's dead."

Brax poured himself a second glass of whiskey and tossed it down.

"I ain't got no gun. That fool deputy took it away from me when I got put in jail."

"Harry, give our new friend a gun and holster," Bramley said. "You'll find one in my office."

Brax started to pour himself a third whiskey, but Bramley reached out to prevent it.

"You'd better lay off that until the job is done. Then you can drink the whole bottle to celebrate."

"Yeah," Brax said. "Yeah, that's what I'll do."

As Bramley had said, Matt Jensen was in the Texas Star, and when Brax stepped in through the front door he walked directly over to the table where Matt was sitting.

"We have some unfinished business, you and me," Brax said.

"How did you get out of jail?" Matt asked.

"That don't really matter now, does it?"

"I suppose not."

"I'm goin' to kill you, Jensen, just like you kilt my two brothers."

"I don't suppose you'll let me stand up, first?"

An evil, triumphant smile spread across Brax's face.

"You mean to make the fight fair? I'm not here be fair, Jensen. Like I said, I'm here to kill you."

"Then maybe I should tell you that I already have my gun out. I drew it when I saw you come in through the door.

"The hell you do. I can see your pistol still in your holster."

"Oh, that. Well, what I have in my hand is a hold-out gun. A double derringer. Not very good for distance shooting, but from here I couldn't miss."

"I don't believe you."

"If you don't believe me, go for your gun," Matt said easily.

Brax stood there for a long moment as he tried to make up his mind what he should do next.

"Go for your gun, or get out of here," Matt said.

Brax looked for a moment as if he were going to try it; then he raised a hand and pointed his finger at Matt.

"This ain't finished," he said.

Matt watched until Brax disappeared through the swinging batwing doors. Then he brought his hands up from under the table. He was not holding a derringer.

"Damn, Matt, what if he had called your bluff?" Hawkins asked.

"It might have gotten even more interesting," Matt said. He stood up. "I think I better check with the marshal. I'm sure she doesn't know Barlow is out of jail."

Matt stood up, but just as he did so, Brax Barlow came darting back into the saloon, this time with his pistol already in his hand.

"You son of a bitch!" Barlow shouted. He fired at Matt, the bullet hitting the iron stove, then careening off with a whine. The other patrons of the saloon dived to the floor when the shooting started.

Matt drew his own pistol and returned fire, and a puff of dust and a little shower of blood flew up from Barlow's shirt where the bullet hit, exactly between the second and third buttons.

Barlow was slammed back against the batwing doors with such force as to tear them off the hinges. He landed on his back at the far side of the boardwalk with his head halfway down the steps. Matt walked to the front of the saloon, where he stood in the wrecked doorway, looking down at Brax's body.

Durbin had been waiting across the street,

watching to see what happened so he could take the information back to Bramley. For a moment, he gave some consideration to shooting Jensen himself. After all, if Bramley was going to give twenty-five hundred dollars to Barlow, he could just as easily give it to Durbin.

Although Durbin gave the idea some consideration, he gave it up as soon as he saw that Jensen was still holding the pistol in his hand.

"Jensen kilt that Barlow fella," Durbin reported when he returned to the Pig Palace.

"Yeah, I sort of thought he would," Bramley said without showing any reaction. "But I figured it was worth a chance."

CHAPTER THIRTY-TWO

Durbin was eating pickled pigs' feet and drinking beer when he saw two men come into the Pig Palace. He had never seen either of them before, but he could tell by looking at them that they weren't ordinary cowboys. One of them was a Mexican, and as long as Durbin had been here, he had never seen a Mexican come into the place, because unlike most Texas towns this close to the border, Shady Rest had no cantina, and no Mexicans. Sensing trouble, Durbin walked over to Bramley's table.

"Boss, there's a couple of men just come in that look like they could be a problem," he said.

Bramley didn't look up from his table, but he smiled.

"They aren't a problem, Durbin. They're a solution."

"A solution? What are you talkin' about?"

"They're goin' to do a job for us. Go ask

them to come over to talk to me."

Nodding, Durbin walked over to the door. "You here to talk to the boss?" he asked.

"We don't talk to the law," the Anglo said.

"Law?" For a second, Durbin didn't know what they were talking about. Then he realized they had seen his badge, and he laughed. "Ha! Don't let this badge fool you. Come on, if you're here to talk to Mr. Bramley, he's over there at his table."

When the two men reached the table, Bramley looked up at them and, seeing them for the first time, he frowned. "I didn't know that one of you would be Mex," he said.

The Mexican had obsidian eyes, a dark, brooding face, and a black moustache which curved down around either side of his mouth. He was wearing an oversized sombrero.

"I don't work with Mexicans," Bramley said.

"Bustamante is a good man," the Anglo said.

"How do you know?"

"Me an' him have done a couple of jobs together."

"All right, I know his name is Bustamante. What is your name?"

"Baker."

"Baker. That's your last name. What is your first name?"

"Why do you need to know?"

"I reckon you're right, I don't need to know," Bramley said. He looked at the Mexican again. "All right, I'll use the Mexican. But to him, I'll pay only half what I offered."

Bustamante didn't reply to the comment. Instead, he turned and started to walk away.

"Wait a minute," Bramley called out to him. "Where are you going? You ain't even heard yet what I want you to do."

"It does not matter, señor. I get the full amount, or I don't do *mierda.*" Bustamante said.

"Mierda?" Bramley asked.

"Shit," Baker translated. "He gets the full amount, or he doesn't do shit."

"He would just walk away?"

"Yeah, and so would I."

Bramley laughed. "All right. That's the kind of man it's goin' to take to do this job anyway. I'll pay full amount."

"What is the job?" Baker asked.

"You mean you came here without even knowing what the job was going to be?"

"I heard that you was payin' twenty-five hundred dollars. That's all I heard, and that's all I needed to hear."

"What will you do for twenty-five hundred dollars?" Bramley asked.

"Anything you say."

"I want you to kill someone. No, I want you to kill two people," Bramley said.

"Yeah, well, twenty-five hundred dollars is a lot of money, so I sort of figured it meant you wanted someone kilt."

"You don't have a problem with killing someone?"

"No problem," Baker said.

"What about you, Bustamante. Do you have a problem with killing?"

"No tengo ningún problema."

"What the hell did he say?"

"He says he has no problem."

"Good, then you are in."

"Who do we kill?" Baker asked.

"Like I said, there are two people I want killed. A man, and a woman."

"A woman?" Bustamante asked. "You want me to kill a woman?"

"Yeah, I thought you said you didn't have a problem with killing."

"You did not say you wanted me to kill a woman. It is bad luck to kill a woman."

"This isn't just any woman," Durbin said, speaking for the first time. "This woman is wearing a badge. She is the law."

"A woman sheriff?" Baker asked. "You've

got a woman sheriff?"

"She isn't a sheriff, she is a city marshal."

"Oh," Bustamante said. "If she is a *mariscal,* then she isn't a woman. I will kill her."

"What is the woman's name?" Baker asked.

"O'Callahan."

"And who is the man you want killed?"

"He is her deputy."

"What is his name?"

"Jensen. Matt Jensen."

"Matt Jensen?" Baker turned toward the door. "Come on, Bustamante. Let's go."

"Wait!" Bramley called. "What's wrong?"

"I'm not going to go up against Jensen for twenty-five hundred dollars," Baker said.

"What would it take?"

"Five thousand."

Bramley drummed his fingers on the table for a moment before he answered. "All right," he said. "Five thousand dollars. But I want both of them killed, and I don't pay a cent until they are both dead."

Baker nodded. "We'll do it."

Matt and Annabelle were strolling down Railroad Avenue, responding to the greetings from the townspeople.

"Miss O'Callahan, my wife wants to know

when you're goin' to open your shop back up," one of the citizens said.

"Why, Mr. Peabody, are you that anxious to spend some more money with me?" Annabelle asked, flashing a smile.

"Yes, ma'am. I mean, no, ma'am. I mean, well, my wife does like the dresses you make, and I don't mind admittin' that I like the way she looks in 'em."

"Jensen!" someone called. "Jensen!"

Turning toward the sound of the voice, Matt saw someone standing in the street.

"I'm callin' you out, Jensen!"

"Annabelle, get out of the way," Matt said.

"I'm the marshal here," Annabelle said. "I'm not goin' anywhere."

"Annabelle, please," Matt said, and there was something about his voice, a pleading desperation, that made Annabelle listen.

"All right," Annabelle said, and she stepped back to the corner of the building.

Upon hearing the issued challenge, the pedestrians and riders moved quickly to get out of the way and in less than a moment the street was empty, except for Matt and the man who had challenged him. But though they were alone in the middle of an empty street, the drama wasn't without an audience, for scores of people, from the safety of buildings, were watching to see how it was about to play out.

"I've waited a long time for this, Jensen," the man in the street said.

"Have we met?"

"The name is Baker. Does that mean anything to you?"

"I remember a Lynn and Harry Baker."[2]

"You killed them."

"Yeah, I did. They needed killing."

"They were my brothers."

"So you plan to get some revenge, do you?"

"Somethin' like that."

"I know your mama must be proud."

"Now!" Baker shouted loudly.

Matt heard a gunshot from behind him, and turning quickly, he saw Annabelle holding a smoking gun in her hand. Turning back, he saw a man with a rifle fall from the roof of the mercantile. All that had taken Matt's eye off Baker, who, taking advantage of Matt's distracted moment, drew his pistol and, in a rare event, actually had his pistol out and fired before Matt drew. Matt's draw, once he started it, was instantaneous, and he returned fire.

Baker missed.

Matt did not.

2. See the book *Snake River Slaughter.*

With his pistol still in hand, Matt made a quick perusal of all the roofs of the other buildings, and seeing no further threats, he hurried over to Annabelle.

"Did I . . . did I kill him?" she asked, timorously.

"You sure as hell did," Matt replied with a little chuckle.

"Oh!"

"Annabelle, if you hadn't shot him when you did, I would be dead now."

"I saw him aiming his rifle at you so I aimed at him. And I remembered what you said about squeezing, rather than pulling, the trigger."

"Annabelle, from my point of view, that may be the most valuable lesson I've ever taught. It, and you, saved my life."

"Jensen killed both of them?" Bramley asked.

"No, and that's the hell of it," Durbin said. "Jensen kilt Baker, but it was the woman that kilt the Mex."

"What the hell is it goin' to take to kill that son of a bitch?" Bramley asked in disgust.

CHAPTER THIRTY-THREE

There were five men who rode into town, then stopped in front of the Pig Palace. The five were Prichard Crowley, Bill Carter, Lenny Fletcher, Dax Williams, and Titus Carmichael.

"Come on in," Carter said. "I'll introduce you."

As the men started into the saloon, Prichard turned to Carter. "I believe you said that Bramley is the one who is generally in charge?"

"Yeah," Carter said.

"Then he is the one I wish to meet."

Durbin was surprised to see Carter and Fletcher, and he hurried back to Bramley's office.

"Boss, you ain't goin' to believe who just come in," he said.

"Who?"

"It's Carter and Fletcher. I didn't think

we would ever see them again. I'd be willin' to bet they was the ones that kilt Lila."

"They probably are. I wonder what they are doing back here."

"I don't know, but they ain't alone. There's three others with them."

Bramley got up from behind his desk, then stood in his doorway and looked out over the floor of the saloon. He saw Carter, Fletcher, and three more men whom he had not seen before, standing at the bar. Bramley walked out to see them.

"This here's the one I was tellin' you about," Carter said to Prichard.

"You are Mr. Bramley?" Prichard asked.

"Yeah, I'm Bramley. Who are you?"

"I could give you a phony name, but as a show of trust, I will tell you my real name. I am, sir, Prichard Crowley, at your service."

"Crowley?"

"Mutt Crowley was my brother. I believe you knew him."

"Yes. But I knew him as Morgan. What are you doing in Shady Rest, Crowley?"

"It has come to my attention, Mr. Bramley, that you and I share a mutual interest."

"Like what?"

"The demise of Matt Jensen."

"You got that right."

"I am also led to believe that you are willing to pay to see that come about."

"Why should I pay you for it, if you also want him dead?"

"As far as you are concerned, the fact that I want him dead should serve only to provide me with motivation to see the job done. That has nothing to do with whether or not I should be paid for the work."

"All right, twenty-five hundred dollars, but there are two who must be killed. Jensen, and Annabelle O'Callahan."

"Annabelle O'Callahan? Ain't she the woman that runs the dress shop?" Carter asked.

"Yes. But now she is also the city marshal."

"Ha! Ain't that somethin', though?"

"Five thousand dollars," Prichard said. "Payable, when the job is completed."

"All right. Five thousand dollars," Bramley agreed.

"Good. Now, Mr. Carter tells me that this street is called Plantation Row, is that correct?"

"It's actually First Avenue, but yeah, people call it Plantation Row."

"I wonder, Mr. Bramley, you being a man of some importance on this street, if you could empty all the buildings along Plantation Row, so that the street would be completely deserted?"

"Why would you want to do that?"

"Because it is my intention to lure Jensen onto this street, where I will have my men strategically positioned. We will have him in a cross fire, and it will be easier to do that, if no one else is here."

"How will you get him to come down here?"

"You empty the building. I'll take care of the rest," Prichard said.

Half an hour later, despite protestations from Foster, Gimlin, and the proprietors of the dance hall, gambling house, and even the pawnshop, all the buildings were emptied except for the Pig Palace. And even the Pig Palace was emptied of its customers.

During the process of emptying the street, Prichard had been sitting at a table at the front window of the Pig Palace. He had a pencil, and he was marking something on a sheet of paper. When he was finished, he called his men over and pointed to a map he had drawn.

"All right," he said. "Dax, you and Fletcher go on the other side of the street. Dax, you'll be on top of this building, Fletcher you'll be on this one," he said, pointing to each building as he made the assignments. "Carter, you and Titus will be on top of these two buildings on this side of the street. I will get Jensen to come down here. . . . Dax, Titus, he will come by your positions first. Let him pass by you before you start to shoot. Once he passes you by, he'll be in the middle of all four of you, in the street without cover. He'll be easy to kill."

"How are we going to get him to come down here?" Carter asked.

"I'll be with the woman marshal," Prichard said. "She'll help me get Jensen down here. It's going to be hot up there on the roofs of these buildings, so you may as well get yourselves a beer now to hold you over. As soon as you finish your beer, get into position. Oh, and use rifles — that will give you the advantage."

"Are you sure you know what you're doin'?" Bramley asked.

"The ambush, Mr. Bramley, has been a classic military maneuver ever since a numerically inferior force of Gothics defeated the Romans in the Battle of Adrianople in the year 378. I think that tactic will work well here, especially as we will not only have the advantage of the ambush, but will also be superior in numbers."

Bramley walked back over to the bar and

poured himself a whiskey.

"He's a dandy, ain't he, boss?" Durbin said.

"Yes. Durbin, after he kills Jensen, I want you to kill him."

Durbin smiled, then finished the beer he had been drinking. "It'll be my pleasure," he said.

Even though Annabelle was still the city marshal, she realized that she was going to have to get back to running her shop, if she intended to keep it open. She was in her shop now, and though her appearance — she was still wearing denim trousers with a belt and holster — was very different from what it had been before she took on the marshal's position, it didn't keep her from doing the things that needed to be done. She was draping fabric on a clothes dummy when she heard the front door of her shop open.

"I'll be right with you," she called and, still holding a tape measure in her hand, moved toward the front door. Expecting to see one of her woman clients, she was surprised to see a man standing there. He didn't look like any of the habitués of Plantation Row. He was six feet tall, clean-shaven, with blond hair, and, Annabelle had to admit, he was rather attractive in a somewhat foppish way. "Oh!" she said.

"I'm sorry, miss. It was not my intention to startle you," Prichard said.

"I'm not startled, just a little surprised. I expected to see one of my lady customers. Is there something I can do for you?"

"I certainly hope so, though I am calling on you in your capacity as an officer of the law, rather than seamstress. And it is quite fortuitous that you are a woman, because I believe the situation can best be handled by a woman."

"Well, I'll do what I can," Annabelle said. "What is it?"

"Ah, I must say at the outset, that this entire thing is embarrassing. As a matter of fact, Martha Jane has been an embarrassment to our entire family, but" — here, Prichard looked down and paused for a moment before he continued — "my father — that is, our father, Martha Jane's and mine — is dying. And despite the fact that he once turned Martha Jane out, he wants to see her one more time before he dies. I've come here to get Martha Jane and take her back to Norfolk, Virginia, with me."

"Oh, I'm so sorry to hear about your father, mister . . ."

"Bixby. Jay Peerless Bixby."

"Mr. Bixby. What, exactly, do you want me to do? Do you need me to convince Martha Jane to go with you?"

"No, Martha Jane wants to go, but she is a — I told you this was embarrassing — Martha Jane is a prostitute. And she owes money to the man that she works for. He has told her that she can't go. I would like for you, as an officer of the law — and as a woman — to help me convince Martha Jane that the man she works for cannot keep her there against her will."

"He most definitely cannot keep her there," Annabelle said. "What is his name?"

"It is Bramley. Jacob Bramley. I'm told he is fairly well known in this community, though I suspect that it is more a matter of infamy than a positive reputation."

"You certainly have that right," Annabelle said. "He is a perfect beast of a man. Come, I'll be glad to talk to him for you and your sister."

"My, this is strange," Annabelle said a few minutes later as they walked up First Street.

"What is strange?"

Annabelle looked up and down the street, and through the windows of the buildings. "I've never known Plantation Row to be this quiet before. It's almost like a ghost town."

"It does seem a little quiet, doesn't it? Oh, this is the place. The Pig Palace," Prichard said as they approached the saloon.

"Oh, yes, I know this place well," Annabelle said.

"After you," Prichard said, stepping back to let her walk through the batwing doors first.

The saloon was completely empty, with not even a bartender in place.

"What's going on here? This is very odd," Annabelle said.

Suddenly Prichard reached out from behind her, and jerked her pistol from the holster.

"What? What are you doing?"

"Upstairs, my dear," Prichard said, his voice losing its dulcet tones to take on a more menacing character.

When they reached the top of the stairs, Annabelle saw Bramley, Durbin, the bartender, and three women. Unlike some of the prostitutes who worked at Suzie's Dream House, Annabelle had never met any of the women who worked on Plantation Row, but she was fairly certain that these three women were prostitutes.

"You," Prichard said to one of the women. "I want you to go find Matt Jensen, and tell him that Prichard Crowley is holding Annabelle O'Callahan in the Pig Palace."

"No, I won't do it," the woman said.

Prichard switched the pistol to his left hand, and with his right hand took out a knife. He made a sweeping slash across the woman's throat. With a look of total shock and fear, she put her hands to her neck, but could do nothing to stop the gushing blood. Her eyes rolled up in her head, and she fell to the floor, where she lay with her eyes open wide in terror, until the light of life left them.

"You," Prichard said pointing to one of the two remaining women. "Do be a good girl and go tell Matt Jensen that Prichard Crowley is holding Miss Annabelle O'Callahan prisoner in the Pig Palace. Tell him if he wants to see her alive again, he had better come down to Plantation Row."

The woman's eyes were wide open in terror; then, nodding, she left, hurrying down the stairs.

"Mr. Jensen! Mr. Jensen! Please, someone, call Mr. Jensen!" a woman screamed as she started running up Railroad Avenue. "Mr. Jensen!"

Matt was in the leather goods store, looking at a pair of boots, when he heard the woman calling his name. He went out into the street and saw her running, screaming, and flailing her hands about.

"Mr. Jensen! Oh, please, where is Mr. Jensen?"

"Miss! I'm Matt Jensen!"

The woman stopped, then ran toward him. "He killed her! He killed Karla!"

"Who killed her? Bramley?"

"No, he said his name is, uh, Richard? Richard Crowley."

"Do you mean Prichard Crowley?"

"Yes, that's it! He sent me to get you, Mr. Jensen. He said to tell you that he has Miss O'Callahan."

"Annabelle? Has he done anything to Annabelle?"

"No, sir, not yet. But he said if you wanted to see her alive again that you had better come down to Plantation Row."

"Thanks," Matt said.

Matt hurried to the stage depot, where he saddled Spirit.

"Goin' out for another ride, are you?" Tobin asked.

Matt pulled his rifle from the sheath, then opened the loading tube and found that he could put two more shells in. He did that; then he jacked a round into the chamber.

"What's goin' on, Matt?" Tobin asked.

"I'm not sure yet," Matt answered. "But I'm about to find out."

CHAPTER THIRTY-FOUR

Swinging into the saddle, Matt rode up to the intersection of Railroad Avenue and First Street.

"Sorry to get you into this, boy," he said. "But we've been in spots like this before."

Turning up First Street, he started riding slowly toward the far end of the road. The way was completely empty, and at first he thought it was just that everyone had gotten off the street. But he quickly learned that it was more than that. Not only the street, but every building on either side was empty.

He could feel a tingling on the back of his neck, and he knew that someone was aiming at him. Then he saw him — not the actual person, but his shadow on the ground in front of him. He saw the false front of a building, and he saw the silhouette of a man, holding a rifle.

"Go!" he shouted, slapping his legs against Spirit's sides. Spirit leaped forward like a cannonball, just as the man on the roof fired. The bullet whizzed behind him, and plunged into a watering trough.

With Spirit still at a gallop, Matt twisted in his saddle, raised the rifle to his shoulder, and fired. His would-be assailant dropped his own rifle, then tumbled over the edge. Matt heard the crash of him hitting the ground.

"Ahh," Prichard said in an oily voice. "The game has started."

Annabelle was lying spread-eagle on a bed in one of the rooms used by the prostitutes. Her arms had been tied by her wrists to the headboard of the iron bedstead, while her legs had been tied, by her ankles, to the footboard. She had also been gagged. The one remaining prostitute was sitting in the corner, as frightened as Annabelle.

"My dear," Prichard said. "Do you have any idea how lovely you look that way? So delightfully vulnerable. I must confess, I have rather a weakness for attractive young women. It's more than a weakness — I dare say it is a pathological disorder that I'm quite unable to resist. When this is over, I'll show you exactly what I mean."

Prichard reached down to grab himself. "Yes," he said. "It will be — so good."

403

Because of the gag, Annabelle was unable to respond, but her eyes grew wider in fear.

From outside she heard more gunfire, and though she knew that the gunfire was being directed toward Matt, she drew some comfort in the realization that if they were still shooting, that meant Matt was still alive.

Matt killed his second assailant on the opposite side of the street from where the first had been.

"Carter? Carter, you still alive?" The shout came from the Crooked Branch Saloon, and Matt turned Spirit toward the saloon. Riding hard, Spirit leaped up onto the boardwalk; then, with Matt bending low over the horse's head, Spirit crashed through the batwing doors and went inside the saloon.

"Hold up here, Spirit. You'll be safer here."

"What the hell! Where did he go? Carter, did you see where he went?"

Matt ran up the stairs, then down the upstairs hallway to the back window. The window was raised, and cautiously, Matt looked out, then up. He saw that he could stand on the windowsill and reach up to grab the edge of the roof. He could pull himself up that way, provided there wouldn't be someone on the roof waiting for his head to pop up. But, if he did climb up, he would have to do so without his rifle. He stood the rifle in the corner, climbed out onto the windowsill, then reached up to grab the roofline.

It wasn't as easy as it looked, but he was able to pull himself up until he could improve his position so that, now, he was pushing down on the roof rather than pulling up, and, leaning the upper half of his body onto the roof, he threw up his right leg onto the roof, then rolled the rest of his body over.

He was still on the edge of the roof when someone came running across the roof toward him.

"You son of a bitch! How did you get up here?"

The man who was coming toward him was armed with a rifle rather than a pistol, and that made it awkward for him to get into position to shoot Matt. Matt reached up to grab the barrel of the rifle; then he jerked it down, and putting the muzzle onto the roof, caused the would-be shooter to vault completely over the edge. The man screamed on the way down, though the scream lasted less than a second.

Matt looked down into the alley below and he could tell by the way the way the body was twisted on the ground that the man was dead.

Bending over at the waist, Matt ran across the roof until he reached the upright part of the false front. Pulling his pistol, he looked around the edge cautiously.

"Fletcher! Fletcher, what happened? Who was that, that screamed?"

The shout came from the roof of the Pig Palace, which was just across the street.

"Fletcher? Dax? Where are you?"

He called two names and Matt knew that he had now killed three. Was this the only one left? Was this Prichard? No, he had heard the name Carter being called. That meant there had to be at least two left, Carter and Prichard. And they were probably in the Pig Palace, which meant that was where he was going to have to go.

It was easier coming down from the roof than it had been climbing up because he was able to use the ladder that was built in to the side of the building. He climbed down, then went back into the saloon, where Spirit was standing, patiently waiting for him.

"All right, Spirit, we're going try and trick them. You just go real slow, and do what I tell you to do."

Across the street, on top of the Pig Palace, Carter was getting worried. He had seen Titus killed, but he hadn't heard anything from Fletcher or Dax. Had they also been killed? Was he the only one left? He wasn't going to face Jensen alone, no way.

Then he saw something across the street. It was the horse, the horse Jensen had been riding. He had seen Jensen ride into the Crooked Branch; now his horse was coming out.

He raised his rifle to be ready, but there was nobody on the horse. The horse came slowly out into the street, turned to Carter's right, then just ambled on up toward the other end of the street as casually as if grazing in a pasture.

"What the hell? What happened to Jensen?" Carter asked aloud. "Maybe he's dead!" he said, hopefully.

When Spirit reached the far end of the street, Matt, who was hanging to the side of his horse, totally out of view, turned him so that he crossed the street, still doing so in a way that kept him hidden. Then, Matt jumped down, led Spirit in between two of the buildings, and found a brace to tie him off. That done, he darted quickly up the alley until he reached the back of the Pig Palace. Again he climbed to the roof, but this time he was able to use the ladder.

When Matt reached the roof, he saw Carter looking cautiously around the false front of the building.

"You must be Carter," he said.

"What the hell!" Carter spun around, firing as he did so. He came close, closer than anyone had in a long time, because the bullet passed so near to his ear that Matt could feel the wind pressure. Matt fired back. Carter grabbed the wound in his belly, fell forward, then slid down the slope of the roof and off.

Quickly, Matt climbed back down the ladder. He tried the back door of the Pig Palace, but it was locked. That meant he was going to have to go in through the front.

He had been inside the Pig Palace before, so he had an idea of how far he would have to go from the door to the edge of the bar. So, taking a deep breath, and with a good grip on the pistol, he dashed through the door and dived across the floor toward the bar.

Durbin was holding a shotgun, and he let go with both barrels as Matt slid across the floor. The ball and buckshot passed over

Matt's head and took out the window with a loud crash. From his position on the floor, Matt looked into the mirror. He saw Durbin with the shotgun broken open, trying to reload.

Matt raised up from behind the bar and fired. Durbin went down.

Upstairs, Annabelle watched Prichard pull his pistol and step up to the door. He was trying to see what was going on downstairs without exposing himself. Then, unexpectedly, Annabelle felt something at her right wrist, and turning her head, she saw that the prostitute was untying her.

With her right hand untied, she was able to quickly free her left hand, then her ankles. Free now, she looked around for a weapon, and seeing a heavy water vase on the chest of drawers, she picked it up, stepped up quietly behind Prichard, and brought it down, hard, on his head.

Prichard went down, and Annabelle grabbed his pistol, then ran out to the overhanging balcony to look down on the floor. She saw Matt moving slowly across the floor; then she saw Bramley behind the piano. Bramley was aiming at Matt, who hadn't seen him!

Annabelle raised the pistol and squeezed

the trigger. She hit Bramley, but it wasn't a killing shot, and with a bellow of rage, Bramley turned his gun on her. Matt shot Bramley before he could shoot; then, looking up toward Annabelle, Matt shot again.

Annabelle let out a little squeal, wondering if he had shot before he looked. Then she heard a sound beside her, and saw Prichard tumble over the banister to crash down onto the piano, the instrument giving off a loud, discordant sound.

Matt had to stay a week longer for the five-thousand-dollar reward money to be paid for Mutt Crowley. The five-thousand-dollar reward for Prichard Crowley was going to Annabelle. The rewards for Bill Carter, Lenny Fletcher, Dax Williams, and Titus Carmichael came to six thousand dollars, and Annabelle divided that money up between Barb and Monica, the two surviving prostitutes who had worked at the Pig Palace. She did that for two reasons: to give them a new start in life, and because she believed that Monica and, to a degree, Barb had saved her life.

With his money in his saddlebag, Matt stopped by to tell Annabelle good-bye. No longer the city marshal, Annabelle was once more dressed in the finery that she wore to

410

advertise her work.

"You could stay here, you know," Annabelle said.

"I can't."

A slow smile spread across her face. "I know you can't," she said. "And I even know why you can't. But do me a favor, will you?"

"What's that?"

"Think of me from time to time."

"I always do," Matt said with an enigmatic smile.

Annabelle chuckled then, because she knew exactly what he was talking about.

"I don't mean think of me when you think of the other women. I want you to give me my own space in your memories."

"I will," Matt said. "I promise you, I will."

As Matt rode out of town, he gave Spirit his head, and Spirit started north.

"It figures, you dumb horse," Matt said with a little laugh. "You brought me south in the heat of summer. Winter is coming on, so which way do we head? North.

"One of these days, I'm going to have to give you a lesson in weather and geography. It's hot in the summer, and it's hotter in the South. It's cold in the winter . . . and it's colder in the North."

Spirit whickered.

"I know, I know, you keep telling me. You can't talk."

Horse and rider rode north until they could no longer be seen by anyone in the now peaceful town of Shady Rest.